The Billionaire's Christmas Castle

A Silver Fox Holiday Beach Town Romance

Sadira Stone

H is billions can't buy what he craves most—her love.

Battling between his career and his conscience, tech investor Michael Garwood escapes the holiday madness and flees to Trappers Cove, the kitschy Washington State beach town he loved as a child. All he needs is an ocean view, a crackling hearth, and a little solitude to figure out his existential crisis. Is that too much to ask?

After too many painful snubs, Annie Scott loathes snooty rich people, not that she encounters many in her beachside antiques shop—until Michael walks through her door. When the gorgeous grump bares his human side, Annie decides that sharing small-town holiday fun is the perfect distraction from her lonely Christmas blues.

When Michael's deluxe accommodations flood, Annie persuades him to rent a quirky clifftop castle and host a Christmas party for the whole damn town. Can a frustrated tycoon and a fiercely independent entrepreneur cross an ocean of differences to forge a love that lasts past the holidays?

Come to Trappers Cove for a holiday billionaire romance that'll steam up your windows and warm your heart!

The Billionaire's Christmas Castle: A Silver Fox Holiday Beach Town Romance

SADIRA STONE

To Duncan, my HEA.

Thank you for your patience, kindness, and support.

Contents

Chapter One

♥

Trying his damnedest to shut out the raucous holiday party outside his corner office, Michael Garwood propped his elbows on his mahogany desk, cradled his aching head in his hands, and willed this looming disaster to disappear.

All he needed was a Christmas miracle. Was that too much to ask?

His two best friends and founding partners in GRA Capital slumped in the leather armchairs opposite him, both looking just as miserable.

"Man, we hear you." Rick Roth laced his fingers over his slight paunch. Not easy to keep up regular workouts with their crazy hours and three teenage kids—a problem Michael almost envied. "Change is hard, especially when it clashes with your values. But not everyone has the privilege of idealism."

Jose Alvarez chugged coffee from his mug emblazoned with "World's Best Dad." His kids had gifted Michael a similar mug with "World's Best Uncle."

Wincing, Jose clawed his fingers into his curly salt and pepper hair. "Look, Mike, I wish I was as comfortable with risk as you are, but I can't afford to be cavalier about this."

Rick nodded. "It all boils down to family responsibilities. We've got 'em. You don't."

"Yeah, and we don't have your resources to fall back on.," Jose added. "The board is overwhelmingly in favor of the change. If we stand against them, we'll lose their trust."

So there it stood. Growing GRA Capital from a trio of tech-savvy finance geeks to one of Washington State's largest venture capital firms had provided rich rewards, but sharing control brought risks. And now, those risks threatened to tank the business he and his two grad school buddies had built from the ground up.

Rick and Jose, both brilliant investment strategists, didn't have Michael's vast personal wealth to fall back on. He couldn't in good conscience ask them to risk their future, and their families' future, for his principles.

His mouth Sahara dry, Michael reached for his mug and gulped cold coffee, which did nothing to ease his knotted stomach. "So I'm on my own."

Rick and Jose exchanged a fraught glance.

Finally, Jose spoke. "You know we love you, Mike. It kills us not to back you on this. If you can find a way to convince the board, we're in. Otherwise, we've gotta protect our livelihood."

Michael's throat tightened until he could barely scrape the words out. "I understand. Go enjoy the holidays with your families. We'll talk as soon as I figure out a plan."

Rick and Jose rose silently and shuffled out, leaving him alone to tackle the impossible.

A reminder flashed on his computer screen. "Board meeting set for January 4, 9 a.m."

Countdown to the end.

He squinched his eyes shut, pinched the bumpy bridge of his nose, and fumbled through his desk drawer in search of ibuprofen. A lone tablet rattled in the bottle—woefully insufficient to quash the pounding behind his brow.

"Argh!" He slumped in his butter-soft leather chair and mashed the intercom button. "Nancy, I need you."

"Of course you do." Chuckling, his assistant bustled into the office, resembling a very businesslike Mrs. Claus in her red tweed suit and blinking Christmas tree pin. "You need me to pry your workaholic behind out of that chair. Come join the party, Michael. Where's your holiday spirit?"

Through the open door, laughter and obnoxious holiday pop tunes invaded his chamber of gloom. He curled his lip at the din. "Painkillers, I'm begging you."

Nancy set her load—a paper plate of cookies and a cup of eggnog—on his desk, then crossed her arms and tutted. "Look at you, Ebenezer, in here sulking while everyone else is making merry." She strode to the floor-to-ceiling windows and switched on the lighted Christmas tree she'd installed despite his protests. "That's better."

Bright points of color against the gray Bellevue sky, the damn twinkle lights only intensified his headache.

Nancy pulled a bottle of pills from her jacket pocket, then tapped her foot while he downed two, chasing them with cloyingly sweet eggnog. "Now, get out there and join the crew. If you stay holed up in here, they'll suspect bad news is brewing. That's no way to start their holiday break."

Michael snorted. "Trouble is brewing, and you damn well know it." He pushed back from his desk and stalked to the window, glaring into the twilight. Rain pattered against the glass, blurring the Christmas lights far below.

Nancy chuckled and shook her head. "Quit perseverating and try to enjoy yourself."

"I'm not perseverating, I'm just—"

"Spinning your wheels. You have a tell, you know." Imitating his unconscious gesture, she rubbed the bridge of her nose.

With a frustrated grunt, he dropped his hand. After twenty-plus years of working side by side, Nancy could read him like a book.

Her lips curved in an indulgent smile. "Coffee?"

"Please."

A few minutes later, he gratefully accepted a steaming mug of perfection, brewed to his precise preference in a Chemex pour-over, strong and clean and smooth, mellowed with the ideal blend of cream and sugar. Closing his eyes, he inhaled the steam.

Nancy's soft hand gripped his shoulder. "They're asking for you out there."

Music drifted through the open door, shrill chipmunk voices warbling about hula hoops.

"Shut the door, will you?" His poor ears had been assaulted by saccharine Christmas tunes since the day after Halloween, and he faced ten more days until December 26th cut off the drivel.

Preoccupied with saving the firm, the last thing he wanted was sickeningly sweet, spiked punch, a pile of cookies, and a wet kiss from the accountant who'd ambush him under the mistletoe—just like last year and the year before.

Nancy regarded him with a sympathetic smile. "Still brooding about the expansion?"

He mimicked the young presenter's chirpy tone. "You mean 'taking the firm to the next level'?" The rest of the board had lapped it up. If not for his intervention, they'd have voted yes on the spot to a one-eighty-degree pivot from the founders' vision, and a total disaster, as far as Michael was concerned.

Nancy sat on the corner of his desk, her brow furrowed. "Can they really change the firm's mission like that? You're the CEO, for goodness' sake."

He knuckled his eyes. "If the majority of the board votes to shift focus, I have no choice but to go along. Or quit."

And quitting was out of the question. Angel investing wasn't just his very lucrative career, it was his calling, his raison d'être. He'd started solo with the seed money his parents gave him after earning his MBA. Then, when the number of start-ups he supported grew beyond what he could manage on his own, he brought in Rick and Jose.

When management duties took too much of their focus away from their mentees, a business consultant convinced them to hire other C-suite officers to take over the boring parts. And it had worked—so well, in fact, that now GRA Capital was attracting the attention of big-league players who invested in larger, more stable tech companies for a slice of the very profitable pie.

But for Michael, what made this punishing work schedule worthwhile was fostering talent and brilliant innovations that, without angel investors, would never see the light of day. Unfortunately, the board had other ideas, prioritizing profit over innovation and the people who make that innovation possible.

And they expected Michael, with his "superior institutional knowledge and experience," to cull less profitable investments, including ninety percent of the start-ups he'd so carefully nurtured into the black. His gut churned at the thought.

Instead of heading back to the party for a well-deserved break, Nancy sank into a chair, crossed her legs, and dangled one sensible pump from her toe. "You should take the holidays off. Christmas is for friends and family, not for slogging through business negotiations." She waved toward the communal workspace beyond the glass wall. "For the next two weeks, this place will be a ghost town."

"Perfect. I'll be able to think for once."

She leveled her sharpest Mom Stare. Only ten years older than Michael, she had that superpower down pat. "You hate this, don't you?"

"Christmas? Hate's a strong word, Nance." Not inaccurate, though. All the holiday season ever brought him was endless rounds of boring parties.

"Don't be obtuse, dear. You hate the expansion proposal."

He heaved a weary sigh. "Business is all about growth, right?"

"And the holidays are about togetherness, yet here you sit, chewing your cud."

"Thanks for that flattering image." He closed his laptop.

"Your tux is ready, by the way. Should I have Jeffrey pick it up?"

Michael glanced through the glass wall and spotted his driver canoodling with a cute data analyst. "Nah, let him enjoy the party. Have it sent to my apartment." He sipped his coffee, then winced, remembering why he needed the damn monkey suit in the first place.

"Something wrong with the coffee?" Nancy looked slightly affronted.

His faithful assistant knew to the molecule the perfect balance of strong brew, organic cream, and raw coconut sugar. From the contents of his mug to the impeccable management of his schedule, she kept Michael's day humming smoothly and cushioned him from disturbances and interruptions. He'd be lost without her.

He gave her a frazzled smile. "No, the coffee's sublime. I'm just dreading tonight's holiday gala." Sponsored by the Rain Coast Arts

Council, one of his mother's pet charities, this gathering of tech bros, finance wonks, and socialites promised as much fun as a root canal.

Nancy leaned forward, eyebrows raised. "So don't go."

"Don't go?" He'd never even considered that option. This gala, and the other glitzy social events crammed into the week before Christmas, were vital networking tools for the firm.

Nancy's pink-frosted lips quirked to the side. "Hmph. Only fifty-four, and losing your hearing already." She raised her voice, over-enunciating each word. "I said, DON'T. GO."

He scowled. "You feeling all right, Nance?"

"As a matter of fact, I'm feeling better than I have in a long time." Her smile held a wistful tinge. "Michael, you've been a wonderful boss, and it's been an honor to work with you."

His stomach plummeted like a runaway elevator. "Nonono! You can't leave me. You're my rock, my guardian at the gate, my voice of reason. I need you."

Straightening in her seat, she folded her hands in her lap. "I'm almost sixty-five. Who knows how many healthy, active years I have left? I want to travel, spend more time with my grandchildren."

Panic tightened his throat. "Is it the money? I'll give you a raise."

She arched an eyebrow.

"I'll double your salary. Think of all the Disney trips you could buy for your grandkids."

She laid her soft hand over his fisted one. "What's the point if I'm too exhausted and stressed to enjoy them? Money can't buy time, Michael. I'll stay through January. That'll give you a month to find my replacement."

He collapsed into his seat. "Merry Christmas to me."

Nancy tutted and pushed to her feet. "Look at you. Wallowing in stress while everyone enjoys the holiday spirit."

"Spirit schmirit. All this phony fa la la makes me want to..." He trailed off on a groan.

"Makes you want to what?" She waited, hands on hips.

He stared into the rainy gloom. "Escape, I guess."

"Aren't you spending the holidays with what's-her-name?" Though she memorized every detail of his work needs, Nancy stubbornly refused to remember the names of his girlfriends. Not that he could blame her—they never lasted longer than a year or so.

"Crystal. And no, she's got a Christmas ski trip in Vail with her family."

And even if she were staying in Bellevue, Crystal wasn't the type to spend a cozy holiday à deux. A high-level financial consultant, she was as work-obsessed as he was. Chic, attractive, smooth as glass, she accompanied him to events like tomorrow's charity gala and scheduled him in once or twice a week for a restaurant meal and an hour of pleasant, if uninspired, sex. She always left afterward so as not to mess up her tight schedule. To be fair, he also rose early for his pre-dawn home workout as he watched the sun rise over Lake Washington—alone.

Not that he minded. His clearest thoughts came during those peaceful morning hours.

An idea tickled his brain and stretched his lips in a grin. "You know what? I'm going to take your advice."

"You always do, in the end."

He threw back his head and laughed. "Rub it in good, Nancy."

She fanned herself with her hand. "Enough dirty talk, boss. My old heart can't take it."

"Old heart, my ass. You'll outlive me by decades."

She speared him with a pointed glance. "I will if you don't deal with this work stress somehow."

"Okay, you win." Rising to his feet, he rubbed his hands together. "I'm taking the holidays off. Do you have time to book me a rental?"

"For two?"

"No, for one. Something nice, cozy, with a fireplace. I want to get away and clear my head." He tapped his pursed lips. "How about on the coast? Trappers Cove would be perfect." Only three hours by car if the traffic wasn't too bad, his favorite Washington coastal town would offer soothing surf, solitude, and sweet respite from all the holiday bullshit.

She wrinkled her nose. "That kitschy beach town?"

"Hey, I love that place. Spent every summer there when I was a kid."

Nancy shrugged. "I'll make some calls—" She hitched a thumb over her shoulder. "As soon as you join the party."

"Yes, ma'am." He snapped a salute, then pecked Nancy's cheek. Squaring his shoulders, he entered the holiday fray, feeling lighter than he had in ages.

Christmas on the beach—long walks on the windy shore, a roaring fireplace, a stack of spy thrillers to read—perfection. Two weeks would give him plenty of time to figure out what to do about the expansion, his life, everything.

Chapter Two

♥

Before opening her antiques and vintage emporium for another day of holiday shopping, Annie Scott pulled out her earbuds, faced her gilt cheval mirror, planted her fists on her hips in a superhero pose, and declared, "I am strong. I am beautiful. I bravely embrace the changes that reveal my life's purpose."

From the depths of her soul, a sour little voice snorted. *Enough? Hah! You're going to die alone, a well-dressed, unloved prune.*

"Argh!" She snarled her fingers in her hair, mussing her carefully arranged waves. Her inner critic was especially mouthy this holiday season, unmoved by a steady stream of self-help audiobooks. Those silver-tongued gurus simply weren't strong enough to squash the nagging self-doubt that had been building long before last night's bad news bomb.

"You understand, don't you, Annie?" Brian wheedled through the phone. "This is a huge opportunity for Wendy and the kids. You could even come with us, if you like."

He knew damn well she was terrified of flying. Determined not to squash his family's happiness, she'd scraped the bitter disappointment from her voice. "It's okay. We'll get together after the holidays."

How could a decent person be anything but happy for her baby brother and his darling wife, finally reconnecting with her estranged parents back East? So what if his good news cancelled the holly, jolly family holiday they'd shared every year since her long-ago divorce? She had plenty of friends, and male companionship wasn't hard to come by, so why was the prospect of a solo Christmas so damn depressing?

All these you-go-girl mantras were just a vain attempt to fool herself. The carefree, single-and-fabulous life she'd built in Trappers Cove just wasn't doing it for her anymore. And the town wasn't the problem. She was.

Back when she and Matt first split up, limiting her love life to casual hookups felt like self-preservation. Even if her ex-husband didn't want her, lots of other guys did. Fun, interesting guys who offered flattery and companionship in convenient, bite-size doses. Over the years, with the shop taking up most of her time and energy, the friends-with-benefits deal became a habit. Who had time for lazy walks on the beach, romantic meals for two, and all the effort it took to keep a guy interested? Not her.

Besides, if she never let anyone get close to her shredded heart, it might slowly heal. And it had, sort of.

But recently, when she read an article about those seaside houses built on stilts to weather high tides and storms, a jarring gong rang in her skull—what a perfect metaphor for her life. Her business made up one stilt—probably two, to be honest, since keeping it afloat took most of her energy and time. Her family was another stilt, as were her friends, including a handful of out-of-town guys who offered physical pleasure and comfort from time to time. But were they really friends, or were they just relative strangers using her to scratch an itch and being used in return?

Lately, their encounters left her feeling empty and vaguely grubby. At first, she'd tried to rationalize it as sexist conditioning, but the more deeply she examined her heart, the sharper the truth became. It was time for a change.

That's the trouble with a house on stilts—if you remove one support, the whole thing topples. So with one stilt already rotting, losing the family Christmas she'd been looking forward to sucked all the joy out of her holidays and frosted her usually sunny mood.

"Snap out of it," she scolded her reflection. "You love Christmas." She smoothed her 1950s tweed skirt, fluffed the bow on her satin blouse, and adjusted the jeweled combs holding back her hair.

Meh. Still needs something.

From the jewelry case beneath the glass counter, she selected a vintage brooch, a green enamel wreath dotted with rhinestones. Perfect. She pinned it above her left breast, struck a pose, and smiled.

"I look fabulous. I *am* fabulous."

You're fifty-six and alone at Christmas. No outfit will ever fix that.

She'd like to punch her inner critic right in its sneering face, but with only six more shopping days till Christmas, she had to focus on practical matters, like finding a dress for the Sons of Italy holiday banquet—preferably a red one, all the better for drowning her sorrows in Chianti and marinara sauce.

Damn it, struggling under these Christmas blues, even that fun holiday ritual felt like just another chore. No fair, after putting so much work into leading the decorations committee. This would be the town's most gorgeous holiday ball ever, thanks to the teamwork of six phenomenal women, and she couldn't let them down by moping through the party.

"I *will* have fun, damn it." She gave her reflection a grim, unconvincing smile, slicked on another coat of scarlet lipstick, then strode to the front door and flipped the sign to *Open* before popping her earbuds back in.

"Change is life's only constant," the audiobook narrator intoned. "A wise soul learns to float on the current of change rather than swim against the tide."

Ignoring the doorway bell's tinkle, Annie closed her eyes, drew a deep, centering breath, and visualized herself floating on a warm current, soothed, supported, buoyant...

Until a sharp poke on her shoulder snapped her attention back to real life.

She forced a smile. *Customers are good. Mustn't snarl at them.*

Especially this time of year, when most customers were also friends and neighbors in search of Christmas gifts or the perfect holiday out-fit.

"Sorry, Cassie. I was lost in an audiobook."

Cassie's warm grin bracketed her mouth in deep parentheses. "You and your self-improvement books. I don't know anyone less in need of fixing. Which one are you listening to now?"

"*The Courage to Change.*"

"Oh yeah, I heard about that one on *Good Morning Northwest.* The author did a TED Talk, right?"

"Mmm hmm. Very inspiring. What can I help you with, hon?"

"I plumb forgot about Secret Santa. We start Monday, and I need a week's worth of presents for a grumpy waitress. Help me out?"

Annie tapped her pursed lips. "Let's see—Lulu likes dogs, doesn't she?"

"Yeah. Especially little yappy ones." Cassie's phone tootled. She glanced at the screen and huffed. "Shoot. Another server down with flu. Gotta run. Could you—"

"I'll scope out doggie-themed tchotchkes. Stop by after you close."

"You're my Christmas angel." She stuffed her phone into her apron pocket. "Glad you're joining us for Christmas Eve."

Annie's smile tightened. "Can't wait. What can I bring?"

"Just your gorgeous self and a white elephant gift. I'll bet yours will be a doozy." She waved a hand, taking in the overstuffed shop filled with vintage clothing and accessories, furniture from Victorian to mid-century modern, artwork, tchotchkes, toys, collectibles, and beachy knick-knacks for the tourists.

"Oh, I'm sure I'll find something."

Cassie's sharp eyes peered right through her phony cheer. "It's hard, I know. But you'll see, friends can be family too." She patted Annie's hand, then trotted back across the street to her bustling café.

"I am an ungrateful Scrooge," Annie muttered as she set to work unpacking a carton of ornaments purchased at an estate sale. Who would willingly part with these delicate glass figures? She ran her fingertips over a blue-robed angel, a slender Saint Nick, and colorful birds with real feathers for tails, remnants of family Christmases past.

Anne blinked back annoying tears. Embarrassing, how her brother's news had scraped all the shine off her holiday. She should be stronger than this.

Brian, his adorable wife, and their three teens were all the family she had left. Ever since her nieces and nephew were tiny, she'd shared a cozy Christmas in their Olympia home and showered them all with carefully selected gifts, relishing her role as the cool, bohemian auntie.

But without their food- and gift-stuffed celebration, how on earth would she spend Christmas Day? Long, solo beach walk? Holiday movie marathon? Romance novel therapy?

Really, she ought to be ashamed of herself. So many single women would envy her the rich, happy life she'd built in Trappers Cove. She lived a few blocks from the ocean, for goodness' sake, in an adorable cottage that twinkled with Christmas lights. She fell asleep to the whisper of surf and woke to the cry of seagulls. She walked to work along Main Street, picture postcard pretty in its holiday finery. And she had no business feeling lonely when she was surrounded by such good friends.

"Friends can be family too." She fluffed the satin bow on Roscoe, the life-size ceramic panther beside the cash register. "Right, puss?"

Her sleek mascot stared with flat, glittering eyes.

"I should get a real cat." She clutched her sinking stomach. "Oh God, I'm becoming a lonely cat lady."

The doorway bell jerked Annie from her doom-spinning as her bestie Cheryl Rossi bustled in. Since few tourists came to Trappers Cove during the cold months, Cheryl often popped over from her vacation rental business next door. "More fun to kill time here than stare at an empty computer screen, right?" But today, a hungry gleam shone in her eyes.

"Whew, it's toasty in here." Cheryl unwound her sparkly red scarf and unbuttoned her tweed blazer—both pieces she'd purchased from Annie's shop. "Nearly froze my nipples off in the thirty seconds it took to walk here."

Annie chuckled. "Don't you look cute today. And predatory."

Cheryl's grin widened. "Just got a call from some rich finance guy's secretary. Wants a two-week rental with an ocean view. Says the boss has the holiday blues and needs some alone time to stew in his feelings."

Annie's face screwed up as if she'd chomped a lemon. "Rich finance guy? Ugh. They're the absolute worst. Them and their snooty wives." Too many sour encounters with their ilk had sent her running from Bellevue back to Trappers Cove—which turned out for the best. She could never have built this kind of success among those stuck-up socialites.

Cheryl rolled her eyes. "That again? It's been years. Isn't it time to let go of that silly prejudice? Rich people are just like you and me, only with fatter wallets."

"Easy for you to say. I bet you've never had a whole table of country club matrons give you the cut direct."

Cheryl's loud laughter drew stares from the customers. Ignoring them, she poked Annie's arm. "Okay, Ms. Austen. Just don't go insulting my client. I really need this commission."

"Hmmf." Annie crossed her arms. Cheryl wouldn't understand. She'd never tried to insert her working-class self into the posh set and been smacked down hard. Those old wounds to her dignity still stung. "So, where will your rich client do this stewing?"

Cheryl bounced on her toes. "The Randall house. That's my priciest property—except for the castle, of course."

Annie fanned herself. "Niiice. Kudos to you."

Still beaming, Cheryl flipped through a rack of sparkly tops. "Can't really take credit for it. Seems the client spent summers here as a kid." She held up a seventies sequined tank. "This would be perfect for the Sons of Italy holiday banquet. This year, I'm getting some of Sal Verducci's manicotti if I have to stab someone to do it." She bumped Annie's hip with her own. "Sure you don't want to bring a date? I've got an extra ticket."

"I'm positive." The downside of living in a close-knit small town like Trappers Cove was knowing too much about the few single guys in her age range—no chemistry, no mutual interests, no sparkling personality... just no thanks.

Cheryl held a glittery black cowl-neck to her chest and regarded her reflection. "Bob says you're welcome to come for Christmas Eve supper. It'll be kind of a noisy mob. The grandkids get a little hyper, but they're so stinkin' cute."

A trio of customers entered the shop, chatting and laughing.

With an eye on the newcomers, Annie lowered her voice. "Thanks, but I'm looking forward to a quiet Christmas."

Cheryl scrunched her lips to the side. "Right, keep telling yourself that." She brightened. "Hey, you should invite one of your hookup buddies. Shame to let all those holiday decorations go to waste."

Annie stiffened. "Friends with benefits, you mean?" The falsehood of that phrase made her inwardly cringe. None of those guys would come running in a crisis or offer a shoulder to cry on. Hell, none of them really knew much about her beyond her tastes in bed.

"Tomato, tomahto." Cheryl nudged her. "You wild woman, you."

"Hmph." Right now, Annie felt about as wild as a pet bunny.

Cheryl squeezed Annie's arm. "I hate to think of you alone at Christmas. Who will you kiss under the mistletoe?"

Annie patted the ceramic panther. "I'll kiss Roscoe."

Cheryl's phone rang, ending her interrogation. "Well, crap on toast. Hold these for me, will you?" She dropped both tops on the counter and hurried out, shoulder-checking a scruff-jawed man with steel gray hair on his way in.

Though she hadn't seen him in a year or so, Annie recognized that frayed fisherman's sweater. After all, she'd sold it to him.

He strolled in, hands in his pockets, grinning. "Annie, me girl, how are ya?" He grasped her shoulders and planted a wet kiss on her cheek.

"Nolan. Long time no see."

"Too long, lassie." Leering, he wound a length of her hair around his callused finger, and she caught a whiff of stale pipe tobacco. A commercial fisherman like her dad, he had that same crinkly smile, lines deeply etched around mouth and eyes by months out at sea. The first time they met, she was charmed by his weird movie-pirate way of talking. Now, the phony accent grated on her nerves.

He raked his gaze up and down her body. "You're looking sweet as a sugarplum, darlin'. What say you and I share a pint at the Salty Dog Saloon tonight?"

She consulted Nolan's card in her mental Rolodex: Funny guy, mediocre kisser, decent dancer, never called her by the wrong name in bed...

Nope. His unannounced appearance strengthened her resolve. She deserved better than a so-so roll in the hay. She deserved a man who appreciated her for more reasons than being—what had he called her last time? Oh yeah, 'a good sport.' And if she fell back into her old patterns, she'd never find the love she deserved.

Love? Even thinking the word made her a little queasy. But you know what they say about shooting for the stars... or was it the moon?

She patted Nolan's arm and slid away toward the customers pawing through her hat display. "Actually, I'm pretty busy this time of year."

The doorway bell tinkled again, signalling a new male customer who headed for the rack of coats on the far wall. Tall, dark hair, sharp jaw. Definitely not a local—she'd have remembered this stunner.

Nolan pursued her through the clothing racks. "But Annie, sweetheart, can't you make time for an old friend?" He waggled his wiry eyebrows. "A friend who knows your deepest, darkest desires?"

Nothing dark about my desires—just a good man who cherishes me. But what were the chances of a woman in her fifties finding that rare bird?

"Friend, huh?" Annie lowered her lids. "What color are my eyes?"

"Why, they're, uh, sort of green-grayish hazel?"

She opened her decidedly blue eyes and glowered. "What do I like to do when I'm not at work?"

"Well now." Leering, he waggled his eyebrows. "I know one thing you enjoy."

Ugh. "Sorry, I've got plans tonight." *An audiobook, bubble bath, and dinner for one.*

Unfazed, he leaned closer. "How about tomorrow?"

"Going out of town." *To Westport, for a dentist appointment.*

His lower lip protruded. "Aww, Annie. Surely, you're not giving your old pal the brush off."

She patted his scratchy cheek. "We've had fun, but lately, I'm craving something different." *Something more satisfying than a booty call.* "I hope you have a happy holiday season." Squaring her shoulders, she strode toward the new customer. "Can I help you find anything, sir?"

Nolan trotted after her. "Hold on, now. I can do different." He snatched a feather boa from the accessories display. "Maybe a little role play?" He grabbed a leather belt. "Or some bondage? You know, like that *Fifty Shades* book? I hear the ladies love that."

The other customer made a choking sound.

Flushed from chest to hair, Annie pointed to the exit. "Goodbye, Nolan."

Shoulders drooping, he trudged toward the door, but turned back for one last try. "Another time, then?"

"We'll see." She should've given him a decisive no, but she didn't want to make a scene in front of a shop full of customers.

Grumbling, Nolan left.

Annie allowed herself the slightest shudder. *Good riddance.*

Chapter Three

♥

She turned her attention to the man rifling through the coats, his movements sharp and brisk. "Can I help you find something in particular?"

He faced her, and her heart stuttered.

Elegant was the first word that leapt to mind. *Yes, please,* were the second and third.

Tall, fit, and near her age, judging by his laugh lines and the furrows bracketing his full lips. His chestnut hair was touched with silver at the temples, and a sexy salt-and-pepper scruff covered his sharply angled jaw. Heavy lids shaded bright eyes the color of cognac. The only flaw on his otherwise model-perfect face was a bump on his nose. Her fingers drifted to the slight protrusion on her own, the result of falling off a beach pony when she was ten.

Quelle coincidence.

His clothing didn't reveal much—just a typical well-off Northwest male wearing a down vest over a flannel shirt, crisp twill pants, and hiking shoes that probably cost more than the new set of tires her van so desperately needed.

His lips quirked in a playful grin, and he inclined his head toward the door. "Don't know what I expected to find in Auntie Annabelle's Antique Attic, but it damn sure wasn't that."

Of course, he'd have a deep, smokey voice that prickled her skin with goosebumps. And of course he'd overheard every word of Nolan's sleazy proposition. Annie's face erupted in flames.

His brow furrowed as he stepped closer. "Are you okay? Should I call someone?"

She smoothed her damp palms over her skirt. "I'm, uh—" There was no graceful way to explain, so she might as well be honest. "Embarrassed, actually. My friend lacks a certain—"

"Respect for a beautiful woman?"

She spluttered, her throat suddenly too tight to emit words.

Mr. Handsome winced. "Sorry. Cheesy flirtation is probably the last thing you want to hear right now." His sheepish smile reeled her in like a hooked salmon.

And then his oh-so-kissable lips formed words to break the spell.

"I'm surprised to see this many customers in a secondhand shop."

So much for attraction. Just another wealthy snob.

Stiffening, she bit back a scathing retort.

He straightened and cleared his throat. "Sorry. I didn't mean to sound snooty. I don't have much experience with this kind of place. Lots of...erm..."—his gaze darted from display to display—"interesting merchandise in here."

At least he was trying. Though her tongue itched to give him a verbal smackdown, it was better to educate than obliterate.

With effort, she softened her tone. "Many people prefer to shop second hand because it's a more sustainable choice. Some folks come here to construct the warm, homey past they never had. Others appreciate well-made merchandise that lasts. Nowadays, things are made to be disposable." Stepping closer, she fingered his chic but flimsy vest. "Like this piece. It looks nice, but it won't hold up to dry cleaning, much less a real winter storm."

His startled gaze fell to her fingers.

Yikes! She dropped her hand and backed out of his personal space. What had gotten into her?

Even his self-conscious laugh reverberated with sexy vibes. "Well, as soon as I remove my foot from my mouth, perhaps you can help me find a coat. Didn't expect it to be this cold in Trappers Cove. Of course, I've only ever been here in summer, and it's been years, so..." He lifted the sleeve of a heavy motorcycle jacket.

This guy didn't seem like the biker type. But what type was he?

Her shoulder brushed his as she rifled through the coats on the upper rack. "We haven't had a cold snap like this since I was a little girl. Old folks used to call it an Alaska Clipper. I've seen photos of icicles on the cliffs at Ivan's Hollow. Hard to imagine, eh?"

She snuck another glance at his sculpted profile and hoped the flush heating her cheeks wasn't too visible. *Wowza, this guy is gorgeous.*

She cleared her throat. "So, what brings you here in winter? Family Christmas on the beach?"

He scoffed. "With family is the last place I want to be this Christmas." He reached past her, and his sigh stirred her hair. "I'm taking a little time to breathe, get away from all the holiday bullshit." His deep, rumbling chuckle sent delicious chills down her spine. "Sorry, I mean holiday nonsense."

His breath smelled like a candy cane. A fleeting vision of that sweet, minty exhalation against her lips revved her pulse—until the obvious smacked her upside her lust-addled head.

This was the finance tycoon who'd come to Trappers Cove to stew in solitude.

Fabulous. The first guy to light me up in ages, and he turns out to be one of them.

Cheryl's chiding words rang in her ear. Her bestie might have the tiniest sliver of a point. After all, the guy apologized for his snooty remark. Besides, no one should be alone at Christmas, not even grumpy billionaires. Helping this attractive stranger enjoy a cozy small-town Christmas was just the distraction she needed from her own holiday blues.

She squared her shoulders and flashed her best saleswoman smile. "Well, Trappers Cove is an excellent place to spend the holidays."

He examined a 1940s trench coat. "When I spent summers here with my aunt and uncle as a kid, I used to wish I could live here year round."

"Oh yeah? Who were they?"

"Great-aunt and uncle, really. Arnie and Ruby Garwood. He was a retired banker. She made quilts, and shortbread cookies, and the best blackberry jam I've ever tasted." Happy memories lent his grin a boyish tinge.

"I remember Ruby. She and my Granny Grace were friends. I think I may have one of her quilts at home."

"Really? I'd love to see it." His shoulder rose in a sheepish half-shrug. "I mean, if you don't mind a stranger in your home."

She patted his arm. "Strangers don't stay strangers for long here. Besides, my granny and your great-aunt were besties, so we're practically related." She stuck out her hand. "Annie Scott, of the Trappers Cove Scotts."

His big, smooth palm enfolded hers, warm and dry and perfect. "Michael Garwood, of the Bellevue Garwoods."

She tried hard to scrape the distaste from her tone. "I know the area well."

Fresh out of college, she took a job as assistant to a private stylist in that swanky Seattle suburb. Their filthy rich customers displayed zero originality or creativity—a bunch of pampered sheep gobbling up the trend du jour. Her passion for pre-loved couture went over like a fart in church.

Once, she made the unforgiveable mistake of suggesting a gorgeous vintage Dior gown to a client. Not only did the woman turn up her nose at the idea of wearing "castoffs," she badmouthed Annie to all her socialite friends.

If Michael Garwood was used to that snobbish crowd, he was in for a surprise. Probably do him good to loosen up and meet some down-to-earth people.

"Well, you won't find any holiday galas here, just friendly folk, a little extra glitter, and too much food. Plus blustery weather. And the sea, of course."

"Sounds perfect." He unhooked a retro raglan coat. "Wow. My grandfather had one exactly like this."

Moving to Michael's side, she sized up his trim body. "Let's see, you're a forty-two long?" Time to flex her skills. She flipped past a vintage trench coat, a puffy down parka, a fleece-lined corduroy car coat, an army field jacket...

"How about this one?" She unhooked a navy pea coat. "The cuffs show a little wear, but the lining's intact, and it's very warm and windproof." Smiling wistfully, she stroked the heavy wool. "Think of the stories this jacket could tell."

"Stories, huh?" Leaning closer, he gave it a discreet sniff.

Just when I thought you might have some redeeming qualities.

She curled her lip. "Don't worry, you won't get cooties. Every garment in the store has been professionally cleaned."

A becoming shade of pink stained his cheekbones. "Sorry. I didn't mean to imply otherwise." He slid out of his too-thin vest and handed it to Annie, who cuddled it to her chest, secretly enjoying the residual body heat while he pulled on the pea coat.

Placing her tingling hand on the small of his back, she directed him to the cheval mirror.

He shoved his hands into the pockets and turned from side to side. "Makes me look like a sea captain from the adventure books I read as a kid."

A very hot sea captain. For a self-indulgent moment, she imagined the two of them cuddled up in a narrow berth, their bodies rocked by the waves while Michael rocked her world.

Whoa now, enough of that. She shook off the naughty fantasy.

A slow, dazzling smile stretched his lips. "I'll take it. Thank you, Annie."

Her heart's reaction landed somewhere between pitter-pat and cowabunga. The doorway bell saved her from making a complete fool of her horny self as Cheryl hustled back into the shop, her expression tight. "Um, Annie, could I talk to you for a minute?"

Michael retrieved his vest, stepped back, and bobbed a courtly bow. "Don't mind me. I'll just browse for a bit."

Annie scooted closer to her jittery friend and lowered her voice. "What's up?"

"That's him," Cheryl hissed, "the tycoon."

"Duh. Seems decent for a rich guy."

Cheryl clutched Annie's arm. "The Randall house sprang a leak!"

"Huh?"

"It's been ages since we had such an extreme cold snap. The pipes froze, then burst, and now the whole ground floor is soaked." Jiggling from foot to foot, she bit her lip. "I really need this client. What am I gonna do?"

Yikes. Trappers Cove was long on charm, but short on swanky accommodations. Not likely someone used to luxury would be satisfied with a cramped B and B, a tiny cottage, or a faded seaside motel. Scowling in concentration, Annie tapped her lips, then brightened. "Didn't you say the castle is available?"

Cheryl crinkled her nose. "Sort of. The renovations aren't quite done, and the owner's not sure if she wants to rent it or sell it."

Annie squeezed her friend's shoulders. "Call the owner and leave the rest to me—I've worked with his type before. They love anything with snooty cred, and how many can boast a holiday spent in their own private castle?"

Pasting on a salesy smile, she glided between racks and shelves toward the toy section where Michael clutched a rubbery action figure, his handsome face wreathed in delight.

"Stretch Armstrong! I always wanted one for Christmas, but my parents said it was tacky." He gave the superhero's limbs a tug.

Annie's eyes prickled at the image of Michael as a sweet little boy, disappointed at Christmastime by parents who refused his simple wish.

The words leapt from her lips faster than thought. "It's yours. A Christmas gift from me to you."

"Oh no, I couldn't." His sad sigh twanged her heartstrings as he replaced it on the self.

She seized his hand and pressed the toy into his palm. "I insist."

For a long moment, their eyes locked and held. Her pulse thrummed in her ears. Michael's mouth opened, then closed.

"That's—" With a husky chuckle, he clutched the action figure to his heart. "Very kind. Thank you, Annie."

Talk about tummy flutters. Her middle jiggled and glowed. No doubt she looked like a complete goof, but she couldn't help grinning up at him. "It's a sign. You were meant to come to Trappers Cove. You're going to have a wonderful Christmas here."

His smile sagged. "Honestly, I'm not a Christmassy kind of guy. I came here to escape all the holiday pressure."

And if she didn't convince him to rent the castle, he'd escape right back to where he came from.

"I get it. You want a nice, peaceful retreat. Somewhere comfortable with a beautiful view, a big fireplace, and a bottle of fine—let me guess—Scotch?"

"Bourbon, actually. In fact," He dug his toe into the carpet—"Once I'm settled into my rental, maybe you could share one with me? I hear it's got a firepit on the deck overlooking the beach."

Hoo boy. Cocktails with Mr. Too-Handsome-for-my-own-good?

She sucked in a breath. "Ah, well, as tempting as that sounds, I'm afraid there's a problem with your rental."

His head tilted. "Problem?"

"Of a plumbing nature."

Groaning, he rubbed the bump on his nose. "Just my luck. That's what I get for being spontaneous."

Annie gripped his arm—his solid, warm, muscly arm. "Hold on, Cheryl has an alternative for you—a very luxurious alternative with an even better view, right, Cher?"

Phone to her ear, Cheryl flashed a thumbs up.

Blinking rapidly, Michael gazed at Annie's hand. "I'm listening."

She released him and clasped her hands behind her back to keep them, and herself, out of trouble. "You remember the castle up on Baron's Bluff?"

"Sure, we used to party there as teens." His brows scrunched together. "No way am I staying in that spooky old relic."

"It's not spooky anymore. In fact, it's had a total facelift. Right, Cher?"

Trotting over to join them, Cheryl pulled a tablet from her copious shoulder bag and flipped through a series of photos. "The fireplaces are magnificent. There's one in the primary bedroom, plus a huge, jetted tub, a modern gourmet kitchen, a wet bar, high tech TVs, new parquet floor in the ballroom..."

Michael scoffed. "What am I going to do with a ballroom?"

"Roller skate?" Annie suggested. "Work out? Invite a few hundred of your closest friends?"

Groaning dramatically, he swiped a hand down his face. "I told you, I came to Trappers Cove for a peaceful, solo vacation."

Damn it, he was slipping away.

Cheryl's face froze in a combination of bug-eyed alarm and desperation. Her friend needed this sale, and Annie owed her for a thousand kindnesses, big and small. What would it take to close the deal?

She arched an eyebrow. "Aren't you curious? I sure as hell am. And if you hate it, you've lost, what, an hour? Cheryl can find you something else like that." She snapped her fingers. "Right, Cher?"

Cheryl drew a finger across her throat.

Okay, so she was stretching the truth a little, but after all, this was a business negotiation.

Michael grunted, an oddly sexy sound. He paced away, then back. Then away again. Finally, he pushed a hank of hair off his forehead. "All right. What the hell. It might be amusing."

Beaming, Cheryl bounced on her toes. "Give me a few minutes. Want to wait in my office?"

He glanced toward the window. "I'd rather stretch my legs after the long drive. See you in half an hour or so."

While Cheryl tapped her phone, Michael paid for his peacoat and tucked Stretch Armstrong into his pocket. Before leaving, he paused, his hand a millimeter from Annie's on the counter. His warmth seeped through the sliver of air between them.

"It was a pleasure to meet you, Annie. And thanks again for the superhero. I'll need his help with—well, boring work stuff. I hope to see you again soon."

Throwing caution and common sense to the wind, she gave his fingers a squeeze. "You're very welcome. And I may take you up on that offer of a bourbon."

"Excellent." Grinning, he backed into a rack of Hawaiian shirts, nearly toppling an artificial tree hung with novelty socks before pivoting and ambling out the door.

As soon as he disappeared from sight, Cheryl clutched Annie's arm. "You've got to come with us."

"Me? Why?"

"Because he *likes* you. And if I can pull off this rental, my commission will keep the lights on this winter. Besides, you could sell snow to Alaskans. Help me out, pleeeease?"

Annie heaved a sigh. "Of course I'll help."

"You're my Christmas angel!" Cheryl pecked her cheek, then dashed out the door.

For a long moment, Annie chewed her lip. Figures—the moment she swore off meaningless hookups, a walking, talking temptation strolled into her shop.

Maybe just one more fling? A little self-indulgent holiday joy?

He'd probably be an excellent kisser, a great conversationalist, and amazing in bed—and then he'd leave, and she'd feel twice as lousy.

Nope, nope, nope. She pulled a feather duster from beneath the counter and attacked a shelf of tchotchkes.

This Christmas would be tough enough without getting her hopes up.

Hands off the billionaire.

Chapter Four

♥

With visions of Annie Scott dancing in his head, Michael strolled up Main Street, hands stuffed in the toasty pockets of his new pea coat. Pausing beneath an old-fashioned lamppost, he gazed up at the strings of twinkle lights crisscrossing the street. Bright against the approaching dusk, they swayed in the icy sea breeze like tiny angels boogying to the Christmas music that blared from hidden loudspeakers.

Funny, these hokey holiday tunes didn't grate on his nerves like they did in downtown Bellevue. In fact, his Christmas allergy seemed to have subsided. Weird.

Back home, sleek high rises and swanky storefronts gleamed with perfectly coordinated, tasteful décor—metallic, sophisticated, cold. But this little town was a riot of glitzy, goofy holiday chaos. He sucked in a deep breath, teasing out the layered scents—candied almonds, petrichor, fir branches, and ocean. His satisfied sigh formed a puffy cloud.

"Fuckin' perfect," he declared to no one in particular as he ambled down the sidewalk past shops and businesses, each with its own quirky take on the holiday—paper snowflakes in Cassie's Coastal Café, a gingerbread village in the bakery window, and in the snow-flocked window of Gelateria Paradiso, a giant upside-down ice cream cone hung with tinsel garlands and glass ornaments.

His grin widened at the memory of all the frozen treats he and his sister Violet gobbled in that very shop during their long-ago summer visits. He should tell her he was spending the holiday here. Perhaps she'd stop by on her way to wherever the hell she was spending this Christmas. You never knew with Violet.

Of course, that would defeat the purpose of a solo retreat from the holiday madness. He needed to solidify his own thoughts before braving his baby sister's barrage of opinions and advice.

Baby sister, hah! What was she now, forty-seven? Forty-eight? How had they gotten so damn old?

He turned toward the north end of Main Street and collided with a sharp, bony shoulder.

"Oops, sorry." The lanky young man slung his arm around his pink-cheeked girlfriend and tugged her out of Michael's path.

"My fault entirely." Michael nodded to them both. Cute couple. Married? Engaged? Must be nice to have a sweetheart at Christmastime.

Of course, he technically did have someone—sort of. Right now, Crystal would be squeezing her yoga-toned body into a sleek cocktail dress and heading out to the arts council gala he was playing hooky from. Try as he might, he couldn't summon up the tiniest sliver of guilt for leaving her to face that yawn fest alone.

Who was he kidding? She wouldn't be alone. And why should she be? It's not like they had made any promises. Each found the other's company pleasant, and their connections useful. How sad that a relationship of ten months boiled down to convenience.

As if drawn by a magnet, his gaze flicked back to Annie's shop, its display window filled with mannequins dressed for the holiday, heaps of gift boxes at their feet. And there it was—a keen zing of guilt, wrapped up in an ache of longing. Because damn if he didn't want the saucy, sexy shopkeeper far too much.

Only an hour into their acquaintance and thoughts of Annie flooded his chest with fizzy warmth. The lady was something else, all right. Funny, with an edge of snark she cushioned with kindness. Her witty clapbacks made him yearn to delve deeper, get to know the woman beneath the old-fashioned clothes and the smile that dared him to drop the bullshit and give her...

"What do you want, Ms. Annie?" he muttered. "A little company? A date for New Year's Eve? Someone to tie up with a feather boa?"

He'd gladly volunteer for any of those roles—if he could manage to keep his new custom hiking shoes out of his mouth. Insulting a woman's livelihood wasn't exactly the smartest come-on.

But what a stunner. Her direct gaze and brilliant smile knocked him sideways and scattered his thoughts like... Oh, how did that old poem go? Dry leaves scattered before a wild... something? And that smoky alto voice—wow. Her laugh could turn a man's bones to jelly.

Annie's natural beauty contrasted sharply with the women in his social circle, with their squeaky-tight faces and gym-toned bodies. Silver threads shone in her amber hair, and deep smile lines fanned from the corners of her startling blue eyes—pale irises ringed with indigo. Her softening jawline pinned her at around his age, but the way she swayed that sweetly rounded rump between the racks and shelves—mmm, mmm. This lady crackled with spirit and sass.

He addressed his reflection in the bank window. "Look at you, all wobbly kneed because a pretty woman gave you a little attention. And a toy."

Chuckling, he fingered the rubbery action figure in his pocket. "What do you say, Stretch? Should we ask her out? Where does one even take a lady in this tiny town?"

The plastic superhero glowered beneath painted-on brows.

"Ugh, you're right. A holiday fling is not on my agenda." Annie deserved a man's full attention, and right now, he couldn't offer her that, not with his firm's future dangling by a thread.

He rolled his shoulders, shook his head, and set off at a brisk pace toward the far end of Main Street. Already, the bracing cold had numbed the tip of his nose. A little exercise and deep breathing would disperse these pointless, mopey musings.

Even crowded with shoppers, Trappers Cove felt wide-open, full of possibility. Easier to breathe here without towering high-rises to hem him in. And soon he was smiling again as each storefront triggered another happy memory: trailing Uncle Arnie and Aunt Ruby on their daily errands, his patience rewarded with crumbly fudge, salt-water taffy, corn dogs, shaved ice, games of Skee-Ball, rides on the bumper cars, or—his favorite—a round of mini golf. What a thrill to make a hole in one right into the plaster dragon's mouth.

"Oh ho, Sir Michael." Uncle Arnie had clapped his big, work-roughened hand on Michael's skinny shoulder. "This is a deed for the ages. Your name will go down in history, Vanquisher of Dragons."

How his life had changed. This current batch of profit-hungry dragons would be a helluva lot harder to vanquish.

He paused to examine the artwork in a gallery window—mostly seascapes, whimsical mermaids, and driftwood sculptures. Mother would like that abstract piece. He'd come back tomorrow, once he was settled in, and buy it for her—a peace offering for missing her favorite charity party.

He stopped to check out the window of Crazy Gus's Souvenir Planet, home of "the best fudge in the universe," whose display of bug-eyed aliens in Santa hats drew a laugh.

The urge to buy one nudged him toward the door—but who would he give it to? Neither he nor Violet ever had children, and his friends' and colleagues' kids were grown. Perhaps Nancy's grandkids?

Again, he fiddled with the toy in his pocket. "Funny how one moment can send your life on a different course, eh, Stretch?"

It was on an icy night like this, right before Christmas thirty years ago, when his fiancée broke up with him, their love worn to brittle thinness by his workaholic ways. Broken by her tears, by the bitter truth of her words, he threw himself into work all the harder, and never looked back.

If he'd fallen to his knees, begged her for another chance, sworn to change, would he be walking down this street now with his own kids? Or even—*gulp*—grandkids? Bouncy little squirts entranced by the lights and smells and sounds of Christmas.

He pushed himself forward in a vain attempt to outrun the 'what ifs'. Up ahead, a squat, brick-fronted shop glowed with bright colors.

"Madame Zora's Psychic Emporium." Violet would love this window display. Santa hat on a crystal skull, shiny red and green bows on Celtic daggers, Tibetan singing bowls in a nest of tinsel, incense sticks peeking out of Christmas stockings.

God, he missed her. They texted back and forth and spoke on the phone every month or so, but how long since they'd met face to face? Six months? Longer?

A movement inside the shop caught his eye. A short, sixty-something woman in a colorful caftan beckoned, her round face wreathed in a welcoming smile.

"Me?" He pointed to his chest.

She tossed her turban-wrapped head and laughed, then beckoned again.

He really should get back to the rental agent's office, but something about the friendly hippie mama pulled him through her door.

Immediately, the color-drenched, incense-scented jumble of woo-woo tchotchkes overwhelmed his senses. Wicker shelves teemed with crystals, candles, and figurines from dragons to Buddhas to fairies. Vaguely Middle Eastern music warbled from hidden speakers.

"Here you go, my darling." The woman pressed a steaming paper cup into his icy hands. "Spiced tea. Warm you right up."

"Er—thank you." He sniffed the rich scent and took a sip. "Delicious"

"Madame Zora, at your service." She executed a deep curtsey. "Now, tell me, what are you searching for?"

What an odd way to greet a customer. "Actually, I'm just passing the time while my rental agent finds me a place to stay."

She nodded sagely. "Shame about the leak at the Randall house. Hard to find plumbers over the holidays."

He nearly sprayed her with tea. "You really are a psychic, aren't you?"

Her laughter tinkled like wind chimes. "It's a small town, hon. We don't get a lot of tourists this time of year. And Cheryl's in my Thursday poker group. She was thrilled to land a—how did she describe you? Ah yes—a Seattle finance tycoon."

"Tycoon?" He scoffed. Though quite comfortable, he was hardly a Gates or a Bezos. And most of his capital was tied up in his Angel Investing. Then again, he might be the richest guy in Trappers Cove. Unlike other beach towns with big, modern high rises and luxury hotels, this little town had a decidedly working-class vibe. He'd hoped his outdoorsy gear would help him blend in better.

Zora tapped his lapel. "I see you've already been to Annie's shop. Warmed you right up, didn't she?"

Heat flooded his face, but the old gal turned away with an airy wave of her be-ringed hand.

"Look around, darling. See what calls to you."

While he sipped his tea, he browsed the book section—mostly volumes of divination, from runes to palmistry to tarot and astrology. Not really his bag. Maybe a book about meditation? A bright yellow volume caught his eye: *The Courage to Change*, by Xander Featherstone. He checked the back cover. "*New York Times* Bestseller. Hmm."

Well, why not? After all, that's why he fled to the coast—to find clarity. Maybe this volume would lend him inspiration. He took it to the register.

"Excellent choice." Zora rang up his purchase, tucked a receipt between the pages, then placed a small, polished stone in his palm—bright purple with veins of white like swirling eddies.

"On the house. Charoite, also known as the soul stone. Good for reconnecting to your higher self. Helps declutter your thoughts and find the right path."

The stone felt smooth beneath his thumb, pleasant and somehow comforting.

"Thank you. Truly, that's very thoughtful of you."

A wide grin bunched the woman's tawny, freckled cheeks. "My pleasure."

In the doorway, he turned back. "Say, what's a good stone for forging new connections?"

She arched an eyebrow. "Like... romance?"

Again, Annie's smile flashed through his mind like a shooting star.

He chuckled down at his shoes. "Let's start with friendship."

"I've got just the thing." She bustled away and returned with a shallow basket of royal blue stones as bright as Annie's eyes. "Lapis lazuli. A powerful stone that bonds relationships and helps people express their feelings." She stirred the gleaming stones with her fingertip. "Go ahead, darling. Pick the one that feels right."

He ran his fingertips over the gleaming stones, lingering over one shaped like a heart.

Don't be ridiculous. You've just met the woman. She'll think you're some kind of creeper.

He selected a smooth oval that fit nicely into his palm. "This one, I think." He paid, thanked Madame Zora, and slipped the book into his jacket. As he slid the two stones into his pocket, his phone vibrated.

A text from Cheryl, the rental agent. **We're ready for you.**

Blinking, he looked from the stones to his phone screen. A sign?

He wrapped up tight against the biting cold and hurried back to Annie's shop.

With an impatient tug, Cheryl straightened Annie's silk scarf. "I can't believe this guy just fell out of the sky and landed in our laps." Pursing her hot-pink lips, she plucked a rhinestone brooch from the display. "He's polite, good-looking, rich, and he lit up like a Christmas tree every time you opened your mouth. If you don't snatch him up, I will never forgive you."

Annie pried the brooch from her friend's bossy fingers. "Don't you dare poke a hole in my vintage Hermes. And why don't you snatch him up if you're such a fan?"

"And give up Bob? Not on your life. He's sweet, devoted, sexy, and lives two hours away, so we don't have to deal with each other's day-to-day bullshit. For gals our age, it doesn't get better than that." She pursed her lips. "But seriously, a little holiday romance would do you a world of good. And who knows? Mr. Fancy Pants could be your Bob."

Annie gave a snort. "Right. Like he's going to zip down from Bellevue every time I want a dinner date. Besides, guys like Michael don't go out with women their own age."

"When did our upbeat Annie get so jaded?" Cheryl grasped her shoulders. "Seriously, I'm worried about you. You're usually leading the charge into holiday cheer. But now—you seem so blah."

Annie shrugged. "Guess I'm just not feeling it this year."

Cheryl tapped her lips. "I know what you need. A younger man. That's the ticket."

Annie held her palm up to her friend's interfering face. "Guys my own age are difficult enough. I'm looking for a partner, not a puppy."

Cheryl flashed a grin of triumph. "Aha! She finally admits it."

Annie smacked her forehead.

"You're tired of booty calls. You're looking for a special someone." More lip tapping. "Maybe an older guy?"

"Old guys can't keep up with my energy."

Cheryl flushed and squawked.

Oops!

"Your Bob is an exception, of course. He's a treasure." At least ten years older than Cheryl, he seemed pretty spritely and definitely besotted.

Cheryl leaned closer to the mirror and fluffed her hair. "You know what they say about snow on the roof and fire in the pants."

"Is that really what they say?"

Cheryl shrugged. "Maybe I got lucky. But honestly, Annie, you deserve better than those so-called friends who roll into town for a quick hook up. They're only using you."

Annie stiffened. "Who's to say I'm not using them?"

If only her insistent libido would let her be. If she didn't crave intimate human touch, she could get off this merry-go-round of casual partners with whom she had very little in common besides loneliness.

"Look, Cher, I love you, and I know you're trying to help, but I'm not shopping for a boyfriend. I've had enough heartbreak for one lifetime."

Cheryl gave her arm a soft squeeze. "I wish you'd let me track down your ex-husband and kick his cowardly ass."

"That's in the past. Let it go. I have." Unwilling to layer another coat of regret on an already dreary holiday season, she forced a smile. "I've got a dozen audiobooks to read over the holidays, a full wine cabinet, and a drawer full of battery-operated boyfriends."

A woman in the next aisle snort-laughed. "Amen, sister."

Cheryl clucked her tongue and tugged Annie behind a wicker screen draped with scarves. "Darling, you're hurting. You're lonely. And you refuse to do anything about it. Why?"

Annie's face heated. Her jaw tensed. But what was the point of having a best friend if she couldn't be honest with her?

"Because, at my age, the chances of finding someone like your Bob are too tiny to measure. You'd need an electron microscope to calculate the odds."

"Huh?" Cheryl shook her head. "Listen, Ms. Mixed Metaphors, I'm going to confess something I should've told you long ago."

Annie blinked in surprise. She and Cheryl had been tight for twenty years. She thought they had no secrets. God knows she'd confessed every ugly bit of her past.

"Go ahead."

"My Bob? I met him through"—she lowered her voice to a whisper—"an online dating service."

"I thought you met him at a winetasting thing."

Cheryl heaved a noisy sigh. "I met him on OlderButBetter dot com. We chatted online for a few months before we finally met face to face—at that winetasting thing."

Annie socked her friend's arm. "Why didn't you tell me?"

"I was embarrassed. Looking for love online felt kind of icky—like I was desperate, you know?" She laced her fingers through Annie's and squeezed. "But hon, that idea was just foolish. I took the leap and found the perfect guy. And look at you. You're gorgeous, talented, funny, creative. There are tons of quality men out there searching for someone just. Like. You." She poked Annie's chest with each word. "So I dare you. I double—no, I triple dog dare you." She pulled an envelope from her jacket pocket and waved it in Annie's face.

She flinched backward. "What's this?"

"My Christmas gift to you. A year's subscription to OlderButBetter dot com. I'll help you set up your profile." She grasped Annie's shoulders and squeezed hard. "Be brave, Annie. Go on some dates. You're too young to give up on love."

"Young?" Annie snorted. "I'm—"

"We're the same age, girlfriend." She leveled a stern glare at Annie. "And you're doing this."

Online dating? How embarrassing. Might as well write it across the sky—*Annie Scott is too old and pathetic to find a boyfriend.* But if it worked for Cheryl, who was disgustingly, blissfully in love, maybe it could work for her too? Maybe she could find something more satisfying than a string of short-term visitors looking for a quick lay and a quicker departure.

She heaved a mighty sigh. "Fine. But after the holidays."

A wide grin lit her friend's face. "After Christmas. I'll bet you fifty bucks we find you a date for New Year's Eve."

The doorway bell tinkled.

Annie wriggled free from Cheryl's grip. "And now, if you're done harassing me, I've got customers to tend to."

"You'll be thanking me soon."

Annie rolled her eyes hard enough to inspect the inside of her skull, then turned to greet the newcomers—Michael again, holding the door for her part-time assistant who'd answered a last minute summons to watch the shop.

Teresita glowed in full holiday regalia, her cloud of curls died bright auburn and sparkling with jeweled clips. Glittery Christmas trees dangled from her ears, and a prize-winning ugly Christmas sweater stretched tight over her broad bosom. Rubbing her hands together, the tiny terror marched to the register and gave the two women a wicked smile. "Get a load of Mr. Hunkalicious," she said in a stage whisper loud enough for the whole shop to hear.

Hunkalicious indeed—cheekbones ruddy from the wind, dark hair a little mussed, face alight with boyish joy despite the deep crinkles around his eyes and mouth.

Annie reached for her coat. "Thanks for coming in, Teresita. I'm helping Cheryl with a rental client. Should be back in an hour."

Her assistant's teasing grin twinkled. "Take your time, doll."

"How was your walk?" Annie asked Michael. "Does the old town look the same?"

"It does indeed, though this cold is kind of astonishing. Glad I let a pretty lady talk me into buying this coat." As he unbuttoned the peacoat, a paperback tumbled to the floor.

Annie stooped to retrieve it. "*The Courage to Change.* Hey, I'm reading that too. Very inspiring."

The corners of his lips lifted, and so did her pulse.

"Good to hear. I usually read business books, but the cover caught my eye." He pulled two colorful stones from his pocket. "Of course, you can't leave a hippie shop without a crystal or two."

"Beautiful. And you're right—I always leave Zora's shop with something. May I?" She held the purple stone to the light. "Amazing colors."

"I've forgotten the name already. Supposed to help with making decisions. And this one is for you." The dark blue stone he set in her palm still held his body heat. "A little Christmas present for the blue-eyed lady who gave me a superhero."

For a moment, she stood mute, gawking first at the indigo stone, then at Michael's crooked smile. "What a sweet gift. Thank you."

His thick lashes lowered. "My pleasure," he murmured in a deep, rumbly voice that turned her knees to jelly.

He inclined his head toward Cheryl, who waited discreetly by the doorway. "To be honest, spending Christmas alone in a castle isn't what I had in mind. I just wanted a comfortable place to relax, and read, and think."

Damn it, he was going to back out, which meant no big holiday bonus for Cheryl. She couldn't let her friend down, and if she was a hundred percent honest with herself, she hated the thought of watching his taillights heading back to Bellevue.

Sidling closer, she lowered her voice. "Forgive me for prying, but you seem troubled. Am I right?"

He gave a sexy grunt. "You could say that. I've got a big decision to make."

"So do I, as it turns out. My friend over there wants me to take a big chance, and I'm not sure I'm making the right choice." She laid her hand on his forearm. "But here's what I do know. When I get all tied up in knots, there's nothing to get me untied like a little fun."

A flash of interest sparkled in the sudden widening of his eyes, the flicker of a curious smile. She'd hooked him. Now to reel him in. For his own good, of course. Because Christmas alone in a penthouse? How depressing.

She waggled her eyebrows. "And what could be more fun than your very own castle?"

From beneath lowered brows, he regarded her as if she were trying to sell him a big, steaming load of crap. Which she totally wasn't. Christmas in Trappers Cove was exactly what he needed, damn it. But how to convince him?

Of course—guys like him were competitive. Appeal to his ego.

She fingered his lapel. "In fact, I challenge you to a race. Let's slide across that ballroom floor in our socks and see who goes the farthest."

His grin unfurled like some glorious blossom—and there he was again, that repressed little boy who just needed the chance to let loose and play.

He stuck out his hand. "You're on. And, for the record, I am going to trounce you with my superior sock sliding skills."

"Cocky, aren't you?" She took his hand, expecting a firm, busi-nesslike grip, but his grasp was a gentle caress, and the way his thumb rubbed circles on the back of her hand sent shivers of pleasure dancing up her arm and down her spine.

Yowza! Flirting with Michael was playing with fire. If she wasn't careful, she risked making a ginormous a fool of herself.

He held her gaze for a long, hot, electric moment, then turned to Cheryl. "All right, let's go see a castle."

Chapter Five

♥

Michael winced as another piece of gravel pinged off his Jeep's windshield. Thank God he hadn't brought the Tesla.

Fun, Annie had promised, but that's not how he'd describe this bone-jarring drive up to the castle. Luxurious accommodations, she'd promised, but he remembered the place as a spooky, rotting hull.

He flicked on his wipers to clear away the sleet. As they rounded a bend in the rutted road, he glimpsed the churning sea far below, now dark gray in the gathering twilight. Hardly a good omen. Only the playful challenge in Annie's smile made him determined to see this visit through. After all, if the lodgings proved too dismal, nothing prevented him from heading for home. Chalk it up to bad luck and stupid impulsivity.

Then again, trusting his gut had seldom steered him wrong. Thanks to his knack for spotting diamonds in the rough, he had the financial freedom to spend his holiday where he damn well pleased. And right now, his instinct urged him to take Annie's dare.

Instinct or infatuation? He'd thought himself too old and jaded for the giddy rush he felt in her presence. Her direct gaze and gentle teasing made him want to play along, and the guardedness behind her sass only sharpened his desire to delve deeper.

The rental agent's SUV rounded a corner and passed through a wrought-iron gate straight out of a gothic movie. He followed, gravel crunching under his tires as the castle loomed into view. Up close, it resembled a hastily constructed set piece from a B movie.

He parked in the circular driveway, climbed out, and surveyed the grounds. The burned-out shell he remembered from childhood summers had been sand-blasted clean-ish, revealing a gray stone exterior that brought to mind a Lego castle with architectural elements stuck together willy-nilly. A three-story crenellated tower loomed over the cliff, while mismatched, turreted towers faced land, topped with tattered red and green flags that snapped in the stiff wind.

Pale, wintery sunlight reflected on tall, gothic-arched windows on the ground floor, Tudor style windows with crisscrossed casements above, and circular roof windows like creepy eyeballs staring out to sea. Heavy timbers supported a Spanish tiled roof over the portico.

The architect must've been drunk.

The weed-choked driveway curved around a muddy lawn and a seashell-encrusted fountain with all the grace of a kindergartener's art project.

Behind the castle, a low, blocky brick building hunkered, still boarded up but scrubbed clean of the graffiti he and Violet had contributed way back when.

Gravel crunching under their boots, the two women joined him.

Cheryl planted her hands on her hips. "Now, this is what I call character." She elbowed Annie. "Right?"

"Right, character." Flashing a snarky sideways grin, she dug her toe into the gravel and squashed a weed.

Cheryl continued her sales pitch. "The gardens are still a work in progress, of course, but come springtime they'll be magnificent." She patted one of the cement urns lining the drive, each with an overgrown topiary shrub trimmed like... birds? Fish? Hard to tell, but each sport-ed a red ribbon around its neck. Or was that its tail?

"A green Christmas goblin," Annie muttered.

He gestured toward the sprawling outbuilding. "Local kids told us this place used to be a prison."

"I heard it was an orphanage. Lots of ghost stories."

Cheryl dismissed their musings with a cluck of her tongue. "Over the years, the property has served as a school, a hospital, and a home for unwed mothers. There's been no credible evidence of ghosts." She climbed the stone stairs to the entrance, still reading from her tablet. "This home was built in 1832 by George Arthur Baron, an eccentric Scotsman who made his fortune in the fur trade."

She inserted a key into the elaborate brass lock and, grunting, twisted the handle back and forth. "Baron brought in all kinds of visitors—minor European royalty, opera singers, railroad tycoons. He was famous for his parties." Despite her efforts, the enormous arched door didn't budge.

"Let me." Michael put his shoulder to the door and shoved. It finally scraped open with an ominous creak.

Cheryl nodded her thanks and tapped her tablet. "I'll message the owner about that."

Rubbing her arms through her coat, Annie stepped inside. "Did you ever come up here?" she asked him.

"Once, on a dare. I must've been twelve or so. We pried the plywood off that window and made it as far as the parlor when a bat flew out of the fireplace and zoomed right over our heads." He chuckled at the memory. "I've never run so fast."

Cheryl beckoned them deeper into the foyer. "I think you'll like what the current owner has done with the place."

He inhaled the sharp scent of fresh paint. Elaborately carved oak paneling lined the entry walls and ceiling, and pale stone tiles covered the floor. Heraldic banners hung beside brass wall sconces with light-bulbs that flickered like candles. "Reminds me of those places where you eat chicken with your hands and watch a jousting tournament."

Annie looped her arm through his. "It is rather over the top, but so what? You can pretend all your servants have been turned into furniture." She tugged him through an arched doorway and pointed to an elaborate brass and oak bar. "Look, there's your butler. Martinis, please, Jeeves. Vodka, with twist of lemon."

Cheryl followed, eyes on her tablet. "The castle boasts a cozy front parlor, a library, and formal living and dining rooms. The conservatory is still under construction, but the kitchen's been refurbished with..."

Annie flashed a conspiratorial grin and towed him through a series of dark, wood-paneled rooms, past a huge stone fireplace painted with medieval style lions and dragons, past ornate, uncomfortable-looking sofas and throne-like armchairs. "Look, right there would be the perfect spot for your Christmas tree."

Michael shook his head. "No tree."

Annie's smile slipped. "Sorry—I shouldn't assume. Are you Jewish?"

"Technically, I'm Episcopalian. But I came to Trappers Cove to escape all that phony fa la la."

Her lips compressed into a thin line. "What a shame."

The knowledge that he'd disappointed her sat in his gut like a cold, pointy rock. Interesting.

Still babbling about architecture, Cheryl caught up with them before he had the chance to explore that thought further.

Annie's grin seemed forced, but she shook off the awkward moment and grabbed his sleeve. "Come on. I've never seen a real-life ballroom."

"This way." Cheryl led them down the hallway, opened a tall set of double doors, and they all filed into darkness, groping the walls for a light switch. No luck until Michael stumbled upon a silk rope and tugged. Overhead, a row of crystal chandeliers flickered to life, and one lightbulb fizzled with a loud pop.

"Wow." Annie clapped her hands to her mouth.

Her childlike wonder filled his chest with warm, fuzzy feelings. Most people in his social circle were far too jaded to be impressed by what was basically a big empty room. Sure, the hardwood floor gleamed, and tufted velvet benches dotted the walls, but the chandeliers looked like they came from a big-box home improvement store, and cheap mirror tiles striped the wall opposite the tall, mullioned windows. Whoever designed this room had a small budget.

"Ready to lose, city boy?" Annie gripped his arm to steady herself while she unzipped her boots and kicked them aside, then wiggled her toes in thick, candy-striped woolen socks.

Chuckling, he glanced from her cute feet to her face, now lit with a devilish grin. "Oh, you were serious?"

"As a heart attack." She took an experimental run and slid several feet, arms pinwheeling. Her victory whoop rang out in the empty space. "Okay, let's see what you've got, tycoon."

Laughing despite himself, he toed off his shoes. "What are we wagering?"

Annie's grin widened. "If I win, you put up a Christmas tree. And no scrawny little shrub. We're talking a big, fat, glorious fir. With decorations. And you invite me and Cheryl over for a holiday libation to admire its beauty."

Laughing, Cheryl raised her palms. "Oh no, you two leave me out of it. I'm going to check the fuse box." She backed out through the door.

Though he'd most likely be trounced, Michael removed his shoes. "And if I win?"

She waggled her eyebrows. "Name your prize."

He rubbed his hands together. Might as well shoot the moon. "How about a date at Trappers Cove's finest restaurant? Let's see, would that be the café across from your shop? Or the brew pub at the end of Main Street?"

With a haughty sniff, she lifted her chin. "I'll have you know that Casa Francesca is very elegant. You'll even have to wear a jacket and tie." She crouched like a speed skater about to jet. "That is, if you win. Which you won't. Run to the first chandelier, then slide. On your mark, get set, go!" She sprinted forward, arms pumping, coat flapping, shapely legs flashing beneath her pleated wool skirt. When she slid, she let fly a musical laugh. And man, did he crave more reasons to hear that laugh again.

Jaw set, he tore after her, but when he reached the chandelier, his thin performance socks gripped the floor, and he barely achieved half the distance of Annie's expert glide.

Skirt flying, she pirouetted and pumped her fist in the air. "God, that feels marvelous." She poked out her lower lip in mock sympathy. "Aww, you hardly slid at all. Want to go again? Best two out of three?"

He raised his palms. "I know when I've been vanquished." He stepped back into his shoes and indulged in a good ogle as Annie bent to refasten her boots. "So, where does a person buy a Christmas tree in Trappers Cove?"

"Library parking lot."

"Ugh." He rolled his eyes. "Probably gonna get pine needles everywhere."

"Buck up, Ebenezer." Grinning, she trotted a few steps and slid to his side. "And when you invite me up to admire its evergreen beauty, I expect cookies, too. Try Garrett's bakery on Main Street. You won't be sorry."

"Demanding, aren't you?" So much for quiet alone time. Yet he didn't really mind a holiday To-Do list if it meant pleasing Annie.

Her brilliant blue eyes twinkled as she gave his arm a squeeze. "Speaking of libraries, let's go find the castle's. Maybe there's a hidden doorway behind a bookcase, with stairs down to a dungeon full of bones." She took his hand, her palm soft and satiny against his. "Would that be more to your liking, Mr. Scrooge?"

Before he could answer, she towed him out the door and down a hallway lined with garage-sale portraits.

"There's Uncle Zebadiah." She giggled. "See how his eyes follow you? Very creepy."

A wide grin stretched Michael's cheeks as he let her tug him along, her hand warm in his. When was the last time he did something this silly and pointless and *fun?* After less than a day in her presence, the weight of his looming decision lifted from his shoulders.

It didn't mean anything—how could it? They were from different worlds. Annie had her shit together, and he was adrift in a sea of indecision. But right now, her bossy, over-the-top Christmas spirit was exactly what he needed.

At the end of the hallway, she pushed open a door, dropped her grip, and executed a slow pivot, her jaw relaxed in wide-eyed wonder. "Oh my. This is... wow."

Amen. Forget the ballroom and the stuffy parlor. This was the best room in the house. Floor-to-ceiling bookcases lined the walls. In the corner, a by-God wheeled ladder fit for a cartoon princess. Okay, the Persian rug was fake, and the shelves mostly held mass-market faux leather volumes—but still, the delicious scent of books permeated the room. A stone fireplace took up one wall, and the leather-top desk would be the perfect place to noodle out his next steps. He pictured relaxing in one of the wingback chairs flanking the hearth, his feet up on a tufted ottoman—preferably with Annie beside him, smiling over the rim of her book.

A sudden break in the clouds beamed golden twilight through the mullioned windows, illuminating a cushioned, recessed reading nook.

As if hypnotized, Annie drifted to the window seat, toed off her boots and sank down with a cat's easy grace, tucking her feet beneath her. "I could spend hours here." Sunset's last rays ignited the gold and silver in her hair, burnishing it like a halo—and for a sweet, slow-motion moment, he forgot how to breathe.

She patted the cushion beside her. "Isn't this the most perfect reading spot you've ever seen? Look at the view."

Succumbing to her irresistible enthusiasm, he sat and twisted to peer down at the surf crashing into the rocky shoreline. Indeed, this would be an excellent place to contemplate his future, especially with Annie's warm thigh pressed against his.

But he had important decisions to make, and only eighteen days to figure out his plan of attack. Annie's presence was already a tempting distraction. His fingers itched to stroke the glowing blond waves that shifted over her shoulders. Forcing his gaze away, he plunged his hand into his pocket and rubbed the smooth, warm stone there. Smooth like her satin blouse, like the gleaming skin beneath...

She nudged him with her elbow, and he yanked his focus to her sharp, probing gaze. "So tell me, Michael. Why is a man who can afford to rent a castle spending the holidays alone in a kitschy beach town?"

Kind and sweet and mercilessly direct. She and Nancy must be related.

He sucked in a breath and straightened in his seat. "I, uh, have some big decisions to make. I needed to get away, clear my head of the holiday noise."

When she only stared, he gave a weak shrug. "I guess that doesn't make sense to someone like you."

Her eyes narrowed as she crossed her arms. "Someone like me? Who doesn't need to think?"

"No, no. That's not what I meant. It's just—" he swallowed against a sudden thickness in his throat. "—you love the holidays. And you seem like a happy person who knows who she is and what she wants."

She slumped in her seat. "You're making a lot of assumptions for someone who's only known me for a few hours." Her gaze drifted out to sea. "I have a good life here, but there are changes I would make if I could. I guess some things are beyond our control, no matter how many self-help books we read."

He nudged her shoulder with his. "If I believed that, I wouldn't be rich enough to rent a castle."

Annie's wry smile flattened. Her eyes narrowed. She pushed her feet into her boots and stalked to the fireplace, giving him her back.

With the sickening feeling that he'd just stepped into a big, steaming pile, he followed her. "Wow, that landed wrong. Guess my comedy skills need work."

Her only reply, a huff through her nose. Irritation radiated from her stiff posture, her tight jaw, and the white-knuckled fist she rested on the stone mantelpiece.

Unsure how to repair the mood, he raised a tentative hand to her shoulder and gently touched her, the barest whisper of contact. "Hey,

I'm sorry. I didn't mean to upset you. Can we pretend that didn't happen?"

Her shoulders fell on a sigh—not exactly relaxed, more like... defeated?

Eyeing him warily, she murmured. "To be honest, I've had some bad experiences with people at your income level."

"Okay. Maybe we could talk about that?"

She shook her head. "It's my problem, not yours."

Annie groaned. Leave it to Cheryl to breeze into the room just as she was fumbling for words to undo the sudden awkwardness.

"There you are. Oh my stars, isn't this library to die for?" Oblivious to the tension between them, she clasped her hands to her heart and beamed.

"Sure is." Annie flashed the world's phoniest smile. "Why don't you show Michael the rest of the house?"

Panic glinted in Cheryl's eyes. "Aren't you coming?"

Michael's fingertips brushed her own. "Annie, please." His dark brows furrowed, contrition written all over his too-damn-handsome face.

She knew she was being unfair, but she couldn't stop her reflexive revulsion at his not-so-humble brag. Did he think she'd be impressed by his wealth? That she was some kind of gold digger? How insulting.

And what an idiot she was, flirting with a clueless rich guy. Talk about different worlds—he might as well be from a different planet. They could never become friends, much less have a deeper connection. And now that she'd finally admitted her desire for a real relationship, spending time with Michael was a fool's errand, no matter how strong the spark between them.

He'd made it clear he'd come to Trappers Cove in search of solitude. Time to extricate herself before this got messy.

Lifting her chin, she smoothed the sharp edge from her voice. "I'll be along in a moment." When Cheryl gawked, she added, "Restroom."

Her friend's expression relaxed. Michael's didn't.

"Down the hall." Cheryl pointed. "We'll start with the kitchen, then the primary bedroom." She looped her arm through Michael's and led him down the hallway, chattering a mile a minute. Trudging after her, he kept his gaze on Annie until he bonked into a suit of armor, nearly knocking it off its stand.

She hurried into an ostentatious powder room, opened the tap, and thrust her hands under the faucet until the stinging cold brought her back to herself. After drying off and blotting her temples with the damp towel, she leaned on the marble sink and addressed her reflection in the gilt-framed mirror. "You're fine. Everything's fine. You just got carried away, Ms. Flirty-Pants. Michael is a nice man who needs a little boost. And let's be honest, so do you. No harm done."

So what if his clueless comment rasped her secret sore spot? That didn't make him a monster, just slightly imperfect, like everyone else.

After a spritz of cologne and a lipstick touch-up, her pissy mood dissipated. As long as she kept a level head, she'd be fine.

She found them upstairs, Cheryl's merry babble audible through an open doorway. "Currently, there are four furnished bedrooms on this floor, but this is the primary suite. Fabulous, isn't it?"

Michael's laughter rumbled, an annoyingly sexy sound that rattled Annie's newfound composure. Squaring her shoulders, she strode into the room.

"Holy shit." She clapped a hand to her mouth to stifle further indignities.

She'd never seen a bigger, showier bed. Massive spiral bedposts held up a fringed canopy, and a mountain of satin pillows in gold and burgundy smothered the velvet cover. Clearly, the designer was living out royal fantasies when they furnished this place. Fluffy synthetic fur rugs flanked the bed, and a monstrous wardrobe with carved curlicues and cherubs took up most of one wall.

Michael spun toward her with such a hopeful expression she couldn't help but return his smile. He moved to her side while Cheryl discretely turned her back to fiddle with the fireplace controls. A gas flame leapt to life.

"Truce?" he whispered.

She displayed her open palms. "I come in peace."

"Thank you." Chuckling, he pivoted to take in the scene. "This is really... something."

Annie nodded. "I'd expect to wake up to servants holding a chamber pot and my brocade dressing gown."

There it was again, that baritone laugh that warmed her right to her bones. "Don't forget your tea tray. What does the Lord of the Manor have for breakfast—kippers?"

"Eew." She pinched her nose.

And just like that, they slid back into easy banter—no sign of class warfare.

"Let's see the bathroom." Cheryl pushed open a tall oak door. "Oh my."

Annie hurried to her side, then exhaled a happy sigh at the sight of a huge, claw-footed tub surrounded by little gilt tables holding candles and cut-glass jars of bath salts. "I could spend hours in here, soaking in bubbles and reading romance books until my fingers get all pruney."

From the doorway, Michael emitted a funny choking sound. She turned to find his cheeks stained bright pink.

Cheryl elbowed her and gave a bug-eyed nod in Michael's direction. But no further prompting was needed.

Grinning, he rocked on his heels. "Guess I've found my Christmas home."

Cheryl squealed and trotted toward him, her arms spread wide for a hug. At his startled expression, she seized his hand instead and pumped it vigorously. "I'm so glad! You'll love Christmas in Trappers Cove."

Brow rumpled, he shot Annie a *help-me* glance. How could he know he'd just saved Cheryl's financial bacon?

She gently drew her friend away. "Cheryl's right. Christmas is a wonderful time here. I'm glad you're joining us."

"I'm glad too, Annie." His softy, dreamy smile spelled all kinds of trouble. "After I'm settled in, maybe I could take you out for coffee? You know, to say thanks."

Cheryl gave a little squeak and pinched Annie's arm. Hard.

"Sure. I'd like that," she told him, then glared at Cheryl, who responded with wide-eyed, phony innocence.

"Well, we'll leave you to it." Annie hooked her arm through Cheryl's and strode through the door and down the grand staircase, towing her friend along.

"Don't forget," Michael called after them. "I owe you a bourbon under the Christmas tree."

If Annie shivered as she stepped through the castle's door, it was on account of the icy ocean wind, and definitely not the prospect of cuddling beneath a sparkling Tannenbaum with a gorgeous gazillionaire.

"You lucky girl." Cheryl squeezed her arm and pecked her cheek.

As they started back toward town, Annie threw a last glance over her shoulder. There he stood, silhouetted in the doorway, one hand raised in farewell.

Just my luck, meeting Mr. Perfectly Impossible right before the loneliest Christmas of my life.

Chapter Six

♥

As the towering door scraped closed, loneliness closed in, cold and damp as coastal fog. Michael cranked up the parlor's gas fireplace, hoping the flames would dispel the ache left by Annie's departure.

What the hell happened? Had he imagined the crackling heat between them? Was all her teasing banter calculated to persuade him to sign the rental contract?

Okay, so his lame joke about being rich enough to rent the castle on a whim landed like a splat of seagull poop—but was that enough to extinguish the spark he'd been so sure was mutual?

"I've had some bad experiences with people at your income level." Must've been some damn shitty encounters, judging by her flat tone and sudden stiffness. And now he was paying the price.

Normally, he danced around the topic of his personal wealth because, once that news got out, the balance of conversation shifted. Every word became calculated. Again and again he'd watched a new acquaintance's eyes sheen with that telltale, predatory gleam, their smiles turn over-bright and brittle.

Not Annie. Instead of leaning in with wide-eyed pseudo-fascination, she backed away, shut down, frosted over. And the loss of her warm interest stung—not only his ego, but somewhere deep down where his wealth couldn't protect him.

Which was weird, because they'd just met. So what if a pretty woman disliked wealthy people? He'd never had any trouble finding attractive women who enjoyed his company.

But none of them had teasing, playful smiles that filled his veins with warm honey. None prodded him out of a funky mood like Annie did. And none had ever made him want to embrace the holiday season for her sake.

He raked his fingers through his hair. Must be his work worries that had him off-balance today. If he were in his right mind, he wouldn't be shivering in a big, empty, wannabe castle. He'd be watching the twinkling lights of Bellevue from his penthouse while he brewed a perfectly smooth coffee to clear his muddied thoughts.

Coffee. That's the ticket.

After toting his luggage to the gaudy bedroom and arranging his belongings, he wandered down to the kitchen. An inspection of the cabinets revealed new pots, pans, dishes, and gadgets galore, along with a cannister of ground coffee, an assortment of tea bags, and a tin of butter cookies. But no Chemex, no French press, not even a mocha pot—just an old-school Mr. Java.

While the coffeemaker burbled, he opened his tablet and keyed in the Wi-Fi password. Spotty and slow, but it would have to do. He poured himself a mug, doctored it with powdered creamer and plain white sugar, *double ugh,* and pulled up the financial news.

His phone shrilled in his pocket. Crystal's ringtone.

He ought to feel guilty about mooning over Annie when he had a perfectly comfortable arrangement with Crystal, not that they shared a deep emotional connection. It was an alliance of convenience for both of them—neither had any illusions on that front. But she was a good person. She deserved to be missed.

"Crystal, great to hear your voice. How was the Snow Ball?" Goofy name for a charity bash in the Seattle area, where it seldom snowed.

"Boring but necessary," she drawled. "We missed you."

"Sorry to leave you stranded like that."

"No worries. Malcolm was glad to be my plus one."

"Malcolm?"

"My new assistant. You met him at the Bemelmans' party. Cute kid. Lean and hungry."

Michael braced himself for a pang of jealousy, but none came. He admired Crystal—her sharp wit, her elegance, her impressive knowledge of their social web and where to shake it to draw in her desired prey.

"Listen," she said, her voice crisp and businesslike, "I've got two reasons for calling. First, I wanted to give you a heads-up."

Her serious tone tightened his gut. "About what?"

"Your parents were at the ball, of course, looking fabulous as always. Hard to believe they're both over eighty. Clarissa's gown was stunning. I'm afraid they didn't buy your excuse about not feeling well." She perfectly mimicked his mother's plummy tones. "It's not the Garwood way to neglect social obligations, especially when under fire."

He swiped a hand down his face. So the news was out—GRA Venture Capital was on the verge of radical mission creep, and the odds of reversing that were not in his favor.

"Yeah, Mother and Dad are all about appearances." Even at their advanced age, they still commanded tremendous respect and influence, thanks to skillful networking and strategic donations, a skill set that had become second nature for him as well. After all, he'd learned from the best.

Crystal chuckled. "You know how much our people love juicy gossip. I have no doubt you'll get your firm back on track. And don't worry, I assured Edward and Clarissa you'd be home in time for their New Year's Eve do. Your mother seemed particularly concerned about that."

Shit on toast. In his haste to flee Bellevue, he'd forgotten about that unfun event. Of course, his parents would expect their golden child to attend their annual impress-the-competition extravaganza, where connections were made and deals sealed. What would it be like to just celebrate the new year's arrival with a few friends, eating pizza and wearing jeans—or pajamas!

"Thanks for covering for me, Crys. What's your second talking point?"

She laughed. "You and I speak the same language, don't we?" Her tone softened. "But I'm afraid our merger has run its course, Michael. I'm bowing out."

He blinked in confusion. "You're...what now?"

"I've met someone. He's not from our world, but he's a wonderful guy, sweet and attentive. I want to explore that attraction and see where it leads us."

"Your assistant?"

She laughed again, a big, warm sound he'd never heard before. "No. A boy toy is the last thing I need. Actually, he's our age. Runs the little café on the ground floor of my building. We've been getting to know each other, and...I'm kind of smitten."

He sucked in a breath and let the news sink in, surprised to find himself a little misty—not because he was losing her, but because she'd found the real thing at last.

"Well then, I'm happy for you. You're a special lady, Crystal, and I've enjoyed our time together. I wish you and your café man all the best. Go find your happiness."

"I will. And I wish you the same, Michael. You're a wonderful guy. You deserve happiness."

And that's that. He set down his phone and gazed out the window toward the darkening horizon.

Now was a shitty time to handle his social obligations solo—and his job came with so damn many of them. If he showed up at his parents' party without a date, the vultures would close in, eager to match him up, and he just didn't have the energy to forge a new connection. Crystal would be hard to replace.

The hairs at his nape rose as a weird thought tickled the back of his brain. Would Annie consent to be his New Year's Eve date? Hard to imagine anyone as genuine and relaxed as her enjoying a networking event—because, let's face it, mere celebration was never the reason for his parents' parties. More like cultivating and repaying favors, shoring up their social standing, and harvesting gossip they could use to their advantage. Annie deserved better than to be thrown into that fray.

He heated his now-cooled coffee in the microwave and carried it and his tablet to the library Annie loved so much. Kicking off his shoes, he sat on the padded bench and gazed out at the rocky seascape—churning gray on gray, powerful waves crashing against immovable boulders.

She was right. This was an excellent thinking spot. He pulled his new worry stone from his pocket and turned it over and over in his hand.

"Okay, purple rock. Where do I go from here?"

He sipped his inferior, bitter coffee and grimaced. Eighteen days until the board meeting. They'd demand an answer that would affect not only himself, but all the start-ups he was backing, the company's future direction, two dozen employees, and his place in the Bellevue finance scene.

Option one: chuck it all. At only fifty-four, he wasn't ready to retire, though he could certainly afford to. What would he do with himself all day? His self-image came from contributing to something bigger than his own bank account. The idle, self-indulgent life wasn't for him.

And he loved financing the dreams of inventors, tech innovators, and small businesses with the potential to grow big and profitable. Choosing the right start-ups to back had built his personal wealth to the point where he could afford to work less—but as a founding member of the firm, he couldn't just run off and play on the beach.

He stared out the bay window, searching for answers and finding only wide-open sea.

Chapter Seven

♥

While the last Sunday customers browsed, Annie strolled through her shop, flicking a feather duster over knick-knacks while humming Christmas tunes. All day, she'd been trying to force a happy holiday mood, but thoughts of Michael intruded again and again—his wounded expression when she pushed him away, her clumsy attempt to explain the sudden change in temperature between them, the clanging alarms that warned her crushing on him would only set her up for another round of ego-squashing pain.

And yet, a stubborn, less intelligent part of her craved more of his company, his smile, his intense, heart-thumping gaze. Knowing he was so close and not reaching out was going to be torture—but necessary.

Meeting him at such a vulnerable moment was the kind of unfair cosmic screw-up that happens to everyone. But why did Fate choose this crappy Christmas to deliver a bad news pile-on?

First, her brother's change of plans, leaving her with no family Christmas to look forward to. Then realizing that casual hookups left her feeling unsatisfied and icky. So much for her self-image as an independent, sexually liberated woman. And now Michael...

She couldn't let this run of bad luck tip her into a full-blown midlife crisis. She was too strong for such foolishness.

She'd googled him over breakfast this morning. A venture capitalist specializing in tech startups, his personal net worth was listed in the two-digit billions. Without much effort, she found photo after photo of him flashing that panty-melting smile at posh parties and charity galas, always with a polished, chic woman on his arm.

How stupid was she, flirting with a billionaire? So what if his eyes seemed to twinkle with genuine interest? No doubt he'd honed that skill on his way to the top.

Best to write off their encounter as her good deed of the day—hooking her friend up with a wealthy client. Dusted and done. She'd probably never see him again. Especially after blurting out her dislike of rich people. Which was unfair. He'd never been anything but polite, charming, a good sport, and so freaking gorgeous a battalion of butterflies danced in her chest whenever he aimed that lethal smile her way.

No doubt about it—her picker was definitely broken. Time to focus on achievable goals.

Since no one needed her at the moment, she tucked her earbuds in and pressed *Play* on her audiobook. The narrator's silken voice purred, "The first step toward freedom is questioning the assumptions that shackle you. Take the time to delve into your beliefs. Don't let the lies you tell yourself limit your possibilities."

She pressed *Pause*.

Amen. I will try online dating. I will find a decent, kind, cute man who wants more than just sex. I will—

Behind her, a deep voice said, "Excuse me, ma'am?"

She pasted on her best retail smile, turned, and clapped a hand over her galloping heart.

There stood Michael, wrapped in the peacoat she'd sold him, melted sleet sparkling in his salt and pepper hair. He must've had a rough night too, judging by the slight bags under his eyes. A sexy scruff darkened his jaw.

"My goodness, look at you!" She peered closer. "Bloodshot eyes. Whiskers. Didn't you sleep well?"

"I did not. Noisy wind, spinning thoughts, and there's a seagull colony roosting below my bedroom window." He raked his fingers through his hair, mussing the dark waves.

Her hands itched to smooth them.

"This morning, I made three pots of coffee, but they all tasted like mud." He rubbed his cheek. "And I forgot to pack my razor. My first day in Trappers Cove is not starting well."

She clenched her hand to keep from stroking a finger along his jaw. "I like your scruff. Makes you look less like a suit model, more like a real person."

His eyes narrowed and his head drew back. "I'm not sure if that's an insult or a compliment."

"Sorry." Her cheeks heated. "I shouldn't be commenting on a stranger's appearance."

He leaned both elbows on the counter and lowered his voice to a sexy murmur. "Well now, I might have a few thoughts about your appearance as well."

She braced herself for a well-earned clapback. "Fire away."

One glossy eyebrow crept up. "I think you look like the perfect person to show me Trappers Cove."

"Um..." Her gaze skittered to the customers milling about the shop. "I have to work."

"Right. Of course. Sorry." He set a knit cap on the counter. "I'll take this please." A devilish grin lifted the corners of his plush, kissable lips. "And perhaps you could throw in some advice."

"Erm, I uh—advice?" Hard to form a cogent thought when he snuck up on her, adorably rumpled and sweetly charming. She ought to bell him like a cat, so she'd hear him coming and have time to gird her loins.

"I need a Christmas present for my sister, Violet. She's kind of Bohemian, and I figured—"

"Michael." She smoothed the squeak from her voice. "We close in ten minutes."

"Oh." His lips pursed in a sexy pout.

Quit looking at his mouth!

"Another time? The shop is less busy before lunch."

"Of course. Thoughtless of me. I'll come back tomorrow." He pulled a crisp twenty from his wallet. "By the way, there doesn't seem to be an Insta Shop service in Trappers Cove. How do you get things delivered?"

"What kinds of things?"

"You know, groceries, books, household stuff."

Spoiled little rich boy. She leaned on the counter and let the tiniest tinge of snark creep into her smile. "You see, we have this amazing app for finding pretty much everything you need. It's called Main Street."

The corners of his lips quirked up. "Touché. I don't suppose you know where I could find a proper coffee maker?"

"Define proper. Are we talking mocha pot? French press? Espresso machine?"

"Just a simple Chemex."

Of course, he'd be a coffee snob.

"Check the housewares department, over there behind the toys. You'll find filters at Trappers Market." Thanks to vacation renters who'd rather leave their kitchen gadgets behind than pack them up for the return trip, she stocked all sorts of cookware.

His voice brightened, raising her core temperature several degrees. "Annie's magic shop to the rescue." He stuffed the hat into his coat pocket and trotted off in search of his fancy coffee pot.

Annie flicked her feather duster over Roscoe, her ceramic panther. "Rich people have weird priorities, am I right?" She smacked the antique hotel bell beside the register and called out, "Ten minutes to closing, my darlings."

Customers lined up, exchanging news and friendly greetings as they waited for Annie to ring up their purchases. She couldn't help feeling a bit like Santa, knowing her carefully curated merchandise would appear under Christmas trees all over Trappers Cove. Mo was going to love that octopus ashtray for his stinky cigars, and Matteo would look dashing in that vintage tux jacket.

The last customer, however, was definitely not a local. And what a damned shame.

Grinning in triumph, Michael set his treasure on the counter. "You've saved me, Annie. I can't think clearly on crappy coffee. Speaking of which,"—his smile widened "—I believe you promised me a coffee date. Since you're closing, how about showing a spoiled, delivery-addicted stranger around Trappers Cove?"

Why did he have to be so damn cute and persuasive? Was that how he built his fortune—charming his way into people's wallets?

He raised his palms. "No pressure. Just coffee and a little stroll down Main Street. What do you say?"

She chewed her lip, searching for an excuse.

"You know,"—he leaned closer—"I started reading that book last night, *The Courage to Change.* The author makes a powerful case for trying new things. Thanks to you, I'm trying out a small-town Christmas, an area where I'm woefully unprepared. I really could use a guide." When she hesitated, he added, "Listen, you surprised the hell out of me yesterday. I'd like to talk about that. One coffee, and if you don't want to hear from me after that, I promise not to bother you anymore."

Should she trade her planned quiet evening for a stroll with a scruffy, flirtatious, under-caffeinated gazillionaire? After all, he was only in town for the holidays. Their banter was a harmless game, a chance to train up her skills for the real dates she'd undertake after Christmas, which was—*gulp*—just seven days away.

Rationalization, thy name is Annie.

"Tell you what, it's pretty late for coffee. How about a drink at the Salty Dog Saloon? It's on the far end of Main Street, and everything you'll need is between here and there." The brew pub was a few blocks from her house, so she could duck out quickly after one drink.

"Sounds great. Now, how much do I owe you for the Chemex? And do you perchance have a coffee grinder too?"

She cocked a hip. "Look deep enough in this shop and you'll find there's very little I don't have."

One corner of his mouth crept up, then the other. "Annie, I have no doubt you've got everything I need."

Ooh, that smile of his was dangerous.

Michael shifted from foot to foot while Annie closed down the register and gently shooed her last customers out the door, exchanging hugs and holiday wishes. He took advantage of the delay to drink in her musical laugh, graceful movements, and outfit—a mishmash of joyful, Christmassy chaos. Her puffed sleeve, curve-skimming red sweater probably dated from the eighties. Her rhinestone brooch reminded him of his grandmother, as did her tweed skirt, whereas her trim ankle boots looked like something off the set of *A Christmas Carol*. She slid into a military-style wool coat and snugged the belt tight around her waist, then popped a fuzzy red beanie over her cloud of silver and gold hair. "Still colder than a snowman's balls out there?"

He sputtered with laughter. "Yes, actually."

She wound a sparkly green scarf around her neck and fastened it with a jeweled candy cane brooch.

Funny how nothing she wore matched, yet it all somehow worked together. "Your outfit is, uh, very unique."

Eyes flashing, she drew up to her full height. "I dress to express myself and please myself, Michael. Is that a problem?"

Stepped in it again! He scrambled to repair the damage.

"Whoa, now. Apologies, Annie. I didn't mean to be critical. I like your style. It's creative and fun." This small-town beauty was touchy about money *and* fashion. What other topics would trigger her trip-wire temper?

She regarded him through narrowed eyes. "I like you, Michael, but let's get one thing straight before we waste each other's time." She drew a hand across her fuzzy hat in a karate chop gesture. "I've had it up to here with snobs. So if you plan to look down your pampered nose at me, my shop, or my town, you can stuff it."

Raising both hands, he backed away from her sudden vehemence and venom. "That's not my attention at all. I have nothing but fond memories of Trappers Cove. And your shop is brilliant. Ditto your style. You're stunning, and creative—a walking, talking Christmas party."

She softened her tone. "I love Christmas." Her shuttered expression didn't match her words, but he wisely resisted the urge to prod, instead offering his elbow.

Her eyes narrowed, probably in distrust. After all, why should she trust a stranger's clumsy flattery? But she slid her gloved hand through his arm. "Right. Let's show you a Trappers Cove Christmas. There's nothing like it." After locking the shop, she added, "By the time we're done, you'll be so full of the holiday spirit you'll poop sleigh bells."

"Sounds painful."

And just like that, they returned to playful banter. Michael wouldn't make that mistake again—when it came to her shop, Annie was a true mama bear. *Don't poke the bear.*

Two hours later, laden with shopping bags, they reached Salty Dog Saloon and Brewery, six blocks from Annie's shop. Darkness had fallen, along with the temperature. Michael's fingertips had gone numb, and his toes ached with cold, but with Annie clinging to his right arm, the whole side of his body glowed with cozy warmth.

He could get used to this.

Despite winter's bite, the bar's front deck was packed with bundled-up people clustered around wooden picnic tables and a large firepit-table. Propane heaters wafted warmth, and strings of old-school Christmas bulbs in every color crisscrossed overhead. Fresh fir garlands wound around the deck railing, and on a low stage snugged beneath the eaves, a young woman wearing fingerless gloves strummed her guitar and sang in a clear alto voice.

Annie grinned up at him, the tip of her nose cherry-red and her cheeks flushed. "Isn't this fabulous? Don't you feel all Christmassy?"

"I'm getting there. Thanks to you, I'm well stocked with fudge, saltwater taffy, paperback thrillers, and alien-themed pajamas. What more could a guy want?"

You. I want you.

She squinted, and for a moment, he wondered if he'd spoken those words aloud.

Those intensely blue eyes did a number on a man's composure. At once pale and bright, they peeled away his practiced suaveness and left him feeling naked despite the thick layers of clothing he wore.

He cleared his throat. "You really take the holidays seriously, don't you?"

Scanning the crowded space, she lifted one shoulder. "You know what they say, fake it till you feel it."

The Christmas queen was faking it? Before he could respond, a thirty-something guy with blond hair and a thick fisherman's sweater strode up to greet them. "Annie, my sweet. It's been too long." He smooched her cheek, then acknowledged Michael with a friendly nod. "I've got two seats opening at the fire table." He led them to a pair of Adirondack chairs covered with fluffy sheepskin throws.

Michael moved to pull out Annie's seat, but their host beat him to it. "Today's special is our spiced Christmas ale, and Quinn's cooked up a kick-ass hot toddy."

They ordered drinks, shrimp-and-bacon-stuffed potato skins, and crab chowder. Before leaving them, the host tilted his head ever so slightly in Michael's direction and gave Annie a quizzical glance. Her answer was a shrug and a cute half-smile.

"That's Ryan Lee, the owner," she told Michael after the guy finally left.

"Seems very fond of you." No doubt, Annie could easily attract younger guys with her teasing smile, her earthy humor, and her lush figure. He bit his lip, embarrassed by his jealousy over a stranger's attention to a near-stranger.

She gave a dismissive wave. "Oh, he's a sweetheart. He bought this place when it was a crumbling old brewery and built it into the most popular hangout in town. His girlfriend Lilo runs the brew operations."

Another couple joined the crowded fire table, giving him the perfect excuse to scoot his chair closer to hers.

"Annieee!" A young woman with bleached, spiked hair poked her head between them, set down two steaming mugs, and wrapped her arms around Annie's shoulders. "It's been ages. Where've you been?"

"Working, doll." Annie pecked her cheek. "Michael, this is Quinn, Salty Dog's bartender extraordinaire. Michael's in town for the holidays."

Quinn's handshake was firm, her gaze appraising. "No better place to be for Christmas. Enjoy."

After greeting their tablemates, most of whom she knew by name, Annie lifted her glass. "Here's to Christmas in Trappers Cove."

He clinked his cup with hers, sipped, then blinked back tears from the intense alcohol fumes. "Powerful!"

"Right?" She coughed and waved her free hand under her nose. "I don't know what she puts in these, but if you drink more than two, you'll definitely have visions of sugarplums—and a killer hangover the next day."

"Will this help you fake it?" he asked.

She pinched her lips together and scowled at her lap.

He laid his hand over hers. "Sorry, was that too intrusive?"

His heart stuttered when she glanced up with tear-sheened eyes.

"God, I'm an utter oaf around you, always saying the wrong thing." He squeezed her hand, half expecting her to yank it away.

Instead, she squeezed back. "You're fine. I'm just feeling sorry for myself because my Christmas plans fell through. I usually spend the holiday with my brother and his family, but that won't be possible this year. I'll miss spoiling my nieces and nephew. They're great kids." She sniffled and gave a wry smile. "I guess the holiday season pulls emotion to the surface." She took a healthy glug from her drink. "What do you usually do for Christmas?"

He snorted. "Work. Go to dull parties. Drink."

"No cozy family get-togethers?"

"No cozy family."

She wove her fingers through his, her expression brimming with sympathy. Something about her gentle touch, the crackling fire—and probably the alcohol—made him want to spill personal details he seldom shared.

"I mean, we get along okay. My sister's great, though I don't see her as often as I'd like. Neither of us ever had kids, so—no niblings to spoil."

"No wife either?"

Poking around for his relationship status—that had to be a good sign.

He shook his head. "Got close, back in college, but my workaholic ways drove her away."

With a sigh, she leaned her shoulder against his. Her hair brushed his cheek. "I wanted kids of my own, but nature had other plans. After the third miscarriage, my husband said he couldn't take any more heartbreak. Now he's married to a nice schoolteacher and has a happy little brood." Her chuckle held a bitter edge. "Don't know why I'm telling you this."

If he hadn't passed his last physical with flying colors, he'd worry about the pressure filling his chest. "Because I'm a good listener?"

"Because you're leaving soon, I guess. I'll never see you again, and that makes you—" She wrinkled her nose. "Safe?"

"Annie." It took every ounce of strength he had not to pull her fingers to his lips. "I'm from Bellevue, not Mars. Now, can we talk about yesterday?"

She blinked rapidly, and for a moment, he thought she'd feign forgetfulness. Instead, she released him and clasped her hands in her lap. "I was pretty rude. Unfair, too. But really, you might as well be from another planet."

"It's the money thing, right? Why is that a problem?"

"Because I've had enough bad experiences to know that people like you don't respect people like me."

"Don't respect you? For God's sake, Annie," he spluttered, "I've been following you like a puppy all evening. You're a shrewd business-woman, a good friend, and from what I've seen today, all the Main Street merchants adore you. Plus, you're fascinating and funny and so damn attractive I get tongue-tied in your presence."

"Cut the crap, rich boy." She poked his chest. "You and I have nothing in common. My dad was a commercial fisherman. Mom was a teacher. Your parents are gazillionaire philanthropists."

"Oho, has the lady been googling me?"

She huffed. "Yeah, okay, I looked you up. Wish I hadn't. It's even worse than I expected."

"Annie." He twisted in his seat. "Look at me, please."

She heaved a sigh, then complied, her chin firm with defiance.

"Can you imagine what it's like to be reduced to your net worth? All your humanity wiped out because other people only see dollar signs when they look at you?"

Her lips parted and her eyes widened. "Wow. I've been a real shit to you, haven't I?" She shook her head. "I'm sorry, Michael. And for the record, that's not how I see you."

If that was true, it would be a refreshing change.

He took her hand again and gently stroked it with his thumb—delicate bones under satin skin. "Let's be real—you see me as a spoiled prince who's gotta have his coffee just so. You remind me of my assistant, Nancy."

A flush painted her cheekbones, but she kept her hand in his. "How so?"

"You don't pull your punches. I like that about you—and your snarky humor. And your laugh that warms me better than hot chocolate. And your rabid Christmas mania. And your determination to help a stranger find a little happiness during a tough time. So thank you, Annie." Finally succumbing to temptation, he raised her hand to his lips and brushed a kiss across her knuckles.

"Gah!" She rolled her eyes heavenward and yanked her fingers from his grip. "Michael, you should know—I've sworn off meaningless hookups."

"Who says I'm looking for meaningless?" His mischievous grin netted him not the tiniest smile in return, so he changed gears. "Tell me, then, what are you looking for?" When she evaded his gaze, he tapped his chest. "I'm safe, remember?"

"Okay, fine." She worried her lower lip between her teeth. "Call me stupid, but I'm looking for a—you know—a boyfriend. Someone who wants more than the occasional booty call. Cheryl made me promise to try online dating." She drained her cup. "To be perfectly honest, I'm dreading it."

"Why? My best friend found his wife that way."

"Feels kind of pathetic. But I guess that's how twenty-first century courtship works. Time to get with the program." She dropped her head onto the back of her chair. "God knows what I've been doing so far hasn't worked."

An idea tickled his brain, probably a stupid one, but maybe...

He leaned in close, brought his lips to her ear, and whispered, "So practice on me."

She jolted in her seat, nearly upending her chowder. "Huh?"

"If you and I have no future, why not use me to practice your dating skills?"

Her brows drew together. "You're just trying to bargain your way into my bed."

Damn it, she saw right through his bullshit. Should've known better than to try and schmooze her, but his flirtation skills were rusty. He seldom had to work this hard to get a woman's attention. Time to recalculate.

"Not going to lie, Annie—I find you very attractive, but I promise I'll never pressure you to do something you don't want to do." He extended his hand for a businesslike shake. "What do you say? Deal?"

She squinted at his palm as if it had grown tentacles. Time for the big guns—radical honesty.

"Since my girlfriend recently kicked me to the curb, I could use the practice myself. With some pointers from a smart, straight-talking lady like you, maybe I won't fall on my ass next time."

The corner of her mouth ticked up. "Just practice?"

"Absolutely." *To start.*

She probably didn't believe this ridiculous proposition any more than he did. But even if she never returned his feelings, Annie was a special woman and well worth getting to know.

He waggled his fingers, silently urging her to seal the deal. For a long moment, nothing. And then—what to his wondering eyes should appear, but Annie's slim hand closing around his for a firm shake. "Okay. Two weeks of practice, then goodbye."

He bumped her shoulder with his. "Unless you decide you'd miss me too much?"

"Don't push your luck, mister." She gave him a playful shove and turned toward the singer, who'd launched into a spirited "Feliz Navidad."

Annie and the rest of their table joined in, bellowing in butchered Spanish. By the end of "Let It Snow," she'd linked her arm through his again, her warmth radiating through his entire body. And by the end of "Have Yourself a Merry Little Christmas," he wondered if he dared kiss her cheek.

But his opportunity evaporated when the blond pub owner stepped onto the stage and took the mic. "Sorry to harsh this happy buzz, but we're gonna have to close early tonight. That Alaska Clipper is closing in fast. Weather service issued a warning for high winds and a hard freeze. Be safe, everyone, and wrap those pipes."

"Well, crap. Better hurry." Annie shoved the last potato skin into her mouth.

Michael signaled for the server. "I'll drive you."

"No need. I live right around the corner." She snugged her knit scarf around her neck and grabbed her purse.

Between her stubbornness and Mother Nature's wrath, their first date seemed destined for an early ending—but he wasn't ready to give up just yet.

He gripped her elbow. "Let me help, at least." When she eyed him suspiciously, he added, "Dating tip number one: Guys like to be helpful. It's in our DNA."

That earned him an eye roll and an indulgent smile. "Fine, if you insist."

Chapter Eight

♥

Michael sorted their bill and followed Annie down the street. When they rounded the corner, a gust of icy, stinging, sand-laden wind smacked him in the face.

"Yikes." She tightened her grip on his arm and lowered her head against the salty onslaught. "Been a long time since we had real winter weather. I'm up there on the left."

She pointed to a pale green clapboard cottage with white trim, its porch posts and railing twined with twinkle lights. Blue ceramic pots flanking the door held miniature Christmas trees decorated in blue and silver. In the sandy front yard, a rope hammock strung between tall pines swayed madly.

"Help me unhook this, will you?"

Together, they rolled it up and carried it to the porch.

While she fumbled in her bag for her key, he peered toward the beach, hidden by dunes at the end of her street. She really was awfully close to the coastline. "Are you going to be okay tonight? Any chance of flooding?"

She waved away his worries with a flick of her wrist. "This old house has stood for a hundred years. Besides,"—she opened the blue-lacquered door—"nasty weather is a risk when you live near the coast."

She hung her coat on a curlicue brass coat tree. "Isn't that how investors like you get rich—by taking smart risks?"

He cocked his head and considered her phrasing. Was that a hint? An invitation to take a risk on her? Normally, he had an excellent radar for subtext and undercurrents, but Annie Scott was a puzzle. With her teasing jibes and snarky smiles, it was hard to tell exactly what she thought of him. Probably hadn't made up her mind yet. Smart of her—in her shoes he'd wait and observe to see if he was worth the investment.

"Still, I'd feel better if you'd spend the night up at the castle."

She smirked. "Sure you would."

"No funny business. There are plenty of guest rooms."

"You got a generator, in case the power goes out?"

"Erm—"

She jutted her chin. "I'll be fine right here."

He watched her bustle around the room, switching on lamps—a colorful, mismatched collection that worked together in fascinating harmony and flooded the space with mellow light. "I'll stow this hammock in the garage. Be right back."

While he waited, he checked out her living room, a cozy space that reflected her eclectic taste: embroidered velvet pillows piled on a squashy leather sofa, assorted bookshelves painted pale blue and green, a sleek mid-century coffee table, and a fluffy flokati rug. Antique birdcages suspended in the corners held trailing ivy, and in the picture window, a bushy Christmas tree glittered with nautical-themed decorations: seashells, starfish, mermaids, and sand dollars—some natural, some glass, some elegant, some homemade. Its rich, piney scent blended with something sweet and spicy—cookies? Tea?

She returned to catch him at the mantelpiece, toying with a silky tassel hanging from a brass reindeer's antler.

"Fondling my tchotchkes?"

Caught me. He turned and shrugged sheepishly. "I love your place. It's so—"

"Chaotic?" She peeled off her knit hat, and her hair crackled with static.

"So *you*. I've never seen a home with so much personality."

She laughed off his compliment.

"No, really. It's cozy and beautiful and surprising. I wonder how you'd decorate my apartment."

Chuckling, she ran her fingers through her flyaway curls. "Ah, but to do that, I'd have to get to know you."

"I hope you will." Stepping as close as he dared, he lifted a strand clinging to her cheek and tucked it behind her ear. The stinging shock he got for his efforts was well worth it.

"Ow" Annie jumped and clapped a hand to her jaw.

Can I kiss it and make it better?

Hoo-boy, keeping his growing attraction under wraps was going to be tough.

She held his gaze for a long, charged moment, then shook her head and stepped back. Way back. "I've got a spigot in the front yard, one in the back, and one around the side. What can we insulate them with?"

"Old towels should work. I'll need duct tape and buckets."

She spluttered a laugh. "Look at you, Mr. Fix-it."

He shrugged. "I haven't lived my whole life in a penthouse, you know."

Actually, he pretty much had, but in college, a spontaneous November trip to a ramshackle cabin on Mount Hood forced him and his buddies to learn a few winter survival skills. They would've frozen their foolish young asses up there if not for the old-timer up the road who took pity on them.

Smirking, Annie left to gather supplies. Together, they swathed her outdoor spigots in cloth and left them slightly open to drip into buckets overnight, like that old mountain man taught him. By the time they finished, his fingers were numb.

Back inside, Annie opened each tap to drip, drip, drip through the night so the pipes wouldn't freeze.

He stooped to open the cabinet doors beneath the sink. "So warm air will circulate around the pipes."

"Aren't you full of useful information?" Hard to tell if her crooked grin conveyed amusement or annoyance.

"I do my best." Biting back a groan when his knees protested, he pushed to his feet and followed her to the tiny laundry room and the powder room. When they reached a door at the end of the hallway, she planted a hand on his chest. "I'll take care of this one, thank you very much."

Damn. He'd love to glimpse her bedroom, her most private, intimate space where she lounged in... silk pajamas? A diaphanous gown? Perhaps—his heart thumped—nothing at all?

She emerged and shut the door firmly behind her. "You feel okay, Michael?" She pressed the back of her fingers to his forehead. "You're all flushed."

"I'm just grand. Now." Turning away to hide his embarrassment, he rubbed his palms together briskly. "What else can we do to keep you safe and warm?"

Her low chuckle raised the hairs on his nape—and other parts further south. "Michael, your efforts to rescue me are very charming, in a medieval sort of way, but at the moment, I don't require rescuing. If that changes, I'll let you know."

"Promise?"

"Absolutely." She stifled a yawn. "Sorry, it's been a long day. Fun, especially this last part, but tiring. This old woman needs her rest."

He snorted. "Old woman? Hardly." He wasn't fool enough to ask exactly how old. Besides, he preferred companions around his own age. Bridging the gap between generations made for awkward, stilted conversation. After working hard all day, he liked to share his off hours with someone who understood what the eff he was talking about.

Annie eyed him from head to toe, then crossed her arms and tilted her chin. "Okay, practice date, let's put our cards on the table. I'm fifty-six. You?"

A slow grin stretched his lips. "Wow. I've never dated an older woman before."

She socked his arm. "And you're not dating one now. We're just practicing, remember?"

"Ouch. Okay, okay, no need for violence." He rubbed the sore spot. "I'm fifty-four."

"Really?"

"Cross my heart." He backed toward the door. "I'll leave you to your beauty sleep—which works really well, by the way. For an older woman, you're a knockout."

She balled her fist again, but she was grinning.

"Right, I'll see myself out." He paused on the threshold. "And thanks for showing me Main Street. I've enjoyed seeing Trappers Cove through your eyes."

Your beautiful, heart-stopping eyes.

She fingered his lapels—not even contacting any part of his body, but still, his nerves vibrated in harmony with that sweet touch.

"You're not bad, for a rich guy."

Taking a risk, he stroked her arms from shoulder to elbow and tugged her a little closer. "See? I'm not so awful. All I needed was a little of your Christmas magic."

She leaned her cheek against his chest and sighed. Her soft hair brushed his jaw, and the ground tilted just a little. Lofted by the wind, tiny snowflakes danced through the open doorway and clung to her hair and lashes. And though the cold prickled his skin, he'd gladly stay in this enchanted snow globe world as long as she let him.

"You're so warm." She nuzzled beneath his chin.

A helpless moan escaped his lips. "Where's the mistletoe when you need it?"

"Oh dear." Chuckling, she planted her forehead on his sternum and pointed up. There, suspended above their heads, a clump of greenery tied with a red ribbon danced in the wind.

Michael blinked up in astonishment. He never got this lucky in love. Never.

She shrugged. "Came with the tree. I figured, why waste it?" She tilted her head back, biting her lip. Her sparkling gaze danced over his face and settled on his mouth.

His pulse galloped as he waited, teetering on a wire between caution and desire.

Annie's lashes fluttered down. "Oh, what the hell," she murmured in a husky voice that flooded his chest with heat. "It's just practice, right?"

"Just practice." He cupped her cheek and lowered his lips to hers, waiting, letting her take control. Because no matter how ravenous he was for her plush mouth, he needed to earn her trust.

Humming deep in her throat, she brushed her lips over his in a brief, sweet kiss that stole his breath and sprinkled his vision with glitter.

"Mmm." Pulling back, she traced her lower lip with the tip of her pink tongue, and he nearly lost control as heat curled up his spine.

She shivered.

"Right." He might be toasty warm, but the temperature outside was falling fast. Gripping her arms, he gently pushed her through the doorway. "Back inside you go. I'll let you know when my Christmas tree is ready for your inspection."

Oh, that teasing smile. "You know where to find me."

"I do indeed. Auntie Annabelle's Antique Attic. My new favorite shop."

Her melodic laughter rang out as she closed the door.

For a long moment, he stood on her light-jeweled porch while the sweet, sensual echo of her kiss flowed through his veins like honey.

"Just practice? Think again, lovely lady." Grinning, hands stuffed deep in his pockets, he trotted back toward Main Street, now empty of shoppers. Overhead, multicolored lights swayed in a syncopated dance, jerked this way and that as the storm sank its claws into the pretty little town. Heated to the marrow by Annie's kiss, he improvised his own merry Christmas carol.

Let it blow, let it snow, I've got my love to keep me warm.

He barked out a laugh, amused by his over-the-top giddiness. It was only a kiss, for God's sake. Tomorrow, Annie would be back to her suspicious, prickly self. But still—he fingered the smooth purple stone in his pocket. What had the hippie mama said? Something about forging new connections.

Tomorrow was soon enough for reality. Tonight, he'd revel in this surprise Christmas gift.

Chapter Nine

♥

Annie knuckled her bleary eyes. "It's ten minutes past closing time, folks." With only five more shopping days till Christmas—well, four and a half, since she'd close early on Christmas Eve—she ought to be grateful for this flood of last-minute shoppers, but right now, she was dead on her feet.

Thank God the storm hadn't taken out power on Main Street. Falling trees had left quite a few Trappers Cove families without power overnight, according to Cassie, who'd brought the volunteer firefighters their breakfast while they worked to repair the damage. And "Crazy" Gus Anagnos had lost a hunk of his souvenir inventory to burst pipes, poor guy.

A harried young dad approached the counter, a toddler on his hip and another clutching his coattails. "Annie, you gotta help me. The cat broke our tree topper."

"Let's see what we can find." She handed each child a piece of saltwater taffy before leading them to the picked-over holiday section. Picked to the bone, as a matter of fact.

"Teresita," she called over her shoulder, "did someone buy that blown-glass angel?"

"Yes, indeed." Her assistant grinned. "Some guy cleaned us out during your lunch break."

The little one in the young man's arms began to wail.

"Hey now." She ruffled the tot's springy curls. "Try the bookstore. Daphne had some cool craft kits. I'm sure you and the kids can build a beautiful angel for your tree."

"With glitter!" the other kiddo squealed.

Their father rolled his eyes and muttered, "Joy, joy, joy" as he wrapped his littles against the biting cold.

Ding, ding, ding. Teresita smacked the hotel bell on the counter. "Come on, people. I gotta get home and make cookies with my grandkids. Get a move on."

Amen. Annie's stomach rumbled and her feet ached—her head too, from the holiday music tapping her skull like a woodpecker. Even an avowed Christmas fan had her limits.

"All I want for Christmas is a bubble bath and Pad Thai," she sang under her breath.

Of course, once she closed up the shop and retreated to her cottage, she'd have to face the consequences of last night.

Way to waffle on your shiny new intentions, Annie.

Just when she finally vowed to put her heart on the line and look for a real boyfriend, along came the perfect short-term fling. And what did this supposedly strong, smart, mature woman do? She kissed a guy who was guaranteed not to stick around. Even if he did, no way could she ever fit into his filthy-rich world.

No matter how soft his lips, how seductive his words, how sparkling his eyes and dazzling his smile, kissing Michael was a huge mistake. Best to laugh it off—why get all worked up over a playful kiss under the mistletoe?

But oh, what a kiss! All night she'd tossed and turned, replaying the moment in her mind. She'd thought that, at her age, there were no new sensual delights to discover. Men were men, lips were lips, penises were penises, and her casual encounters were merely a way to scratch an itch and lower her stress dial. Since her long-ago divorce, she'd had plenty of pleasant kisses and cozy cuddles and perfectly serviceable orgasms, but kissing Michael was a revelation—a too-brief, delectable contact, a quick exchange of breath and touch and heat that blew all other kisses out of the water.

Still, she couldn't let one innocent, delicious kiss distract her from her goals. After helping Teresita ring up the last customers, she drifted over to the eveningwear section. What to wear for the Sons of Italy banquet? As a board member, she had to show up in style—even if only to stuff her loneliness with linguini and rumba with handsy old Italian dudes.

At the mirror, she held a deep blue chiffon gown to her chest. Lovely lines, a little lacking in sparkle, but that was easily remedied with jewelry. Or perhaps this dusky pink cocktail sheath?

It'd be nice to show up with a date as handsome and suave as Michael. Holding a too-large scarlet dress, she swayed to Nat King Cole, imagining Michael's arms around her, his strong, solid body pressed to hers as they twirled beneath a kitschy disco ball.

Maybe it wasn't too late to grab an extra ticket. She fingered her phone, then spun when the doorway bell jingled, and a blast of icy wind lifted her hair. Drat, she'd forgotten to lock up.

"Sorry, hon, we're closed."

"At last." Michael stood framed in the entrance, clutching a slender paper bag. His hair stuck up at odd angles, his face was flushed, his scarf hung crooked, and his smile shone bright enough to light the winter darkness.

"What happened to you?" She set down the dress. "You look like you've been dragged through the shrubbery. Backwards."

"That about sums it up." Stepping inside, he grinned broadly and held up his prize. "The finest bourbon I could find in Trappers Cove. Not my first choice, but it's pretty good."

"Right, because your first choice probably costs more than I earn in a year." She plucked a pine needle from his hair and another from his woolen scarf. In fact, he was peppered all over with needles, and his left cheek bore a long scratch.

He set the bottle down and pulled off his leather gloves to reveal badly scratched hands. "Let's not quibble about details. The point is, I'm ready to pay up."

"Pardon?"

"Our bet. I lost fair and square, so I spent the day scouring Trappers Cove for decorations and bought a twelve-foot noble pine. Those things are vicious." He wiggled his shredded fingers.

"Yikes!" She took his hand and turned it over, inspecting the damage. "Why not hire someone to set it up for you?"

"Because a certain lady I'm trying to impress looks down her pretty nose at entitled rich guys."

She winced. Had she really called him that? Normally, she'd never stereotype a person before getting to know them, but something about extreme privilege brought out an ugly, snarling side of her.

Do better, Annie.

"Let me get my first aid kit."

He stood patiently while she sprayed his cuts with antiseptic and applied a few Band-Aids. When she glanced up, his smile held a dreamy cast, his lids half-lowered. "You're an excellent nurse," he murmured, and happy sparks skittered up her arms and down her spine, right to the juncture of her thighs.

He pulled a blocky bottle from the paper sack. "Thought you'd like something local. Woodinville Bourbon Whiskey, perfect for decorating a Christmas tree. What do you say?"

Annie's cheeks heated. As much as she'd love to share a glass with Michael beneath a towering Christmas tree, hard liquor led to lowered inhibitions, which led to trouble.

"I don't know. I'm kind of a lightweight when it comes to alcohol, and that castle road is tricky."

He pulled a business card from his pocket. "The guy who sold me the tree is also a ride share driver."

Of course. Adalberto, Trappers Cove's Jack of All Trades, was always hustling for a buck.

Annie sighed and raised her palms. "Okay. Fair's fair—since you went to all that trouble." She silenced her inner alarm bells and donned her coat and scarf. After all, she was a sensible, mature woman who could certainly handle a drink or two. Maybe even another kiss—a welcome ego boost. Lord knows dating again at her age would require all the confidence she could muster.

Michael rubbed the sexy, silver-tinged scruff covering his jaw. "What can I add to entice the lady? I've got the tree, the booze, a picnic feast from Trappers Market, and cookies from the bakery."

Annie's stomach growled.

A chuckle rang out from behind them. Shoot, she'd forgotten Teresita was still here. Bustling past, wrapped up like a well-padded mummy in her down coat and wooly hat, she nudged Annie's arm. "Go on, woman. Wasting food is a sin." She rose on tiptoe to whisper, "So is wasting a tasty man like him."

Annie flung up her hands. "All right, all right. Let's go toast your tree, Ebenezer."

But I am not sleeping with you, no matter how tempting you are.

Chapter Ten

♥

The sea churned below, and so did Annie's stomach as they bumped and jolted up the winding road to the castle. Looking over the cliff made her dizzy, so she focused on Michael, who gripped the wheel of his Jeep SUV with easy confidence, his sculpted features relaxed—the perfect distraction from her fear of plunging to an icy death.

"You're letting your beard grow?"

"Maybe." He glanced at his reflection in the rearview mirror. "These days, it comes in more salt than pepper. Makes me feel old."

She stroked a fingertip along his jaw, enjoying the prickly-velvety texture. "I like it. Gives you a dangerous edge."

He huffed a laugh and pulled up against the cliff to allow an on-coming car to pass. While they waited, their eyes met, and the air between them heated by several degrees. Self-conscious, she clasped her hands in her lap. "Glad I don't have to make this drive every day."

"I'm getting used to it." The corners of his wide mouth ticked up. "I'm finding lots of things I could get used to out here."

Biting her lip, Annie stared down at her whitened knuckles until the Jeep began to roll again.

Gravel crunched beneath the tires as they passed through the spooky iron gate. The castle rose up before them, its tall windows glowing. Funny how being occupied, even by one person, gave the old hulk a welcoming vibe.

Michael hopped out and opened her door. Hunched against the driving wind, they dashed up the stairs. He ushered her inside, shed his coat, and hung it on one of the brass hooks lining the campy foyer. "Brr, colder than a yeti's balls out there."

She doubled over with laughter, complicating his efforts to help her out of her coat.

"You lose power last night?" he asked as he hung her winter things on a brass hook near the door.

"Nope. Not even a flicker. You?"

"A few flickers, but the gas fireplace kept me warm."

She took the hand he offered and followed him deeper into the building. When was the last time she'd held hands with a man? His touch conveyed the perfect level of intimacy, connecting them in a sweet, low-pressure way.

She peered through an open doorway. "You didn't put your Christmas tree in the parlor?"

"Nope." He led her past several closed doors.

"The ballroom?"

"Also no." He mounted the grand staircase, towing her behind him.

Her stomach tightened. Having only visited the castle once, her memory of the layout was murky. Were they heading to his bedroom? This could be beyond awkward.

"Come on, slowpoke." He tugged her down the hallway, around a corner, and pushed open a tall wooden door banded with metal. Inside, crackling flames in the fireplace cast a golden glow on the floor-to-ceiling bookshelves. Candles flickered in hurricane lamps on the mantlepiece—she inhaled the spicy scent of Zora's special Christmas blend. Surrounded by boxes and shopping bags, a towering, fragrant fir nestled between the hearth and the window seat. A white linen tablecloth covered the desk, which held an impressive spread. He must've bought out the market's entire deli case—stuffed vine leaves, marinated mushrooms, spiced olives, nuts, an elaborate charcuterie platter with cheese, salami, prosciutto, mortadella, crusty bread, a slab of creamy butter, grapes, figs, clementines...

Annie clapped her hands together, giddy with delight. "A library Christmas tree!"

"It's your favorite room, right?"

No doubt about it, she was dueling with a master of seduction. The only way he could've improved this scene was to drag a bed in front of the fireplace—and thank God he hadn't done that, or her resolutions would be toast.

She stepped forward and stroked the springy needles, releasing even more piney perfume. "But you didn't decorate it?"

Michael gave a sheepish shrug. "Afraid I'm a virgin. My parents always hired a decorator. Once I got my own place, I did the same." He stepped to her side, close enough to feel the heat rolling off his body. "I was hoping you'd lend me some of your creative vision." He nudged her shoulder. "And isn't a tree trimming party a thing?"

"You want me to decorate your tree? I don't know whether to be charmed or annoyed."

With his thumb, he rubbed the bump on his nose. "I was definitely going for charming."

And he'd hit the target like Robin Hood.

She rubbed her palms together. "Well, I guess I don't mind working for my supper. And I'm flattered that you'd entrust me with your first non-professional tree. Let's see what you've got."

Stepping carefully, she poked through the sea of packages. "Wow, you really picked Main Street clean, didn't you?" In addition to the antique blown glass ornaments from her shop, she found tiny dream catchers and astrology-themed ornaments from Zora's Psychic Emporium, origami cranes and hand-cut paper snowflakes from Daphne's bookshop, glitter-dusted aliens from Crazy Gus's Souvenir Planet, gingerbread ornaments from the bakery, plus lights, tinsel garlands, and enough candy canes to give the whole town a toothache.

She clasped her hands over her heart. "Oh my. This is…" She blinked hard, touched to her core by the glorious, glittering chaos of it all. "Making all this work together harmoniously will be a challenge."

Michael rubbed his broad, warm palms down her arms from shoulder to elbow. "If anyone can do it, you can." His lingering gaze simmered with desire, and a whisper of longing unfurled from her center out to her fingers and toes. The air between them developed its own magnetic pulse that tugged her closer, closer…

She gulped hard and stepped back, reminding herself she was done, done, *done* with casual hookups. She'd already made that clear to Michael, but his nearness sapped her resolve.

Seeming to sense her inner struggle, he moved to the table. "But first, I promised you a bourbon." He poured them each a crystal tumbler of liquid amber.

Raising her glass, Annie admired the dancing firelight in its depths. "What shall we drink to?"

His smile bloomed slow and simmering. "To finding my Christmas spirit. I loved the holidays once. With your help, I just might learn to love them again."

Mouth dry, heart racing, she clinked her glass to his. "To finding Christmas." She sipped, then inhaled sharply as a sweet burn spread through her chest. "Wow."

Michael's grin widened. "Right? Now, let's fuel up. We've got a lot of tree to decorate."

An hour later, stuffed to the gills with delicious goodies and replete with holiday stories, they set to work.

"Oof." Focused on unspooling his string of lights, Michael bonked into Annie on the back side of the tree. "Here, let me—" He ducked under her arm, but her lights snagged his.

"No, this way." She twisted toward him and freed one of his bulbs from her strand, only to get caught again until they found themselves roped together, her back pressed to his heated, muscly front.

"Ow, my hair."

"Hang on." Chuckling, he grasped her shoulder and turned her. The gentle tug of his fingers in her hair zapped a shock of arousal through her body. "Got it. Now, how do we get out of here?"

His hand landed on her hip. His rope of lights tightened across her chest, and her nipples hardened to aching points. "Let me just—" As his fingers fumbled at the small of her back, a wicked impulse urged her hips backward.

White-knuckling the reins of control, she wiggled free and slid beneath his arm. "There we are, all good. Now hand me your spool and take mine." They parted ways, heading in opposite directions.

While Michael fetched more decorations, she gulped a breath and rested her damp forehead against the stone mantlepiece. *Damn, that was close.* Clearly, she'd overestimated her strength by miles.

He nudged her arm with a box of glitter-dusted little green men. "Shall we start with the aliens?"

Grateful for the distraction, she took the box. "What kind of theme could we build from all this?"

"Theme?" He tilted his head like a confused puppy. "How about Trappers Cove, since I got something from nearly every shop on Main Street?"

Here was an interesting opportunity. "And how would you describe Trappers Cove, Michael?"

He answered her teasing grin with one of his own. "This is a test, isn't it? Let's see. This town is… Trappers Cove is… quirky." He slid closer. "Colorful." He held her gaze, inching forward with each word. "Welcoming. Surprising. Beautiful."

Her mind blanked as her body took over—all pounding pulse, throbbing core, and simmering anticipation.

He lifted her hand to his lips. "Trappers Cove is…" His other hand kneaded her hip. "Just what I need."

The contrast of firm grip and soft kiss melted her resistance like candle wax.

What's the harm of one last fling? He wouldn't be back for more. As soon as his holiday break ended, he'd return to his Bellevue skyscraper, and she could continue with her plan—new year, new me, blah, blah, blah…

Her audiobook crooned in her memory: *If you want to fly, you've got to jettison what's weighing you down.*

She shook her head, the movement sharp and emphatic, then extricated herself from his tempting embrace.

"Michael, I'm sorry. I can't."

His dreamy smile flattened. "Annie, please don't pretend you don't feel this. We have—hell, chemistry isn't a strong enough word. This is powerful magic brewing between us."

She balled her fists, frustration forcing her voice to crack. "I'll admit I'm very attracted to you, but there's no way this could work. We're from different worlds."

"I see." Dropping her hand, he returned to the pile of ornaments and lifted another box. His broad shoulders rose and fell on a deep breath. He spun back to face her, his dark eyes hard and bright. "Look, I get it. You've had bad experiences with wealthy people. But I'm not some cartoon Scrooge McDuck. I'm just me."

Turning away, he hung a twinkly sequined mermaid on a low branch, then selected a blown-glass surfboard. "Just a tired, confused guy surfing his midlife crisis and trying not to drown." As he attached the decoration, he heaved a sigh that stirred a sympathetic vibration in her chest, despite her determination not to let him in. *Damn it.*

Still averting his gaze, he hooked a glitter-dusted starfish on a high branch. "I'm just a guy who finds you attractive and interesting and wants to get to know you better." With his fingertip, he traced the curled arms of a purple glass octopus—and oh, how she longed to feel that careful caress on her skin.

"Don't I deserve to be seen as who I am? Isn't that what everybody wants?" He knuckled his closed eyes as if in pain. "If I'm wasting my time, please just say so."

Annie's scalp prickled with shame. By projecting her insecurities onto Michael, she'd erased the living, breathing man in front of her and replaced him with a caricature drawn from her own experiences, grudges, and biases. He's done nothing to earn her scorn. In fact, he'd been nothing but kind. And funny. And generous and sweet and—

Lurching forward, she gripped his forearm. "Hey, I'm sorry. I've made unfair assumptions about you. From now on, no more snark. Until you leave Trappers Cove, you're just another guy."

One corner of his mouth quirked up. "Just another in your stable of admirers?"

"Stable?" she scoffed. "You're over-estimating my love life by miles. Leagues. Light years."

He slid closer until they stood toe to toe. "If that's true, all the better for me." His fingertip traced a tingling trail down her arm. His liquid gaze thickened her tongue and sped her pulse.

She planted her palm on his chest—his warm, solid, muscly chest—and grasped her last crumb of inner strength. "Michael, I promised myself no more casual hookups." With a will of its own, her hand rubbed circles over his thumping heart. "As tempting as you are, that lifestyle doesn't work for me anymore."

He huffed an incredulous laugh and gestured toward the enormous tree. "Does this look like casual to you? They had itty-bitty Christmas trees at the lot, you know."

"But you're not an itty-bitty kind of guy, are you?" The unintended double entendre hit her, and her face flamed.

One dark, glossy eyebrow inched up. "Thought you weren't interested in hookups."

"Ungh!" She thunked her forehead onto his chest.

Michael rubbed her back as laughter shook them both. And oh, what the sound of his laughter did to her. Enchanted thunder, it rumbled against her cheek and rolled along her nerves until every cell in her body sizzled.

All this inner strife was exhausting. Affirmations were well and good, but she was closing in on sixty, and the romantic pickings were sparse. Did she really want to let an audiobook narrator bully her out of what might be her very last Christmas treat—a sweet memory to treasure while slogging through online dating profiles?

His long fingers toyed with her hair. "So, about that fancy restaurant you mentioned?"

"I… er… huh?" She blinked up at him, completely thrown by this non sequitur.

"When we made this bet. Casa something?"

Oh, right. The memory solidified—sliding across the ballroom in her stocking feet, Michael's laughter ringing out as he tried in vain to catch up.

"Casa Francesca."

"That's the one." He tapped his lips with his forefinger. "What's something we can bet on where I'm guaranteed to win?"

Annie scoffed. "If you want to ask me to dinner, Michael, just ask."

His hands slid down to cup her elbows. "Annie, would you do me the honor of having dinner with me at Casa Francesca? At the risk of sounding snooty, I'd like to wine and dine you."

She waved a hand toward the feast. "You already have."

"No, this is whiskey and dine. And since I'm useless in the kitchen, someone else will have to do the cooking."

"Michael, I—"

"Please, let's drop this 'practice dating' nonsense. I am sincerely interested in you, Annie. Other than your habit of stomping on my ego, I can't recall when I've had more fun with a woman. And if I have to court you slowly to convince you, slow is how we'll go." He slid his fingertip from her palm to the sensitive underside of her wrist, circling once, twice, before slipping inside her sleeve.

Shivering with pleasure, she nibbled her lip. His gaze zeroed in on the movement. His nostrils flared.

Damn. I am going to end up in this man's bed. We're going to have a marvelous time. And when he leaves, I'm going to miss him so hard.

But if she ignored the powerful magnetism between them, she'd regret it to her dying day.

Tilting her head, she flashed her bravest smile. "I'm free on Wednesday."

"Wednesday," he murmured, as if repeating some magical incantation. "Excellent." He brushed his cheek against hers, the soft scrape of his whiskers indescribably delicious. His hot breath fanned over her ear. "And I'm warning you now. After our third date, I plan to kiss you."

Sweet, aching pressure swelled in her chest, her belly, her sex.

Ah well, the new year was soon enough to launch the new Annie.

"No." She slid her hand up until she cupped the back of his neck, her fingers sliding through the silken curls at his nape.

His eyebrows rose. "No?"

She shook her head. "No. Kiss me now."

Desire darkened his eyes as he sucked in a sharp breath. Strong arms encircled her, pressing her body to his. His thick lashes fluttered down. With a hungry moan, he captured her lips in a deep, drugging kiss.

Her lips parted on a sigh, and his velvet tongue swept inside, gliding, teasing, learning her mouth with each languid slide.

One broad palm rose to cradle her head while the other slid to her lower back and snugged her tight against him. "Annie," he whispered, releasing her mouth to trail hot, wet kisses down her neck. His fingers knotted in her hair, tugging her into a deeper arch. His tongue traced the hammering pulse in her throat. Soft lips nibbled her earlobes, then sharp teeth nipped the sensitive flesh. Gasping, she clutched his silken hair and claimed another frantic kiss. And another, and another...

Michael groaned, gripped her arms, and broke away. Eyes pinched shut, he shook his head. "Wait. Hold on."

"I am." She tunneled her fingers beneath his belt, toward the tempting curve of his ass.

"Annie, please." Seizing both her wrists, he clasped her hands over his thundering heart. "This isn't what you want."

"It is," she insisted, breathless.

"No." Darkened with desire, his penetrating gaze stilled her efforts to escape. "You said you're done with hookups. You want more. You deserve more." Gently prying open her clenched fingers, he rested his cheek in her palm. "I'm trying to prove myself, Annie. Give me a chance. Please."

Never in her life had she been so sweetly refused. Dizzy with confusion, body thrumming with frustrated need, she stepped out of his embrace and turned her back.

For a long moment, the only sound was the fire's crackle and the whoosh of their breathing. He cupped her shoulder, his touch soft and tender. "Are you angry?"

She heaved a lung-emptying sigh. "I don't know what I am, Michael." A bitter chuckle burbled up. "But I know what I'm not—a user. I won't push you to do something you don't want to do."

"Annie." He pressed his cheek to her hair. His breath tickled her sensitized skin. "I don't feel used. And I want you desperately, but not at the expense of what we could be together."

She shook her buzzing head in a vain effort to untangle her emotions. What the hell was she feeling? Ravaged, ravished, furiously aroused, and on the verge of tears. But not used.

"Okay then." He pressed a soft kiss to her temple. "Forgive me for my lack of control?"

Forgive you? I'm the one who tried to climb you like a tree.

She blew out a shaky breath and forced a smile. "There's nothing to forgive, Michael. We're just two horny, lonely humans who got carried away. Now, shall we finish decorating this tree?"

"Sure." He stepped to the table and lifted the bottle. "But first, I need another drink. One for you?"

"Yes, please." The whiskey would burn away the sting of embarrassment and disappointment.

One drink turned into three, way over her usual limit—but two hours later, the giant tree shone with quirky splendor, and they had recovered their easy banter, though the beginnings of a killer headache drummed inside her skull.

When Adalberto's van rolled up, its dented sides now emblazoned with *Rides4Hire*, Michael slipped him a few bills before helping a slightly wobbly Annie into her seat and pressing a chaste kiss to her cheek. "I'll see you Wednesday evening."

"You will?" She tilted her head, and the van tilted a bit as well.

"Casa Francesca, remember? I called for a reservation while you were in the bathroom."

She blew out a long breath. "Right. I look forward to it."

He gently closed the passenger door and waved as she bumped off into the drizzly, icy night.

Adalberto waggled his eyebrows. "So, Miss Annie, you making friends with our billionaire?"

"Mind your business, Berto." She rested her pounding head against the cool window.

Our billionaire? He's not ours. He's not mine. And if it weren't for his common sense, I'd be in his bed right now.

She ought to be glad he cut things off when he did, but deep down, she wished he'd been a little less gallant.

Chapter Eleven

♥

What were you thinking, dumbass?

Michael knotted his fingers in his hair and leaned on his elbows, struggling to concentrate. This room could not be more perfect for solitary work—piney scent of Christmas tree layered with freshly brewed coffee, gas flames dancing in the fireplace, rain pattering on the mullioned windows, crisp new journal at his elbow, tablet fully charged, yet all he'd accomplished so far was a short list of lame arguments that would never convince the board.

Without his intervention, GRA Venture Capital would devolve into another unprincipled dividend mill. Unfortunately, he doubted his cofounders Rick Roth and Jose Aceves would see it that way—they both had mortgages and kids in college.

And how could he build a case with his gut churning over last night's volcanic kiss and the clumsy way he stomped on the brakes? Clearly, Annie had either changed her mind about casual hookups, or she'd changed her mind about him. Either way, he blew it.

He still felt the echo of her heat and softness pressed against his body, the wet silk of her mouth, heard her hungry moans, saw desire turn her eyes to gleaming star sapphires—and instead of accepting the gift she offered, he'd cut her off just as their attraction caught fire.

But if he gave into temptation, a holiday fling was all they'd ever share. And he wanted more—a jarring realization about a woman he hardly knew, but two evenings with her were enough to ignite his keen interest. She was so...

Seizing his Montblanc pen, he scribbled a list in his notebook.

Intriguing

Sexy

Smart

Snarky... but kind

Grounded.

Knows her mind and heart—not a chameleon who changes her colors to catch a wealthy man.

Ripe

Luscious

Tempting

He dropped his pen and snarled through clenched teeth.

What did a workaholic like him have to offer someone so rooted in her community? If he were smart, he'd forget about Annie and focus on the reason he came to Trappers Cove in the first place.

But he had a reservation tonight, a table for two overlooking the sea. And when he texted Annie to confirm, she replied with a cheery "Can't wait" and a winky face emoji. What the hell did that mean?

A jarring alarm tone sent his phone skittering across the desk. Time to get ready for their date. Time to repair the damage if it wasn't too late.

After showering, he picked up his electric razor on autopilot and regarded his scruffy reflection. "It gives you a dangerous edge," Annie had purred as she stroked her finger along his jaw.

"Right, the beard stays." After neatening up the edges, he slid into the suit Nancy express-mailed to the castle—*May blessings shower her like Seattle rain*—then surveyed the ties she'd sent. Red with tiny Christmas trees? Too cheesy. Green with red stripes? Too blah. Deep blue with tiny stars? Good enough. Considering her distaste for showy wealth, he selected simple silver cufflinks and skipped the silk pocket square.

The bumpy ride into town jarred loose some of his angst, but his heart still galloped as he pressed her doorbell.

"Coming!" Footsteps drew closer, and the door opened to reveal Annie in a shiny blue dress that skimmed her curves. Head tilted, she fiddled with her earring. She'd fluffed her honey and silver hair into loose waves and pinned up one side with a jeweled clip. The scent of roses and spice wafting from her cleavage made him dizzily, desperately aroused.

"Shoot, sorry." She beckoned him inside and pecked his cheek. "I'm running late. Make yourself at home."

She trotted down the hallway, her skirt swirling like water around her shapely calves.

Gazing after her, he rubbed the warm spot she'd left on his skin. "Pipes okay?"

"Just peachy." A drawer slammed. "Is it raining?"

"Not at the moment." He wandered to her mantelpiece, where silvery glass reindeer and angels shared space with framed photos—Annie with Cheryl, laughing over cocktails. Annie huddled with three teens, their jeans rolled up as surf eddied around their bare feet. These must be the nieces and nephew she spoke of. Good-looking kids whose wide grins nearly matched the brilliance of their aunt's.

He lifted a solo snap of Annie seated on a rock, gazing out to sea. The photographer had beautifully captured her wind-whipped hair and soft, contemplative smile. An intimate portrait taken by someone she trusted—maybe even loved? A twinge of jealousy furrowed his brow.

A low chuckle sounded at his shoulder. "Snooping?"

He replaced the photo on the mantel. "How did you sneak up on me in those high heels?"

She extended her leg and displayed twinkling rhinestone buckles. "Had my cobbler add non-skid soles after falling on my ass."

"Your cobbler?"

"Old Gus McPherson. He repairs shoes, makes belts, leather gear."

His mouth dropped open.

Laughing, she laid a finger beneath his chin and pressed it shut. "Not that kind of leather gear." She waggled her eyebrows. "Well, perhaps he makes that too. I've never asked. Are you into bondage, Michael?"

Heat flooded his face. "I, uh—"

"I'm just teasing." She sashayed to a small table by the front door, where she pulled a lipstick from her bag. Leaning closer to the mirror, she slicked scarlet over her lips and rubbed them together. "Ready?"

Yes ma'am. Ready to strip that sexy dress from your body and taste every inch of your skin.

"You bet." He helped her into her fur-trimmed coat. "Mink?"

"Faux, of course. Vintage seventies fashion, along with this Qiana disco frock. Not the shoes, though. Didn't want to risk falling off platform sandals. Shall we?"

He held her door as she gracefully maneuvered into her seat, then followed her directions up a rise to another bluff on the opposite end of town. He vaguely remembered this place from his childhood summers, but of course his great-aunt and uncle never brought him and Violet up here. And now he saw why.

Floodlights hidden among fragrant junipers washed the stone façade of Chez Francesca in golden light. Inside, a stiff-backed maître d' with a pencil mustache led them from the marble-tiled lobby into a dimly lit dining room right out of a classic mafia movie—tufted red leather seats, Tiffany lampshades, gleaming white linens, oil paintings of the old country, and potted palms between the tables. Servers in tuxedo shirts and satin cummerbunds glided silently, ferrying giant, leather-clad menus and steaming trays of food. In the corner, an old gent with slicked-back hair played his baby grand with flourishes worthy of Liberace.

"Here you go, Ms. Scott, sir."

Annie flashed their host a brilliant smile. "Thanks, Larry." Her fingertips fluttered to her lips. "Sorry, I meant Lorenzo."

The maître d' cracked a smile. "My pleasure. Your server will be with your shortly."

Once he was out of sight, Annie leaned onto the table and whispered, "He's my neighbor. Great guy, salt of the earth, but up here, he loves playing the stiff butler type."

He opened his menu, forcing his gaze from the distracting spill of her breasts. "So, what's good here?"

"Everything. You can't go wrong at Francesca's."

He flipped to the lengthy list of first courses. "Hmm, the pressure."

"Hey." She placed her soft hand on his arm. "Listen, the other night—"

He lowered the menu. This was it—his chance to make things right between them. "Yeah, about that. I owe you—"

"I want to apologize—" she blurted, overlapping.

He tilted his head. "What for?"

"For jumping your bones, of course. I should've checked in with you before assuming—I mean—" Slightly crooked teeth nibbled her pillowy lower lip. "I realize I was sending mixed signals, and that's not fair. You're so—" She trailed off on a sigh.

Though it cost him great effort, he pressed his lips together until she finished her thought. His own apology could wait. He needed to understand this puzzling beauty—prickly one moment, warm and welcoming the next.

Finally, she slid her hand over his and squeezed gently. "I don't know what to make of you, Michael. Or of my reaction to you. Meeting you has made me question—so many things." She wove her fingers through his. "I suppose it's good for me, but it makes me dizzy as hell."

Warmth blossomed in his chest. "Tell you what—why don't we set aside our prejudices and take this one day at a time? And for the record, I'm sorry too. I've spent the last few days kicking myself."

Her lips curved in the most beautiful smile. Candlelight danced in her mesmerizing eyes.

A discreet throat-clearing broke the spell. "Are you ready to order?"

Annie raised an eyebrow. "Do you trust me?"

"Implicitly."

She turned to the server. "We'll have the antipasti misti and two glasses of Sangiovese Rosé. Then bring us the steak Sinatra and a bottle of Barolo."

"Perfect," the server chirped.

He chuckled. "The lady knows her wines."

She unfurled her napkin and laid it across her lap. "The lady treats herself to dinner here far too often for her budget."

The appetizer platter proved to be as delicious and sophisticated as anything he'd eaten in pricier Seattle eateries—sweet-hot pickled cherry peppers, delicate slices of marinated eggplant and zucchini, olives from tiny to enormous, butter-soft prosciutto, spicy artichoke hearts and mushrooms, and pillowy Burrata cheese that melted in his mouth. Even more delicious was watching the hypnotic swipe of Annie's pink tongue over her full lower lip as she chased the last drop of golden-green olive oil. And when she closed her eyes and moaned, his poor, tortured dick rose to attention inside his suddenly too-tight slacks.

"So," she asked once the server cleared away the empty platter, "What made you flee work, home, and Christmas?"

"Whew. You're mercilessly direct."

"So I've been told." She steepled her fingers and waited.

Quickly, he sketched out his dilemma vis-à-vis the board and his company's direction.

"So there you have it. Do we concentrate our resources on a few high-earning clients, or do we continue to risk investing in start-ups?"

She nodded, her expression solemn. "That's a tough one. You're obviously on team start-up."

He lifted a shoulder and let it fall. "Thrill of the hunt. Besides, fostering innovation is the whole point. Without investors like us, so many brilliant ideas would never see the light of day."

Her eyebrows flicked up. "You love a challenge. Good to know." Reaching across the table, she waggled her fingers. "And you have a generous heart."

Touched by her simple praise, he wove his fingers through hers. Funny how untying this ethical knot felt easier with Annie's fine-boned hands in his. "As much as I crave your approval, I'm in business to make a profit. But yeah, I enjoy mentoring. I never had kids of my own, and these young developers are so bright and eager. They're ready to change the world."

"Tech stuff?"

"Mostly, yes."

Tilting her head, she leveled an appraising glance. "I didn't take you for a computer geek."

"I'm not, really. Can't tell you how many times I've had to call the IT desk to untangle some mistake I made by pushing the wrong button. But I have an eye for potential."

She nodded slowly. "Ever think about investing in other sorts of ventures?

A chill chased over his skin. Here it came, the part he'd been dreading. "You want to expand your shop? Create an Antiques empire?"

Annie waved him off with an airy laugh. "Me? I'll stay right where I am, thank you very much. It took a lot of years to find the perfect work-life balance."

"Uh huh." Stomach tightening, he braced himself for the big ask. Somehow, it always came down to this. And he'd been so sure Annie was different.

She continued, oblivious to his tense posture. "But it's frustrating how few resources we have for locals compared to bigger beach towns. Ocean View recently opened a new community center. Sunset Bay converted an abandoned movie theater to a performance space. I'd love to see resources like that in Trappers Cove." Removing her hand from his, she sipped her wine, her gaze focused out to sea. "It's a balancing act, you know? Runaway development ruins the town for locals, but if there are too few community facilities, locals move away. Either way, the town's spirit dies."

"Hmm. That's a tough dilemma," he murmured, hoping to strike the right sympathetic note without implying commitment.

Her focus snapped back to him. "Why that face?"

"Sorry." What the hell was wrong with him? He was usually better at schooling his features. "It's a reflex. When you have my resources, you get used to being hit up for donations. Not that saving Trappers Cove isn't a good cause."

Eyes narrowed, brows scrunched together, lips pressed in a thin line, her expression darkened to shuttered hostility. If looks could kill, he'd be a smoldering pile of ash. "You think I'm asking you for money?" she hissed, hands white-knuckled on the table as she scraped her chair back.

Fix this, you stupid ass. Just as he was beginning to win her trust, he'd accused the woman he desperately wanted of mercenary motives, and she looked nuclear-level furious.

Raising his palms, he hurried to correct his gaffe. "No, no—you're not that way at all. I jumped to a stupid conclusion. I'm sorry, Annie."

Her eyebrows rose sky high, then slammed down again as she swept a hand down her body. "Do I look like a gold digger to you? Is this how a gold digger dresses? Or talks? Or—" Growling, she ripped the napkin from her lap and tossed it onto the table.

Panicked, he grabbed her fist. She was slipping away, and he had to stop the downward spiral before this fragile connection went up in flames.

"No, Annie. I absolutely do not think you're a gold digger. Your devotion to your community is admirable. It's just—" He winced. "We're all shaped by our backgrounds, right? And more than once, I've been fooled into thinking someone cared for me when all she wanted was money." He massaged the back of her hand with his thumb. "I let a defensive impulse get the better of me. Please forgive me?"

The air between them vibrated with tension. Her nostrils flared on a deep inhalation she finally released through pursed lips. "Okay. I guess I have my reflexes too. Sorry I spoke so harshly. You didn't deserve that."

"Friends?" He pried her clenched fist open loose and twined his fingers through hers.

She rolled her eyes. "Friends, I guess."

Relief flooded him. That was a damn close call. One more blunder and she'd toss him out on his privileged ass—of that he had zero doubt.

Just in time, the wine steward arrived to uncork their bottle. Michael sampled, swished, and sighed. Berries, faint floral notes, and a hint of satisfying earthiness. "Excellent."

"Very good, sir." His face perfectly stony, the steward filled their glasses.

As soon as he finished pouring, their server wheeled a cart to their table and, with a flourish, lifted a silver dome to release a cloud of fragrant steam that made his stomach rumble.

She filled their plates with bone-in rib eye steaks topped with portobello mushrooms, roasted red peppers in balsamic vinegar, crispy roasted fingerling potatoes, and grilled broccolini dusted with parmesan cheese. "Enjoy your meal. Please signal if you require anything else."

Michael nodded his approval. Compared with the constant interruptions and saccharine chirpiness from servers in trendy Seattle eateries, this old-fashioned formality was a refreshing change.

They dined in companionable silence punctuated by soft moans, the clink of silverware, and Christmas music from the piano. Each time their gazes met and caught, the corners of Annie's eyes crinkled, a sweet gesture that gave him hope he hadn't completely blown his chance with her.

Finally, she pushed her plate away and heaved a happy sigh. "Incredible."

"Magnificent." He wiped his mouth and reached for another slice of crusty bread to sop up the last of the velvety sauce. "So, tell me about your holiday plans."

Her smile slipped on one side. "I've never actually spent Christmas in town."

"Oh, right. Your brother. That must be hard."

She hitched a shoulder, but her wry expression betrayed the truth. "There's a singles party at Cassie's café on Christmas Eve. I might take a walk on the beach on Christmas Day, if it's not too windy." She pushed a bit of bread around her plate with her fork. "What does your Christmas usually look like?"

He chuckled. "A stiff, formal dinner with my parents. Catered, of course. Sometimes I escape to go skiing with friends." He reached for her hand. "Perhaps I could join you for that singles party?"

She took it, and her smile gained a little altitude. "Perhaps."

"And New Year's Eve?"

"The VFW hosts a game night. They greet the New Year in their pajamas." She dabbed her lips with her napkin. "I'll bet you do something much more glamorous."

He sighed. "I suppose you could call it that. My parents throw a cocktail bash. More of a networking thing than a real party. I sip expensive bubbly, greet business contacts, and do my best to uphold the Garwood image."

"Sounds grim. Sure you wouldn't rather come to the VFW with me? They have those little cocktail weenies. And at midnight, Asti Spumante in plastic cups."

"I wish. I'm already on thin ice for skipping out on several holiday events. With my business on the line, I can't afford to burn bridges." Recognizing his perfect opportunity, he squeezed her hand. Why not? Worst she could do was shoot him down, and she'd probably do that anyway, after his bone-headed comment. "Annie, would you be my date?"

Her hand went slack. She blinked rapidly. "I, uh—wow. I like you, Michael, quite a lot. But I'd be more of a liability than a help."

"Impossible," he scoffed. "You're gorgeous, stylish, charming."

"Thank you." Her posture stiffened. "But with age, I've lost my ability to let little digs slide off my back like the proverbial duck. And we both know how bitchy rich people can be to outsiders."

Odd that she'd think so. He'd never noticed that kind of snobbery among peers his age. "That's true of some of my parents' friends, but we'll laugh at them behind our cocktail napkins."

Her sour expression tightened. How to convince her?

"Listen, I can't promise you it'll be as much fun as a Trappers Cove party. In fact, I can pretty much guarantee it won't. But there'll be a jazz trio, great nibbles, enough bubbly to float a yacht, and you'd be doing me a huge favor."

Annie huffed a sigh and rolled her beautiful eyes.

"Just one night, then we'll come back to Trappers Cove." He wove his fingers through hers. "I'd love to celebrate the New Year with you."

She pursed her lips and shot him a long, narrow-eyed glance. "I'll do it on one condition."

Elation buzzed through his veins. "Name it."

"The day after tomorrow, I'm going to the Sons of Italy holiday banquet. Pretty much the whole town will be there. It's quite fancy by Trappers Cove standards, and it's always fun—mountains of delicious pasta, funny speeches, raffle baskets, and dancing. How about you be my date? You know, tit for tat."

His gaze flicked to her cleavage, just for a microsecond, but her sharp eyes caught him in the act. She balled up her napkin and tossed it at him. "Michael, be serious." Though she scowled, her shoulders shook with laughter.

He raised his hands in surrender. "Mea culpa. And I'd be honored."

They shook on it, and Michael held onto her, relishing the feel of her soft, delicate hand in his. He'd never considered his palms an erogenous zone, but wow.

When the piano player launched into *Have Yourself a Merry Little Christmas*, Michael pushed his chair back and stood. "Shall we dance?"

She threw a nervous glance toward the piano guy. "Oh—people don't usually dance here."

He leaned in closer. "A certain wise, lovely lady taught me to embrace the fun in life—Christmas trees, windy walks on the beach, pajama parties..."

"Hoisted on my own petard." She let him tug her to her feet and followed him to an empty spot by the piano, where he pulled her into a lazy two-step, because who the hell knew which dance went with Christmas carols? Diners at other tables greeted this unexpected display with laughter, oohs, and ahhs, and soon a few elderly couples joined them, twirling with practiced ease. When the song ended, he spun Annie out, then back in against his chest.

She beamed up at him., and his belly filled with twinkling fireflies.

"That was brilliant, Michael. Thank you."

Back at their table, the server persuaded them to try the dessert special, molten chocolate cake topped with Washington cherries poached in red wine.

Annie took a bite, closed her eyes, and hummed deep in her throat. "Mmm. This tastes the way your voice sounds, rich and decadent and delicious." She licked her fork, and he went iron-hard in his pants.

Think about spreadsheets. Tax audits. The board meeting.

Eventually, that did the trick, and he was able to rise and help Annie into her coat without embarrassing himself.

She looped her arm through his. "Before we go, come see the view." She led him through glass doors onto a cliff's edge patio, where icy cold smacked his face.

"Hard to enjoy the view with frozen eyeballs," he grumbled.

"Look, over there." The tables and chairs had been cleared away, but a propane heater burned in a corner shielded from the dining room—probably where the staff took their smoke breaks.

Nestled in the pool of warmth, he wound his arm around her shoulders and gazed out at the darkened sea. Together, they watched a thick blanket of clouds swallow the moon.

"You know, coming to Trappers Cove was a last-minute decision." He nuzzled her hair. "I'm glad I trusted my gut."

Chuckling, she hugged his waist. "I almost cancelled tonight. After the way I threw myself at you, facing you again was kind of mortifying."

"Hey, that kiss was a hundred percent mutual. And I must confess—all night I've been fighting the urge to grope you through that beautiful disco dress."

"Well, here's your chance." She raised her chin, her impossibly blue eyes sparkling with playful challenge.

Powerless to resist, he took what she offered, claiming her mouth in a kiss that quickly deepened. The contrast between body heat and icy wind was far more intoxicating than Barolo wine, far more delicious than molten chocolate. Mewling softly, Annie unfastened his coat buttons, loosened her coat's belt, and pressed her torso to his, wrapping them both in thick wool.

Mindful of his aching erection, he angled his hips away, but she hooked her calf around his leg and pulled him closer. A cry escaped her lips when he clasped her sweet, soft ass and rocked his pelvis into her belly.

"So good," she murmured and pressed her heated sex against his thigh.

Lowering his head, he feasted on the delicate skin of her throat. Her pulse leapt beneath his tongue. This was crazy, reckless, wild—dry-humping like teens while the surf pounded and the wind tore at their clothing. With Annie panting in his arms, he felt exhilarated, more alive than he had in years.

A clatter behind them startled them apart. "Holy shit. Sorry, folks."

A young man in a server's uniform clutched his vape pen to his chest. "Um, I've gotta check the pipes."

Sure you do, buddy.

Annie clapped her hand over her open mouth to stifle a laugh.

Michael wrapped his arm around her. "We were just leaving."

Giggling, they stumbled to the parking lot, where he bundled her into his Jeep. "Let's get you home before we're arrested for public indecency."

Still laughing, she let her head fall back against the headrest. "You bring out the wild woman in me."

Hope soared in his chest. Maybe she'd invite him in, lead him to her bed, and put him out of this sweet misery.

As they rounded the corner onto Main Street, Annie's phone pinged.

"Who's texting so late?" she muttered, digging into her bag. She tapped the screen, then she squeezed his knee in a vice-tight grip. "Oh no!"

Chapter Twelve

♥

"What's wrong?" Eyes wide with alarm, Michael pulled into a Chevron station.

Annie removed her clawed hand from his knee and gulped a few steadying breaths. No need to startle him into a crash. She couldn't solve this problem from a hospital bed.

"It's the Sons of Italy hall. With the holidays, everyone was focused on their own families, so this guy messaged that guy who messaged another guy who didn't check his messages until it was too late."

"Too late for what?"

"To keep the pipes from freezing and flooding the place. Everything's waterlogged. The decorations are destroyed. There's no way we can hold the Christmas ball there." Her voice wobbled. "This is a disaster! We have less than 48 hours to find a new venue. They've called an emergency meeting in Cassie's café."

So much for following up that hot kiss with even hotter...

She dropped her head against the seat rest and groaned. "I'm so sorry, Michael. I'm on the party committee. I have to help."

He gripped the wheel, released a sigh that went on forever, then tilted his head toward her with a weary smile. "I understand. Your commitment to your community is one of the many things I admire about you." His long fingers drummed on the wheel. "Is there another hall you can use?"

Annie scrolled through her phone, her stomach sinking with each new dose of calamity. "Pipes are bursting all over town. The school gym and St. Sebastian's church hall are the only venues big enough, and they're both flooded."

They pulled into the last free parking space near Cassie's Coastal Café, brightly lit despite the late hour. Inside, at least a dozen people sat in the long window booth, pointing and gesticulating while Cassie refilled coffee mugs.

Michael patted her knee. "Looks like they're arguing."

"More like panicking."

Through the painted picture window she saw club president Sal Verducci push to his feet and fling his hands up in a gesture of frustration. Marquetta stabbed a finger at his chest while Zora tried to tug her back into her seat.

She pointed. "The Sons of Italy leadership." Getting this bunch to agree on much of anything was a chore and a half, even on a good day. Solving this disaster was going to be a painful slog.

Michael raised an eyebrow as he wound a tendril of her hair around his finger. "You're Italian? With a name like Scott?"

"On my mother's side. Annamaria Russo. But that's not the point. This holiday party brings the whole town together. We can't lose it."

An idea flickered to life—a risky one. God, she hated to ask him, especially after their heated exchange over dinner. If Michael thought she was using him for his resources, that would be the end of their budding relationship, fling, whatever this was. Though losing him would hurt like hell, her loyalty to Trappers Cove had to come first, and she was out of options.

Gripping his arm, she poured all her powers of persuasion into her pleading gaze. "You could save Christmas for all of us."

He tilted his head. "You want me to finance the repairs? Fly a crack team of plumbers out here?"

"No, nothing like that. Just host the party. The castle's ballroom has plenty of space. You're not using it, and the pipes are freshly insulated."

Michael's jaw went slack. "Annie, I'm no good at planning parties."

Yup, she was losing him. She gentled her voice. "*The Courage to Change* says the only way to grow is to try something you're not yet good at."

"Great," he muttered to the car's ceiling. "She's quoting self-help books. What's next, motivational posters?"

She covered his fisted hand with her own. "All you have to do is open your doors. The club will bring everything we need—tables and chairs, serving dishes, food, booze, DJ equipment, decorations."

Groaning, Michael massaged his brow. "Sounds like a major invasion." His hangdog expression tightened the knot of tension behind her breastbone. "Annie, do you realize what you're asking? I came to Trappers Cove to escape all that holiday brouhaha. It's a shame about your party, but I'm dealing with a crisis that could destroy my business and affect dozens, no—hundreds of people's livelihood. How am I going to sort it out with the whole town traipsing through my door?"

Well then, she'd gambled and lost. A leaden heaviness settled over her, but she sucked in a deep breath and forced a smile. "Fair enough. It was worth a try." Leaning across the center console, she pecked his whiskered cheek, probably for the last time. "Thank you for a wonderful evening, Michael. I wish it didn't have to end now, but I've got to help fix this."

She climbed out and headed toward the café. Behind her, a car door thunked closed.

"Annie, wait."

Michael stood beside the Jeep, his shoulders hunched against the cold, hands stuffed into his pockets, his handsome face twisted in a grimace. "Just Friday?"

Breath held, she nodded.

The vapor of his heavy sigh wreathed his head. "You really love this place, don't you?"

"It's my home, Michael." She gestured toward the café. "These people are my family."

Her words struck with a painful thud. How foolish and ungrateful she'd been to count her holiday as spoiled because her blood relatives weren't available. She was surrounded by family, and they needed her.

Michael's eye narrowed. His chest rose and fell. He gave a curt nod. "Okay. As long as you get the owner's permission, I'm in."

Heart leaping, she raced to him, threw her arms around his neck, and peppered his face with kisses. "You won't be sorry, I promise."

Chuckling, he pressed his forehead to hers. "Somehow, I doubt that. But you're worth it."

"All you have to do is open your doors," Michael muttered as he waited for his morning coffee to drip through the filter. Annie hadn't mentioned that he'd have to open his doors at six freakin' a.m.! This on top of a very late night pondering his next steps with the firm—because what else was he going to do with all that pent-up, horny energy thwarted by busted pipes? Not that his midnight musings yielded any fruit—just pages of scribbled nonsense. Pathetic.

The sky was still as dark as the inside of a cow when a volley of doorbell ding-dongs interrupted a very sweet dream of dancing with Annie on the beach. Yawning and fuzzy headed, he pulled on flannel pajama pants and his favorite UW hoodie, then stumbled down the stairs to see who was raising that ungodly racket.

It was Sal Verducci, the stocky, mustachioed gelato shop owner he met last night at the emergency Sons of Italy meeting, currently wrapped from knees to chin in a puffy down coat. Behind him on the gravel drive, a couple of delivery vans, three pickups, and an assortment of cars puffed exhaust clouds into the icy air.

"Good morning!" The old guy beamed and rubbed his gloved hands together. "You ready?"

Michael knuckled his bleary eyes. "Ready for what? The party doesn't start until tomorrow."

"Told ya we'd be by this morning with the tables and chairs and such. Most a' these guys have to be at work by nine, so here we are. Bunch a' troopers, am I right? Point the way, son."

So now, here Michael stood in the castle's kitchen, trying to pry his eyelids open while dozens of strangers pushed hand dollies up a makeshift plywood ramp and down the hall to the ballroom. Others toted storage bins full of decorations, chafing dishes, and God knows what. An army of Christmas cheer. At six a.m.

Fa la fuckin' la, la la la la.

A tall woman with gray hair braided snug against her head stepped into the kitchen holding a coffee urn. "Mind if I plug this in for the workers?"

Which one was she? He'd met so many people at last night's meeting, he couldn't keep their names straight.

He pointed to an outlet above the counter. "Sure, uh..."

"Marquetta, hon." She got to work setting up paper cups, powdered creamer, and sugar packets.

"Ah, right. The librarian?"

"Very good." She filled the urn's base with water. "And don't worry, no one expects you to remember all our names." After dumping ground Folgers into the filter tray, she plugged the behemoth in, then flashed a knowing smile. "Pro tip: just call everyone hon. Works for me."

Another familiar face poked into the room—Zora, the old hippie mama who sold him his purple thinking stone, along with the self-help book that got him into this mess. After setting down an enormous bakery box, she wrapped her arm around Marquetta's waist and pecked her cheek, then stifled a yawn. "Not much sleep last night, eh?" Her lips curved in a warm, motherly smile. "But it's for a good cause. Thank you, Michael, for opening your heart."

Marquetta rolled her eyes.

"I heard that." Zora lifted the lid on the pink cardboard box. "Help yourself, Michael. If you haven't had Garrett's pastries yet, you're in for a treat."

Normally, he avoided refined carbs, but desperate times called for desperate calories. With a nod of thanks, he selected a flakey turnover and took a bite. The pastry shattered into buttery flakes, revealing a dark berry filling that hit the perfect balance between sweet and tart.

"Mmmf!" He wiped crumbs from his beard.

Zora grinned. "Good, right? Now, should we send the workers here for their breakfast, or would you like to help us tote this into the ballroom?"

He was cornered either way. While he was tempted to hide out in the library, it wouldn't be right to leave all these strangers unsupervised.

Okay, so he was rationalizing his way out of working on his presentation, but helping these people might lend some new perspective—and it would certainly get them out of his lodgings sooner.

"Send them in here." He pulled the trash bin from beneath the sink, then rubbed his hands together. "Right. Put me to work."

The two women exchanged knowing grins. "Follow me, hon."

Three hours later, Michael's hoodie was plastered to his chest with sweat and his muscles ached from lifting and bending, but the ballroom was arranged with neat rows of rectangular tables, each with twelve chairs.

Matteo Verducci, Sal's buff, thirty-something nephew, clapped Michael on the shoulder. "It'll be a tight fit, but everyone will have a seat."

He wiped his damp forehead. "Great. So we're all done here?"

Though quite a change from his usual home gym workout, the exercise had gone a long way to clear his head. After a meal and a shower, he'd be ready to dive back into his presentation.

Matteo laughed. "All done? Not by a long shot."

From the corner by the tiny dance floor, someone whistled.

"Keep your pants on," Matteo hollered, then tipped his ball cap. "Thanks again, man. Really big of you to step up for the town." He lowered his voice. "Of course, Miss Annie's a pretty powerful incentive, isn't she?"

He trotted away, leaving Michael to gape and splutter. Did the whole town think he was courting Annie? Which he was, to be fair, but having all her friends in on the matchmaking game left him feeling itchy. He wasn't used to this much scrutiny of his personal life.

"Don't let it bother you," Zora said, popping up beside him like a cheerful, curly-haired chipmunk. She wiped her dusty hands on her colorful batik tunic. "We're family here, all up in each other's business.

We have our squabbles, but when the chips are down, no one in this town faces a crisis alone."

If only he could enlist their can-do attitude to address his crisis with the firm. But it would take a lot more than folding tables and baked ziti to convince the board.

Zora patted his arm. "Now, you go on and get back to"—she waved a be-ringed hand—"whatever it is you're doing in Trappers Cove. Oh, and the ladies will be bringing lunch. Be sure to stop by and fix yourself a plate."

He blinked down at the little hippie mama. "Ladies?"

"The decoration committee. Annie lit up that phone tree starting at five this morning. I can't wait to see what she comes up with." She bustled off to bark orders at a group of teens shedding their coats and gobbling pastries. Hell, at their age, he'd have done hard labor for a few of those treats.

Shaking his head, he drifted toward the hallway and was nearly mowed down by a fir tree.

"Coming through," a bearded guy called. "Where you want these?"

"I'm not in charge. Ask Zora." He sidestepped the next tree, and the next. How many Christmas trees were they planning to cram into the ballroom?

"Mo!" The petite boss lady bustled over. "Have you met our host? Michael, this is Mo Abadi, owner of Ali Baba Kebabs."

"Co-owner," a dark-haired woman inserted, setting down her prickly green load and extending her hand. "Nabila, Mo's better half. We really appreciate what you're doing for the town, Michael. Stop by anytime for a deluxe kebab plate on the house."

"Now that's an offer you won't want to miss."

Michael jumped at the sound of Annie's voice so close behind him. He turned to find her in worn jeans, sneakers, and an oversize fisherman's sweater, her arms wrapped around a large chafing dish/Sterno thingy, the kind caterers use.

"Annie!" He lifted the bulky contraption. "What are you doing here? Who's minding the shop?"

"Teresita brought in her daughter and son-in-law. This is an all-hands-on-deck emergency." She rose on tiptoe and kissed his cheek in front of—well, enough of Trappers Cove to cement those rumors. What a sweet way to announce their connection—and quite a bold step, considering her reservations about short-term relationships.

"Besides," she continued as she directed him to the long line of serving tables, "if I'm asking you to make this sacrifice, I need to put in my own share of sweat equity."

"Look at you, flinging around financial terms." He set down his load, then took her hand and pulled her close enough to whisper, "Such a turn-on."

Giggling, she nestled to his side, tilted her face up to his, and purred, "Let's see—rising interest rates, firm bottom line... liquidity." She gave him a saucy hip bump, then stepped into the fray. "Hey Daphne, let's get started on the centerpieces."

Red faced and grinning, he shook his head. What a welcome switch; instead of riding the brakes, Ms. Annie was pumping the gas. Or did she just enjoy stirring him up when he was helpless to do anything about it?

Either way, their flirtation was building up steam.

Look at her, thick hair gathered into a ponytail, schlepping along with the rest of the town, her retro glamour set aside for the sake of friends. *Family,* Zora had called them.

Aside from his sister Violet, a reliable ally against their parents' stifling expectations, family had always meant obligation, propriety, presenting a united front for the sake of impressing people whose opinion affected their social status.

But here he was in the middle of a very different kind of family. Watching Annie buzz from table to table, laughing with friends and neighbors as they spread tablecloths and decked the hall with a mishmash of hastily gathered ornaments, he felt a glow under his sternum. What would it be like, having this kind of ride or die crew?

Sure, he had friends back in Bellevue—golf friends, office friends, college friends he met for drinks or the occasional ski trip. Plus Rick and Jose, business school roommates he'd recruited to build his one-man investment project into a firm to be reckoned with. But he'd never experienced anything like this easy camaraderie where no one was trying to impress or out-maneuver anyone else.

His gaze zeroed in on Annie's firm bottom line, round and lush, as she bent over a carton of tinsel. Man, those hips were mesmerizing. Would he get the chance to see them without jeans or wool skirts or whatever else she wrapped around her glorious body?

As if sensing his heated gaze, she flashed a grin over her shoulder and held up fistfuls of tinsel garlands. "What do you think—a different color on each table?"

"Whatever you create," he called, "it's going to be gorgeous."

But not as gorgeous as you.

Biting his lip, he turned away to hide his wide, foolish grin. *Yup. I'm a goner.*

Chapter Thirteen

♥

Glaring at his reflection in the baroque-framed bedroom mirror, Michael fumbled with the world's slipperiest bow tie, a scarlet number purchased at Annie's shop for tonight's Sons of Italy Christmas Ball. He figured his boring, standard-issue Armani tux could use a little color. Okay, it was a flimsy excuse, but he'd stalled out on his presentation for the board and craved a few minutes of her presence. It had worked, too. Upon returning to the castle, his ideas flowed.

But since Annie had picked this tricky tie, he damn well had to wear it.

"Should've bought a clip-on," he grumbled as it slipped through his fingers again. Already, Christmas music drifted up from the ballroom, along with the heady scent of garlic and cheese. The Italian feast Annie had promised him had been streaming through his front door since four o'clock, and splotches of red, white, and green sauces spattered his kitchen counters. His rumbling stomach urged haste, but he'd never get a taste if he didn't master this cursed tie.

"The things we do for love," he muttered.

His jaw dropped.

"Holy shit! Love?" He goggled at his reflection. "Where the hell did that come from?"

Sure, he liked Annie a lot. Admired her. Enjoyed her company, and her style, her spunk and resourcefulness and intoxicating kisses—but love? Way too soon for that.

All this sudden change had scrambled his brain.

On the dresser, his phone tootled. A text from Annie:

I'm here. How's the tie?

He tapped out a reply, erased it, then sent her an angry-face emoji.

She responded with a winky-face emoji and **On my way.**

A moment later, a knock sounded on his bedroom door.

"Come," he hollered.

She stepped into the room, and his breath hitched. "Mamma Mia, you look—wow."

She dimpled and pirouetted to display her party dress, a snug, scarlet sheath that sparkled all over with tiny glass beads. High-heeled pumps lifted her a good three inches, bringing the top of her head level with his eyes as she sauntered toward him, tsking as she swayed those mesmerizing hips.

"Don't tell me a man with your accomplishments has been defeated by a bow tie. Here, let me help." Her teasing smile sent his heart skittering in giddy directions.

Her gentle fingers brushed the sensitive underside of his jaw as she coaxed the tie into a perfect bow. Her rose and spice perfume filled his nose with delight and his head with wicked thoughts of peeling off that beautiful dress and forgetting the party entirely.

"See?" She gave his lapel a pat. "Elegant and festive. Told you it's possible to be both."

"Annie." He stroked his fingertips down her bare arm. "You're stunning."

A flush bloomed across her cheekbones. When she sidestepped to examine her reflection, he immediately missed her heady warmth.

"I don't often get the chance to pull out all the stops." She adjusted the jeweled clip in her upswept hair.

His fingers itched to stroke the delicate curls at the nape of her neck. "Stick with me, doll," he said in his best Humphrey Bogart voice, "and you'll get lots of chances to pull out the stops. Or is it put on the dog? Puttin' on the Ritz?"

She uttered a low, indulgent laugh. "Ready for your grand entrance?"

"To tell the honest truth, I'm a little nervous about facing a party of strangers." Not that he didn't do that all the time back home, but here he couldn't hide behind his reputation. With no one angling to win his favor, he'd have to impress the locals on his own merits. And for Annie's sake, he wanted to make a good impression.

"Pfft. Are you kidding? Your generosity saved our bacon. That ballroom is full of your personal fan club." She tucked her hand into the crook of his elbow. "And lucky me, I get to make a grand entrance on your arm."

He tugged her around to face him. "Can I get a kiss for good luck?"

Her chuckle bloomed into a rich, musical laugh. "Good thing I'm wearing a non-smear lip stain." Winding her arms around his neck, she offered her softly parted lips.

He pressed his mouth to hers, and a sweet little mewl escaped her throat.

Spurred by the sexy sound, he swept his tongue into her silken heat, tasting her sweetness, letting her taste his need.

After a long, deep, smoldering kiss he never wanted to end, she planted her palms on his chest and gently pushed. "Michael, you are a delicious man. But I've worked too damn hard on this to show up late and bed-mussed. Can we table this for later?"

A laugh burbled up. "There you go again with the business jargon. I tell you, it drives me wild." He lifted her hand to his lips. "But of course, we can't miss the party. Let's go."

Music and laughter drifted down the hallway, growing closer as they approached the ballroom. At the doorway, a gum-snapping teen in a fluffy prom dress and a spangled Santa hat snapped to attention.

"Good evening, Annie." She raked Michael with a head-to-toe appraising glance, then whispered, "This him?"

Annie nodded.

"Noice!" She gave Annie a conspiratorial wink, then bobbed a curtsey. "Pleased to meet you, Mr. Garwood. Thanks for lending us your ballroom."

"Oh, it's not really my—"

"Whatever, man. You coulda said no, but you didn't. That's a stand-up thing to do." She accented her declaration with a loud crack of her gum.

Annie tightened her grip on his arm. "Mr. Garwood is a stand-up guy, Avril."

The girl flashed a wide grin. "Follow me to your table."

As they passed through the crowded ballroom, conversation halted, and a hundred stares followed their progress. Annie glided like a queen, turning this way and that to offer greetings.

"This is amazing." Michael murmured.

Her pink-cheeked smile shone as bright as the glittering decorations that had transformed the tacky ballroom into winter wonderland.

Truly, Annie's decoration committee had wrought a miracle.

Multihued glass balls and fresh fir garlands hung from the chandeliers. More sparking ornaments twinkled from eight, nine...ten Christmas trees scattered around the room's edges and flanking the DJ's station in the corner. Potted poinsettias bloomed everywhere, and each table held a monochrome centerpiece of Christmassy tchotchkes in blue, red, green, or silver…

"Hold up, Avril." Resembling Mr. Monopoly minus the monocle, Sal Verducci trotted toward them, nudging people out of his way with his brass-handled walking stick.

He clasped Annie's shoulders and planted a formal kiss on each of her cheeks. "Annie, love. Let me be the first to congratulate you. This is the prettiest party we've hosted in all my years in with the Sons of Italy."

"And daughters," Avril reminded him, cocking her hip.

"Of course, dear." Sal tapped his cane on the ground. "I'll take it from here." To Michael, he added, "Tweaked my back hauling tables yesterday. My nephew's still giving me hell. But our Annie found me a cane with style."

He straightened his satin lapels. "As president of the Trappers Cove Lodge of the Sons *and Daughters* of Italy, allow me to escort you to your table. Annie, dear?" The old guy crooked his arm, courtly as any medieval knight.

Chuckling, Michael handed her over to the dapper gent and followed them to a large round table beside the dance floor, its center glittering with a gold-painted urn full of gold-tinted ornaments and wrapped in gold tinsel.

"Just your style, Annie." He slid in front of Sal to pull out her chair. Damned if he'd let the old flirt steal that honor. "You transformed a mishmash into a harmonious whole. I'm impressed."

She cocked her head and flashed the most adorable aw-shucks smile. "Well, I had help. But yes, I enjoy creating harmony."

"You're very good at it." He made a mental note to show her the slides he was working on for the board. Maybe she could work her magic there and assemble all his jagged points into something smooth and convincing.

"Crostini?" An apple-cheeked grandmother thrust a tray of little toasts between them. "Eggplant caponata. My nonna's recipe."

"Why, thank you, Vittoria." Annie gracefully lifted one without spilling a drop.

Michael was not so lucky. He dabbed at a greasy spot on his jacket.

"Don't worry," she whispered, "I know a good dry cleaner."

The proud chef lingered until they each took a bite and proclaimed her creation delicious.

Annie pushed her chair back. "Pro tip: pace yourself. The nonnas are relentless. Come, let me introduce you around."

"Nonnas?" He rose to follow her.

"Grandmothers. They get very competitive when it comes to their cooking."

Sure enough, they only made it a few steps before being assaulted by three more matrons wielding tomato bruschetta, marinated mushrooms, and mini pizzas. Following Annie's example, Michael took a tiny bite of each, made enthusiastic num-num noises, and wrapped the rest in a napkin to toss away once the proud chefs departed with triumphant grins.

While Dean Martin crooned from a tall bank of speakers, Annie introduced him to what seemed like the whole town, all of them wearing festive apparel—which ranged from "ugly" Christmas sweaters to old-fashioned formalwear, but everyone glowed with holiday spirit.

He placed his hand on the small of Annie's back to slide her around a cluster of giggling teens. "How many of these people have you dressed?"

She shrugged. "Most of them."

From a podium beside the DJ's station, Sal Verducci tapped his glass with a spoon.

A memory zinged through him—his cousin's wedding last summer—her fourth, the groom's third. Every time the newlyweds picked up their forks, someone would ting, ting, ting, demanding they kiss. By the end of the evening, Vivienne complained of chapped lips.

For a moment, he sank into fantasy—himself and Annie in a ballroom like this, surrounded by friends and family as they accepted hugs and congratulations.

He gave his head a shake. Clearly, some needy part of him liked the idea. Loved it, even.

Sal leaned into the mic. "Let's settle down now." Gradually, the din of conversation and laughter subsided.

"Welcome, everyone, to our fifty-seventh annual Christmas ball. Let's start with a big round of applause for all the volunteers who made this last-minute change possible. There are a too many of you to name, and"—his husky voice wobbled as he patted his chest—"it does this old nonno's heart good to see the way our community came together to save this beloved celebration."

Applause rolled through the room.

Sal raised his glass. "Before we dig into our Christmas feast, raise your glasses, famiglia mia, to the host who generously offered his home, Mr. Michael Garwood."

"Not my home," Michael muttered amidst the cries of "hear, hear." And "To Michael."

"It is tonight." Annie nudged him forward. "Now go say something gracious."

He stepped to the podium and took the mic, surprised to find his own voice a little wobbly. "I want to thank you all for making me feel so welcome in Trappers Cove. To be honest, this trip has taken an unexpected turn." He sought Annie's sparkling gaze and held it. "I came here to hide out and solve a difficult problem. Meeting you..." He scanned the sea of smiling faces, from teens to seniors. "...meeting all of you has been a delight. So thank you." He raised his glass. "To Trappers Cove. Merry Christmas."

After cheers all around, Sal slapped Michael's back and relieved him of the mic. "Mangiamo! Gold table, you're first in the buffet line."

Good-natured grumbling accompanied him and Annie as they made their way to the serving tables. Just as she'd warned him, the merciless nonna squad piled his plate high with pasta, chicken marsala, risotto, gnocchi, osso buco, grilled vegetables, and garlic bread.

While sampling the goodies, they chatted with their table-mates—the mayor and his wife; bookshop owner Daphne Lee, her brother Ryan, proprietor of the Salty Dog Brewpub, Lilo Eisinger, his girlfriend and head brewer, plus rental agent Cheryl and her boyfriend Bob, a charming white-haired gent who clearly doted on her. They asked polite questions about his life in Bellevue but didn't push for details—a mercy for which he was grateful. Their good-natured teasing and banter soon had him feeling like a member of the family—enfolded, accepted, welcome. It was a refreshing new experience, not having to be on guard lest he say or do something that could be interpreted as weakness.

And through it all, Annie was there, her thigh pressed against his under the tightly packed table, her gaze sparkling with holiday cheer, her cheeks flushed with wine—and maybe just a hint of the lust her touch sparked in him.

Across the table, Cheryl lifted her glass. "Looks like our host and Annie are getting cozy. Here's to a cozy Christmas."

Annie rolled her eyes but raised her glass. "To Christmas."

That sparkle in her playful gaze—*Mamma Mia!* More intoxicating than the finest wine, it promised private pleasures to come. Hidden by the tablecloth, her calf slid against his, a slow, sensuous stroke that sent tingles up his leg and tented his trousers.

After adjusting his linen napkin, he raised his glass. "To Trappers Cove. Thank you for making me feel so welcome." He shifted his free hand to Annie's knee and stroked his thumb over the sweet indentation on the inner side.

Closing her eyes, she bit into a hunk of bread and gave a low, sexy moan.

"Delicious, right?" Cheryl grabbed another slice from the basket.

Good cover, but Annie's friend knew what was up, judging by the twitch in her lips.

Better focus on his dinner before he embarrassed them both—along with all their tablemates.

Finally, having polished off far more food than he intended, he groaned and pushed his plate away.

"Here." Cupping his jaw, Annie blotted his chin with her napkin. "You've got a smudge of sauce." Her breath tickled his cheek, and whatever composure he'd rebuilt crumbled as he melted into her touch.

Her plush lips hovered mere inches from his. Her lashes swept low as her gaze dropped to his mouth. She hummed deep in her throat. His hand closed over hers as he slid closer...

"Raffle tickets?" A fat coil of paper tickets was thrust right into their nearly joined faces.

Damn it to hell and back.

"It's for a good cause," the elderly ticket-hawker proclaimed. "The Sons of It'ly scholarship fund."

Michael flashed a tight grin to cover his frustration. "Sure. I'll take twenty."

After scribbling his name on the tickets, he left Annie to drop them into the collection boxes while he excused himself to the restroom. At this point, a cold shower would be best, but a splash of cold water on his face would have to do.

When he returned, the drawing was in full swing.

"And the basket from Sea Queen Spa goes to…" With a dramatic flourish, the old gal plunged her hand into a brightly wrapped box, stirred, and then squinted at the winning ticket. "Michael Gar—something?"

"You won!" Annie squealed and smooched his cheek.

It took every ounce of strength he had to keep from deepening that kiss in front of all her friends and neighbors.

The same gum-popper who greeted them at the door paraded toward their table holding an enormous, cellophane-wrapped basket.

Cooing with delight, Annie dove into the goodies. "Ooh, look at this. Sea salt body scrub, nourishing kelp mud mask, jojoba oil body butter, and a certificate for a foot massage." She waggled her eyebrows. "You lucky duck."

An image flashed in his mind's eye: Annie's nude body face-down on a table, her skin glistening with oil as a masseuse's hands glided and kneaded, eliciting soft groans of pleasure.

He pushed the basket toward her. "Please, keep it. I'm not really a spa kind of guy."

"Oh, I couldn't." But she gripped the handle tightly.

If anyone deserved some pampering, it was Annie. She must be exhausted after scrambling to pull this party together.

"I insist."

The DJ cranked up the music again. Sinatra invited everyone to have themselves a merry little Christmas—and Michael intended to do just that.

He rose to his feet and extended his hand to Annie. "May I have this dance?"

Smooth as butter, they glided across the dance floor. Annie matched his every move, sensed each turn, and—when the floor grew too crowded, nestled into his hold. She draped her arms around his neck and swayed, humming along to Old Blue Eyes in a rich, sexy alto.

A man could only resist temptation for so long.

He dipped his head and brushed a kiss over the shell of her ear, then took the tender lobe between his lips.

"Ohhhh my." She shuddered and arched her throat in a gesture so enticing he couldn't help tracing her leaping pulse with his mouth.

Her fingers clutched his nape, then raked into his hair, sending shivers of pleasure over his scalp and down his spine.

"Want to get out of here?" He murmured. *Please, please, please...*

"I really should stay."

"But baby, it's cold outside," Dean Martin crooned, right on cue.

Annie threw her head back and laughed, loud and free. "You know, I do believe that's a sign."

Thank you, Dino.

Spotting a gap in the throng, he fox-trotted her off the dance floor. Perfect timing, as everyone was occupied with either dancing or attacking the dessert table.

Spurred on by a different hunger, they bypassed the platters of cannoli, tiramisu, panna cotta, and Christmas cookies. Annie scooped up her evening bag and wrap, then nudged her raffle basket toward Cheryl. "Hang onto this for me, would you?"

Cheryl's eyes widened. Grinning, she socked Annie's arm and whispered, "Good for you!"

Hand in hand, they sidled between tables and slipped out the door.

"Quick, before someone tries to stop us." She trotted up the stairs, her ass jiggling alluringly in her snug dress.

Halfway up, his control snapped. He looped his arm around her waist and pressed his aching body into her softness. Finally, he indulged his desire to nibble those baby-fine curls at her nape. Delicate as duck down, just like he knew they'd be.

"Michael," Annie wiggled her sweet ass into the cradle of his hips. "You're so scandalous."

"And you love it, saucy wench."

"Oh, are we back to Medieval Times again?" She slipped from his grasp, turned to face him, and beckoned, a sultry smile on her lips. "In that case, sir knight, let us adjourn to yon tower before I am compromised."

Holding his gaze, she grasped his lapel and backed up the stairs. The air between them crackled.

Heat curled down his spine as he stalked after her. "Make no mistake, fair lady. I intend to compromise you until your bones melt."

Chapter Fourteen

♥

As soon as they reached the top step, Michael caught her around the waist and buried his face in the sensitive crook of her neck, drawing a squeal from Annie's gaping mouth.

With soft lips and agile tongue, he wrought magic over her collarbones, her throat, the tender skin beneath her ear, all the while inching her closer to his bedroom. Christmas music from the ballroom faded to just the bass line, an echo of her pounding pulse.

With a sexy grunt, he pressed her up against the door. Its rustic finish snagged her dress, but what were a few sequins compared to this dazzling sensation? Never before had she felt so deliciously melted by desire.

And I never will again.

She let her head loll back and raked her fingers in Michael's silky-soft hair, refusing to allow fear of a future without him spoil tonight's bliss. She would enter his ridiculously ornate bedroom with her eyes wide open, take the pleasure he offered, and face the morning like a grown-up.

"You're tensing up, Annie." Pulling back, he gently gripped her shoulders. Though hunger smoldered in his dark eyes, he held himself apart. "Have you changed your mind?"

If she had an iota of common sense, she'd stop now. The more she indulged this foolish yearning, the deeper the pain when he left. And he would leave—of that, she had no doubt. Trappers Cove might lure him for a brief getaway, but he'd never build a life here, and she could never give up her home.

But common sense be damned. Call it a Christmas present to herself—a final fling before she gave up casual connections for good.

Heart fluttering, she licked her suddenly dry lips.

His gaze followed the movement, desire darkening his chestnut irises to sable.

She flattened her hands over his chest. "No, Michael, I haven't changed my mind. I want this. I want you."

"Thank God." Spearing his fingers into her hair, he sealed his mouth to hers in a fierce, mind-numbing kiss and fumbled for the door handle.

As they tumbled into the room, her heel caught on the fluffy faux-fur rug, catapulting them toward the enormous bed. She flung out her arms to brace for impact, but with swift grace, he twisted so he landed on the mattress, his muscled body cushioning her fall. She landed half atop him, her thigh resting over both of his.

"Good catch." Laughing, she shifted to untangle herself, but he gripped her knee and held her fast, staring up at her with glittering eyes as he flexed his hips and pressed a hard ridge into her inner thigh.

Desire crackled and zapped between them, electrifying every inch of her skin. He slid his long fingers around her nape and tugged her forward, oh so slowly, until only the tiniest sliver of heated air separated them.

"Annie," he murmured, his voice rough with lust, "I have wanted this from the moment I set foot in your shop. When we're together, I feel..." He pressed his lips to one corner of her lips, then the other.

"I don't even know how to describe it. I feel *more*. I want more." He claimed her mouth again, sweeping his tongue inside in a silken caress.

Her last sliver of caution sent up a feeble protest. This wasn't just a meaningless fling. Her heart was in serious danger.

When his hand slid up her thigh-high stocking to stroke the bare skin above the lace, her resistance crumbled to ash. She had to see what lay beneath his crisp tuxedo, had to feel his warm body beneath her palms, had to know his scent and taste and rhythm. Now.

She rose to her feet, turned her back, and with her best over-the-shoulder smolder asked, "Unzip me?"

A slow, devilish smile bloomed across his face. "Yes, ma'am."

His breath hot on her neck, he slooowly dragged the zipper down. Cool air whisked over her bare skin, raising goosebumps—or perhaps it was anticipation that prickled her skin.

Either way, Michael noticed and lunged for the nightstand. "Where is that remote?" She heard a click, and the gas fireplace whooshed to life.

"That's better. Now, what does the lady have on underneath this stunning dress?" He slid the snug cocktail sheath off her shoulders and eased it over her hips.

Biting her lip, she sent up a silent prayer of thanks to the lingerie gods. Anticipating tonight's possibilities, she'd chosen a red satin bra and panty set trimmed in white lace. Especially at her age, that first unveiling of bare flesh was a nerve-wracking moment, and she hoped the beautiful underthings would distract him from time-wrought dimples and bulges.

Biting her lip, she waited for Michael's reaction—a hissed intake of breath. "Sweet Jesus," he whispered, and skimmed a finger down her back, sparking heavenly shivers of pleasure. He eased a fingertip beneath the elastic of her satin panties and stroked the swell of her bottom. Humming deep in his throat, he glided his palm up to her hairline.

"May I take down your hair?"

"Yes please." She braced herself, but he dexterously coaxed the pins from her updo without the slightest pinch. When the last curl tumbled down, she shook her head, fluffed her spray-stiffened locks, and faced him.

Oh my. His lips were softly parted. His chest rose and fell on rapid breaths. His nostrils flared as he drank her in with lust-darkened eyes. Whatever doubts she'd had about baring herself floated away, lofted by the sizzling heat of his gaze.

She always found a man's naked desire the most potent aphrodisiac—and at this moment, basking in his rapt focus, every inch of her craved him.

"My turn." She planted her palms on his broad chest and pushed him onto the mattress, then grasped his bow tie. One little tug released it. Next, she unfastened his shirt buttons to bare his throat and chest, bending to kiss each newly revealed patch of skin.

His palms slid up her ribs and grazed the outer curve of her breasts. "Is this okay?"

She grasped his hands and placed them where she craved his touch—well, the first of several places. His palms smoothed over the thin satin of her bra. When his thumbs circled her nipples, bright sparks of pleasure danced along her nerves and ignited an answering pulse in her clit.

If he kept up this sweet torture, she'd come before he even touched her between the legs.

With an impatient huff, she slid out of his grasp, kicked off her toe-pinching shoes, and climbed onto the bed. On her knees, she scooted behind him and peeled his shirt off his shoulders. Now it was her turn to explore the wide angles and muscular planes of his magnificent back. His satin skin felt so delicious beneath her palms, she had to taste him. Purring with delight, she peppered kisses and tender nips down his neck, over the curve of his shoulder, down the groove of his spine.

He arched his back on a gasp.

She chuckled. "Not expecting that?"

"Annie, you are full of surprises."

She inhaled his hair's spice and cedar scent. "And you enjoy surprises?"

Reaching back, he grasped her hands and placed them over his thundering heart. "I wasn't expecting you, Annie. I'm not a young man, but you make me feel like a star-struck kid."

She stroked slow spirals over his chest, relishing the scrape of crisp hair on her palms. Angling her head, she kissed the shell of his ear. "And you make me feel luscious." She nipped the soft lobe. "Thank you for that."

His head lolled back onto her shoulder as she stroked down his firm belly, following the dark happy trail. Good thing he couldn't see how comical she must look, squinting over his shoulder to find his belt-buckle.

"Allow me." He deftly unfastened it, then leaned back into her embrace.

He enjoys being teased. How utterly splendid.

She popped the button at his waistband and slid her fingertips inside, stroking his trembling muscles, lower and lower, until she reached a hard ridge.

Her fingertip traced his length and circled the plush crown once, twice—

With a roar, he sprang to his feet, kicked off his shoes, toed off his socks, and danced a goofy jig until his trousers dropped to the floor.

Eyes gleaming, he pulled her hands to his flat belly, above his silky boxer briefs. His rigid cock strained against the thin cloth, angling toward his hipbone. When she curled her fingers around his shaft, his abs jerked and his eyes fluttered closed. For a long, sweet moment they breathed in tandem, sunk into pure sensation.

She pressed a kiss to his sternum, then circled his flat nipples with the tip of her tongue, trailing feathery kisses over tight muscle...

"Wait," he yelped. For a moment, he squinched his eyes shut as if in pain. When he opened them again, his dark irises shimmered with sexy promise. He lifted her onto the mattress and knelt at her feet, kneading her calves.

"Annie, I can't remember when I've wanted a woman as much as I want you right now." His touch feather-light, he teased the sensitive skin behind her knees. "But before I sink into your beautiful body, I want to feel you coming apart under my hands, my mouth." Bending low, he pressed a wet kiss above her stocking and traced the lace with the tip of his tongue.

Her sex thrummed with every touch. Her breath grew quick and shallow.

"Is that okay with you?"

Blinking back from the brink of nirvana, she found him gazing up at her, awaiting her response.

"Yes," she whispered, "please."

A feral grin stretched his lips. "Excellent."

Gliding his hands up her sides, he pressed her onto the mattress, then skillfully unfastened the front hook of her bra and slid the straps down her arms before—*God help me!*—pressing a wet kiss to the crook of her elbow.

Who knew elbows could be such a potent erogenous zone?

He plumped her breasts in his warm hands, his rapturous expression as arousing as his touch.

"So beautiful," he murmured before lowering his head and sucking her nipple deep into the wet heat of his mouth.

Pleasure danced along her nerves with each deep pull. After worshiping her other breast, he slid lower, trailing kisses over her belly. His breath heated the satin of her panties.

"Even your underwear is stunning." He chuckled against her mound. "Yup, I'm a poet."

She sank fingers into his gleaming hair. "Your words are sweet, Michael, and your touch is pure magic." She gave the thick salt and pepper waves a tug. "And if you keep me waiting much longer, I may have to tackle you into submission."

"A challenge?" He nipped her hip. "I accept."

Hooking his fingertips into the elastic, he tugged her panties oh-so-slowly down, drawing them over her stockinged legs and tossing them away. His eyes burned with sexy mischief as he spread her thighs and gazed down at her bared sex. His fingertip traced her folds in languid, whispery strokes, up and down, cruelly skating around her aching clit. Each pass heightened her need.

"Michael, please," she gasped, arching her hips.

"So impatient," he teased.

One long stroke of his tongue, another, and a bolt of bliss jolted her body and pulled a harsh cry from her throat.

"Mmm. Almost there, beautiful?" Raising his head, he flashed a lascivious grin and dove in again, driving her right to the edge with merciless tongue flicks and dizzying circles around her clit. When he eased two long fingers inside her, the world spun away.

Racked by ecstasy, she writhed and bucked until he finally released her with a lust-drunk laugh. "I swear, Annie, you are the most amazing woman." He stood and gazed down at her, eyes glittering, his distended cock tenting his tight shorts. A dark spot of pre-cum bloomed at the tip.

At the sight, her sated desire flared to life again. She reached for him. "Come here, please."

"Oh, I intend to." He grabbed a foil packet from the nightstand, then let her peel his boxer briefs down his lean hips and muscular legs. Freed at last, his fat, ruddy cock bobbed up to smack his stomach.

Annie's mouth watered as he rolled on the thin sheath. He climbed onto the bed, his muscles flexing as he prowled toward her like some glorious big cat.

"Are you ready for me, beauty? Or would you like some lube?" He slid two fingers between her sopping folds and hissed. "Mmm, never mind. You're so wet for me."

Despite the delicious tension, she had to laugh. "Were you a boy scout? 'Cause you sure are prepared."

"Well, I was hoping we'd end up here, and I wanted to be ready with whatever you need. Or whatever you want." He kissed the tender crook of her neck, and the contrast between hot, wet mouth and rough beard drew a moan.

Braced above her, he nudged her knees wider, lowered his hips to hers, and notched the plump crown at her entrance.

Holding her gaze, he penetrated her in one smooth glide.

"Ohhh, Annie." He dropped to his elbows so his taut body covered her from tingling breasts to throbbing core.

Could sex feel this good for a man? Could he even understand the delicious satisfaction of being filled, stretched, pressed into the mattress, rocked by his thrusts?

Pleasure swelled in successive waves, each plunge bringing her closer to bliss. Mindless, breathless, she twined her arms and legs around him and undulated to meet each heavenly stroke.

Shifting higher on the bed, he claimed her mouth and swept his tongue inside to caress hers in rhythm with the fierce digs of his cock.

Bright bolts of sensation jerked her body within his cradling arms.

"Michael, yes, right there…" She canted her hips to increase the delicious friction.

Growling deep in his throat, he speared her deep and ground his pelvis against her. Rapture flashed through her nerves, pulling a ragged cry from her throat as she tumbled over the edge into a blinding climax.

He followed with a roar, his body shuddering as he rode out the last waves of his release.

Sweat-slicked, panting, he rolled onto his back, carrying her with him. Clutching her ass with one hand and her bed-snarled hair in the other, he sealed his mouth to hers, chuckling into their kiss.

"Holy angels, Annie. Did we both die just now? Are we in heaven?"

She nipped at his lower lip. "Hope not. I have a lot of living left to do."

He scooted into a sitting position and arranged her legs to straddle him, then pressed his forehead to hers. "Do it with me, Annie."

Laughing, she lifted her chin to accept the kisses he feathered across her throat. "I believe we just did."

"Not the sex—though that was by far the best ever. I mean the living part. I want that. With you."

Annie's heart skittered to a stop. Was he asking her to move in with him? In Bellevue? Unthinkable. "Michael, I—" she choked out, but no more words came, because what on earth could she say to such an outrageous—

"Hey now." He gently cupped her cheek in his broad palm. "Forget whatever scary thing you think I meant. I just want more of this." He took her hand and pressed it over his heart, its rhythm a steady drumbeat beneath her palm. "I want to know you, Annie. I want to share good times with you. I want to show you my home, my people, the way you've welcomed me into yours."

The artless, hopeful gleam in his dark eyes quieted her panic. Breath by breath, calm descended over her.

Maybe she'd been too quick to write their connection off as a mere holiday fling. Maybe, just this once, listening to her heart might be worth the risk of pain.

She wiggled her hips in his lap, and his softened cock slithered out of her still-tingling sex.

Michael groaned and looked down. "Way to ruin the vibe, little dude."

She laughed. "Is that what you call him?"

Gently, he untangled his limbs from hers. "He goes by many names—little dude, the CEO, Mr. Happy. Sometimes he steers me wrong, but this time, he got it perfectly right." He dropped a kiss on her nose. "Now, if you'll excuse me, I'll go clean up." He peppered her bare, damp chest with kisses, giving each cold-pebbled nipple a suck. "Will you be here when I return?"

She stretched like a cat, wiggling into the sheets. "Well, I'm sure as hell not going to parade downstairs past all of Trappers Cove. Not looking like I've been dragged through the bushes backwards."

"Annie..." His fond gaze raked over her nude form. "You have never looked more beautiful. No matter what happens next, I will never forget this moment."

Standing there, his glistening cock encased in latex, his hair poking up at odd angles, and the sweetest, goofiest grin on his sex-flushed face, he outshone any lover she'd ever welcomed into her bed. Or her heart.

Heat swelled in her chest, making it hard to breathe. "Go on, flatterer. Clean up the little CEO, then hurry back and keep me warm."

She watched his lovely, lean ass and broad back as he retreated to the en suite bathroom. As soon as the door closed, she snuggled into the silky sheets and gave herself a good talking to.

"You've made your bed, missy." With a wry chuckle, she ran her hand over the velvet coverlet. "Might as well enjoy the ride." Groaning, she rolled onto her side and traced the dent in Michael's pillow. "And what a ride. When it ends, I'll face it like a grown-ass woman, not some simpering, lovesick girl."

When Michael returned, smelling of sandalwood soap and bearing a fluffy towel for her sticky lady bits, she let him gently blot up the messy aftermath of their passion.

Reclining beside her, he wrapped her in crisp sheets and warm eiderdown and strong, gentle arms. But she lay awake long after his breath deepened to the slow rhythm of sleep. Watching the flames crackle and dance in the fireplace, she let herself pretend, just for this night, that this was where she belonged.

My Christmas gift to myself—a pretty lie.

Chapter Fifteen

♥

Michael awoke to silvery dawn, those damn squabbling seagulls, and Annie's gold and silver hair spread across his pillow. Beneath the covers, her curves undulated like rolling coastal hills.

A memory flashed to life: Trappers Cove in summer, the dunes between his great aunt and uncle's house and the sea. He and Violet—they couldn't have been more than twelve and six—clutching flattened cardboard boxes to their chests and running full-tilt to launch themselves at the dune's crest and sled down its silken-sandy face, whooping and laughing.

That's what pulled him back to this place—the memory of joy, that giddy, carefree sense of summer stretched out before him, sheltered from their school-year grind by a kindly, childless old couple who'd donated their share of the family fortune to charity and wanted nothing to do with their Bellevue relatives.

No sandy belly flops on this trip, yet once again, he'd somehow landed in soft, cozy bliss.

After her initial prickliness, he hadn't expected Annie to lay down her arms this easily, much less to melt in his arms and kiss him breathless and take him into her glorious body.

Truly, Trappers Cove was a magical place.

Loath to wake her, he wound a lock of honey around his finger and sighed into a dreamy smile. His body hummed with remembered pleasure. How many times had they made love last night? The moon had been high when he woke to her lips on his chest, his belly, then lower…

He huffed a silent chuckle into the pillow. *Making love.* He used to wince at that corny phrase. But in this case, it rang true. Something new and giddy and impossible to deny flickered beneath his breastbone, and this medieval-schlocky bedroom gleamed like a king's chamber—all because Annie lay asleep beside him.

Until those execrable seagulls started squawking.

Naked, pricked with gooseflesh, he tiptoed to the window, opened it, and leaned out.

"Psst. Shoo. Get outa here." He waved his arms.

A dozen gulls flapped away, cursing him in their raucous language.

A cold hand gripped his ass cheek. "What a sight to wake up to."

Head thrown back in laughter, he turned around and gathered Annie into his arms. "Your hands are like ice."

"Well then, shut the damn window." She pressed her soft breasts and belly to his front and goosed him good with her frigid fingers.

"Yikes! My poor hiney." He danced her backward toward the bed.

"Hiney?" She spluttered a laugh.

He rubbed the sore spot with his palm. "That's what Aunt Ruth called it. 'Oh, hon, did you fall down and bruise your hiney?'"

Annie gave his ass another squeeze. "Sounds like my kind of woman."

"Come to think of it, she was."

Annie's sweet derriere hit the bedpost. He tried to maneuver her around it, but she held fast. "Hold on, are you saying I remind you of your great aunt?"

He lowered his head and nipped at the soft crook of her neck. "In all the best ways. You're kind." He soothed the bite with a tender kiss. "And sweet. And funny. And smart and independent and resourceful..." He trailed kisses up the pale column of her throat.

"Well, in that case—" She scooted to the side, sat on the mattress, looped her arms around his neck, and fell backward, pulling him on top of her. Horny mischief sparkled in her bright blue eyes.

"Again? Miss Annie, you must have mistaken me for a much younger man."

"Oh, pshaw." She wiggled her hips against his growing erection. "I have to get to work soon. Now quick, give me something to remember you by while I battle the last-minute shoppers."

He rocked his hips against her softness. "This medieval setting inspires so many bad jokes about riding to your rescue." Grasping the silken flesh of her inner thigh, he spread her wide. "And jousting. With lances."

"Zounds and gadzooks, Sir Knight. Thou hast made my lady bits grow hungered." Undulating beneath him, she slid her slick folds along his shaft, and the top of his skull nearly lifted off. A faint fruity odor reached his nose. Clever girl, she'd helped herself to the organic, strawberry-flavored lube in the nightstand.

Shivers of pleasure danced over his skin as he canted his hips and nudged the head of his cock between her folds.

Annie's eyes drifted shut, then flew open again as she groped toward the drawer. "Condom."

Close call. He tore open the foil packet and sheathed himself. As desperately as he wanted to feel her silken grip on his bare cock, he'd play it safe until he could get tested and ask her to do the same. Because inside Annie was where he planned to spend every available moment from now until...

"Come here," she hissed in his ear as she wrapped her calves around his hips.

Breath held, body thrumming, he drove into her liquid heat and grasped her tight, his lungs emptying in a whoosh of rapture.

"Give me your hand." She slid his palm down her belly to her thatch of soft curls. "Feel how good this is, joining with you. Michael, you're—" She trailed off on a whimper as his fingers found her clit and caressed the firm nub with a light, teasing touch.

This was heaven, watching her surrender to their shared pleasure. Eyes and mouth and thighs and heart wide open, her breath mingling with his, she clung to him as if she, too, yearned to prolong this sweet connection. How lucky, how perfect to find what he needed so desperately right here in Annie's arms. Joy fizzed in his veins and danced along his nerves as he drank her in.

"Please," she moaned, "I need to feel you moving inside me."

He withdrew to the very tip and then plunged into her again and again—all the while circling her clit. Fighting for control, he kept up a steady in and out rhythm until Annie dug her nails into his shoulders and cried out his name as her inner walls fluttered around him, plunging him into a vortex of wild pleasure.

Soft as falling snowflakes, reality slowly descended, bringing him back to their love-rumpled bed, his sweat-slicked body atop hers, their panting breaths, the goosebumps prickling his skin. He pulled the covers over them both, but Annie wriggled from beneath him and tossed them aside.

"Nooo," he whined, his arm thrown over his eyes. "Don't leave me."

Giggling, she retrieved her red satin panties from where they'd landed, shrugged into her bra, then trotted back to the bed and kissed his lips. "You might be on vacation, but I'm not. Can't keep my customers waiting, no matter how much I'd like to spend the day right here with you."

She held up her dress from last night's Christmas ball and chuckled. "First time I've taken the walk of shame in vintage Dior."

He propped himself up on his elbow. "Are you ashamed, Annie?"

Her mouth curved in a contented smile. "Not in the least." She pulled the dress over her head, gathered her snarled hair up with one hand, and turned her back. "Zip me up?"

He complied, dropping a kiss on the tender curve of her exposed nape. "You'll freeze in this. Let me fetch you something warmer."

A moment later, having wrapped her in his cashmere V-neck and Burberry scarf over her cocktail dress, he walked her to the front door and looped his arms around her hips. "Sure I can't make you breakfast first?"

"I'll get takeout from Cassie's café." Rising on tiptoe, she pecked his lips, then pinned him with her intense blue gaze. "I'm not brushing you off, Michael. Christmas Eve shoppers count on me, and I count on their cash. It's purely a business decision. You understand, don't you?"

"Of course." He returned her kiss and deepened it, memorizing her taste and softness. "But I still hate letting you go." He pressed his forehead to hers. "Spend Christmas with me?"

Her summer sky eyes crinkled at the corners. "I'd love to. My place? I'll cook."

"Oh." He shuffled his feet on the stone tiles. "I, uh, took the liberty of ordering food from Casa Francesca—spaghetti con vongole, shrimp scampi, roast salmon. You know, feast of the seven fishes. I'd hoped we could share it in the library." He'd imagined the whole scene: candles flickering from every surface, a linen-decked table for two, soft music, delicious food, gifts under the tree—the perfect setting to plead his case. And if they happened to end up fucking on the window seat with the sea roaring below, so much the better.

"Hmm." Annie tapped her pursed lips with her forefinger. "A seafood feast or the singles' potluck at Cassie's café. Tough choice." A teasing sparkle lit her eyes.

He cupped her elbows and tugged her a little closer. "You know, you're not technically single at the moment."

Up flew her eyebrows. "I'm not?"

Had he overstepped again? It wasn't easy, respecting her autonomy while making his intentions clear. Getting past her well-earned defenses would take all his negotiating skills.

"Look, we don't have to put a label on this if that's how you want to play it, but here's fair warning, Annie. I'm courting you." He skated his palms up her arms and massaged her stiff shoulders. "In whatever manner you'll permit. And I get it—you have no reason to trust me and plenty of reasons not to. But I want more than just a holiday fling. You and I met for a reason, and I'm not going to waste this opportunity." He pressed a kiss to her lips. "This gift."

She cocked her head, a trace of playful challenge lighting her smile. "We've spent a lot of time in your place, Michael. I mean, in the castle. I'd like to spend some time with you on my turf." She patted his chest. "So, yes to sharing Christmas. Let's say Christmas Eve dinner is on you, and Christmas dinner is on me. It won't be as fancy as Casa Francesca, but I can promise it'll be good."

How did she manage to make everything sound so deliciously dirty? "You drive a hard bargain, Ms. Scott."

She kissed him, then nipped his lower lip. "Oh, I intend to. Now, are you taking me to town?" Releasing him, she backed toward the door. "That's not a dirty pun. I need to get to work."

A wide grin stretched his lips. "Yes, ma'am. Let's go." He grabbed his jacket.

Happiness filled his chest with fizzy lightness as he drove her down the bluff and back to her Christmassy cottage. She was giving him a chance. He had to make the most of it. Now, what to get the lady for Christmas? He needed the perfect gift stat.

After a far-too-brief goodbye kiss, he pulled his phone from his pocket and dialed Violet's number. Miracle of miracles, she picked up.

"Sis, I need advice."

Her husky chuckle tickled his ear. "Oh Lordy, what kind of trouble have you got yourself into this time?"

"The very best kind."

Chapter Sixteen

♥

Annie yawned and stretched her arms high overhead, dislodging the heavy comforter. Brilliant winter sunshine streamed through her bedroom curtains, illuminating the rumpled bedclothes disarranged by last night's midnight tumble.

Grumbling, Michael tugged the satin comforter up to his chin. "Five more minutes." He threw his arm across her waist and nuzzled her shoulder, tickling her neck with his warm breath.

So beautiful, the way his dark lashes fanned across his cheekbones, the gentle rise and fall of his ribs, the sleepy-soft weight of his arm. His unguarded beauty melted her heart.

Stupid heart. All the warm fuzzies in the universe couldn't bridge their differences. Michael would see that as soon as he returned to his high-finance, high-rise world.

Which was all the more reason to enjoy today, right? Knowing this joy was the fleeting kind lent a bittersweet edge, but that didn't erase Michael's warmth from her bed, or the memory of their passion from her soul—a treasure she'd hold tight after he was gone.

The audiobook narrator had said, "A wise person learns to let go of future worries and enjoy the moment, because now is all we ever have."

With a sexy groan, Michael stirred and cupped her bare breast. Soft lips feathered over her shoulder. "Merry Christmas, angel," he croaked, his voice roughened by sleep.

"Merry Christmas to you." She kissed the top of his head and inhaled his spicy-woodsy scent. "Did you sleep well?"

"Never better." His fingertips circled her nipple, a light, teasing touch that stirred an answering throb between her thighs. "If I didn't have to piss, I'd show you just how energized I feel." He rolled to his feet and trotted to the bathroom, his morning wood bobbing.

What would it be like to have him here whenever she wanted? To know he was a phone call away? And why was she such a masochist, indulging in pointless daydreams?

He returned, yawning and scratching his flat belly. "Man, that was some feast last night. I dreamt I was swimming in a sea of scampi and calamari."

"It was marvelous, Michael. Thanks again."

He chuckled. "Thank Francesca. So… coffee?" He bent to rummage through his overnight bag, gifting her a stellar view of his taut rear.

"It may not be up to your refined standards." She kicked off the covers and crossed to the closet, giving his adorable butt a swat as she passed. "But it's hot and comes with waffles, eggs, bacon, grapefruit…" She pulled on the red satin pajamas she'd set out for Christmas but never got around to wearing last night.

"Let's see—what's the dress code for Christmas breakfast?" He pulled out well-worn jeans, flannel pants, and a gray Henley shirt.

Her lips twitched. "I believe it's traditional to wear pajama pants, a sexy Henley, and—this is crucial—no undershorts."

"Funny, I've never heard the commando commandment, but since you're the fashionista, I'll obey." He tossed the fresh undies aside and stepped into his PJs.

"Ooo, I like the sound of that." Wrapping her arms around him from behind, she trailed a fingertip over his enticing, unrestrained bulge.

He goosed her satin-covered ass. "Woman, make up your mind. Do you want breakfast or sex?"

"First coffee, then breakfast, then sex."

He wriggled his rear. "And Christmas presents."

After a flurry of phone calls yesterday, she'd tracked down the perfect gift for Michael, something to help him remember their time together. Perhaps those memories would pull him back into her orbit one day. A foolish hope, but Christmas is prime time for miracles, right?

Though he claimed to lack basic kitchen skills, Michael handled the waffle iron like a pro, humming along with Christmas tunes on her smart speaker while Annie fried bacon and eggs. After stuffing their faces, they freshened their coffee and adjourned to the living room.

Gazing at the pile of gifts spilling from under her beach-themed Christmas tree, she felt a pang of guilt. She'd saved these gaily wrapped packages to give her spirits a boost on her first solo holiday, but that was before Michael. Now, his measly two presents looked sad tucked amongst her stack of loot.

"I can open these others later," she told him.

"No way." Flashing an adorable, childlike grin, he propped his bare feet on her coffee table. "I want to see what your friends and family got you."

She cocked her head. "Why?"

"Because I want to know you better. Now, chop chop. Get to opening."

Her self-consciousness melted away as Michael laughed over comical trinkets from Trappers Cove friends, including hats and accessories for her ceramic panther Roscoe, plus books, a faux-mink blanket, and framed photos from brother Brian and his family. Cheryl gifted her a dating kit—a jeweled tackle box filled with Love Goddess cologne, "Because I know you'll never buy it for yourself," a selfie stick, a book of humorous affirmations, and a pair of red lace panties.

Michael plucked the latter item from her hand. "Are these—oh my, they are!" He wiggled his fingers through the empty space where the crotch should be.

She snatched them back. "Be good, and I'll model them later."

He folded his hands on his lap and fluttered his lashes. "Yes, ma'am. Good as gold."

"You goof." The time had come, and she found herself embarrassingly nervous. Never before had she been tasked with choosing a gift for someone who could buy a whole freakin' town and not even feel the pinch. "I hope you like my present."

Leaning close, he cupped her cheek. His dark eyes glimmered as his thumb stroked her cheekbone. "Annie, you didn't have to get me anything at all. Just sharing Christmas with you is the greatest gift I could ask for."

She blew out a breath, hating this prickly, defensive feeling. "Michael, let's face facts. You're rich. I'm not. That makes for some awkward moments. Let me do what I can to even things out between us."

His brow rumpled. "You really don't—"

"Hush." She squeezed his hand, then rose to fetch his gifts. If there was ever a moment for 'It's the thought that counts,' this was it.

When she returned to the sofa, he clutched a glittery gift bag full of tissue paper in his lap. "Confession time. I had to enlist help with your present."

"From who?"

"Your friend Cheryl. I hope that's okay. Also, my sister and my assistant." With a sheepish grin, he scratched the back of his neck. "Nancy usually takes care of my holiday shopping, but a generic diamond watch wasn't going to cut it this time." He set the feather-light bag on her lap, and she placed the first of two packages on his.

"You go first," they both blurted.

Annie held up a fist. "Rock, paper, scissors?"

Her rock smashed his scissors, so he gently tore the glitter-snowflake wrapping paper from her first gift, a painting she'd found at Janice's art gallery. Its simple brushed steel frame would probably fit in well with his corner office or penthouse.

He held the canvas up to the light. "It's beautiful. Wait—" He peered closer at the glossy beachscape. "Is that the castle?"

"It is indeed. This was painted from Ivan's Hollow, looking up at the bluff. It was still a ruin back then, but I figured you might appreciate a souvenir of your stay." She cleared her throat to ease a sudden tightness.

He ghosted a fingertip over the painted whitecaps and rough stone cliffs. "As if I could ever forget." He laid it down on the table and gathered her into his arms. "What a beautiful memento of a special time. Thank you, Annie." His voice cracked, probably at the reminder of how little time they had left together.

Sadness rolled through her, weighting her limbs.

Michael rubbed his cheek against her hair and murmured, "Yesterday, after you left, I read a few more chapters of *The Courage to*

Change. Have you reached the part where the author says how change is like a horse?"

Annie chuckled into his solid warmth. "I wrote it down." She pulled her journal from a drawer in the coffee table. "Here it is. 'Change is like a horse. You can take the reins and guide its path, or you can hang on and let it run. The latter choice is exhilarating but increases the chance you'll get bucked off and break your ass. So develop your riding skills, darling, and consider the path before you.'
"

"That's the one." He kissed her temple. "Kind of feels like we're riding bareback, doesn't it?"

Immediately, her mind flew to riding Michael's cock without a latex sheath between them. But asking him to get tested implied a future connection she doubted they'd ever share.

"Whoa now, that's not what I meant." He tilted her chin up and kissed her through a wide grin. "But loving you with nothing between us would be a dream come true."

Loving her? Why did he have to phrase it like that and set her heart racing? She socked his arm. "Let's get through the holidays first."

"Deal." He smooched her nose, then tapped the bag in her lap. "Open your present."

Beneath the tissue paper, she found three envelopes. She tore the first open with her nail and unfolded a heavy sheet of sea green stationery. "Reserved for Ms. Annabelle Scott, a full day of pampering with hot stone massage, cool gemstone facial, nourishing algae mask, sea-flora hydrating wrap..."

Michael squirmed in his seat. "That one was Cheryl's suggestion. Is that okay?"

"Okay? It's brilliant!" A full day at the Sea Queen Spa was a luxury she'd never permitted herself—too expensive, too time-consuming.

His grin widened. "I'm so glad. Open another one."

The next envelopes revealed certificates for a wine tasting and dinner for two at the Seafoam Winery in Aberdeen, and VIP tickets to the Olympia Jazz festival in March.

"Michael, these are—I don't know what to say."

He lifted his shoulder in a half shrug. "Cheryl and my sister agreed that someone with your refined taste would appreciate experiences over physical objects."

"I'll have to thank them both." She pecked his lips. "Two tickets, huh? Is this a hint?"

His gaze fell to his lap. "Well, I'd love to share these experiences with you. And lots more. But it's your choice." He raised his eyes and pinned her with a look so full of longing her heart squeezed hard.

A less jaded woman might see these incredibly sweet, thoughtful gifts as proof of love. Though Michael had money enough to buy her a stable of horses or a Maserati, he'd taken the time to learn her tastes and choose something personally meaningful. But love? Like the real deal? They'd only known each other for a week.

Head out of the clouds. Feet on the ground.

She forced a chipper grin and fetched his last present from beneath the tree. "This one took some hunting. Found it in a trunk in the attic."

He chuckled as he tore the paper. "Feels too soft to be a skeleton." Splashes of color peeked through, some bright, some faded. As he uncovered more of the cloth, his mouth fell open. "Is this... Aunt Ruby's?" The astonished sparkle in his eyes filled made her so happy she'd tracked down this childhood keepsake.

She nodded. "She gave my granny this crazy quilt years ago. I remember napping on it when I was little." She traced the irregular scraps. "Recognize anything you wore as a kid?"

He unfolded the quilt across their laps. "God, that was so long ago. Wait." His eyebrows shot up as he tapped a triangle of T-shirt cloth printed with tiny dinosaurs. "I remember this one. Wow." He clutched the quilt to his chest, his eyes glistening. "I'm touched, Annie. What an amazing gift. You've given me back some very precious memories."

She patted his cheek, then thumbed away a tear from the corner of his eye.

His self-conscious laugh crackled with emotion. "Ruby was a whiz with a sewing machine. She made her own clothes, and she mended the jeans Violet and I tore scrambling over that rock wall to Ivan's Hollow." His voice hitched. "Look at this one. She taught us how to tie-dye T-shirts." He rubbed the cloth to his cheek. "What a great old gal—creative, resourceful, and always patient with our shenanigans."

Annie regarded him, her mouth scrunched to the side.

"What?"

"Looking at you now, so polished and suave, it's hard to imagine you as a scrappy little kid tearing his jeans on the rocks. I wonder if we met as kids. My brother and I were agile as mountain goats back then, always racing over that rock wall."

He draped his arm around her shoulders. "Just goes to show you—even a snooty rich guy has layers."

"Not so snooty." She toyed with a button on his wear-softened Henley. "I'm glad you let me see your sweet, nostalgic side."

He gathered her against his chest and nuzzled her messy morning hair. "You bring out all kinds of feelings in me, Annie. I'm so glad we met. Without you, I'd be holed up in that castle perseverating over PowerPoints."

She pecked his lips. "Well, we can't have that, not on Christmas. Say, did you want to go to church?"

His mouth quirked in a wry smile. "To tell the truth, I'm not really religious."

"Neither am I, but I like the music." She glanced at her antique mantel clock. "Too late, anyway. How about a walk on the beach?"

He drew her into a slow, sweet kiss. "How about we make our own music first?" His soft lips skimmed her jaw, then he nipped her earlobe, sending a bolt of sensation straight to her clit. "I love the way you sing when I tease you with my tongue."

"You're on." She arched her neck, inviting more of his seductive touch.

He pulled her to her feet, then folded the quilt over his arm. "Come on. Let's infuse this with some new memories—a bridge from happy past to happy future."

Chapter Seventeen

♥

As he floated back down to earth, arms wrapped around Annie's sweet, soft body, Michael trailed gentle kisses over her sweat-dewed forehead, her closed eyelids, the bump on her nose.

"That tickles." She squirmed in his embrace while he continued his lazy exploration, memorizing every detail.

He kissed the bridge of her nose. "How'd you get this bump?

Her lips curved in a drowsy smile. "Fell off a horse. Just a pony, really. I was ten. Landed right on my noggin."

"Ah." He smooched her lips. "That explains a lot."

With a yelp of outrage, she flung her thigh over his middle, rolled him onto his back, and pinned his arms above his head. "Okay, smart-ass." She nipped the tip of his nose. "How'd you get your bump?"

He grinned up at his feisty queen. "My one and only bar fight. Some drunk frat bro insulted my fiancée. I didn't think, I just punched." He winced at the memory. "He punched harder."

"Quite the gallant hero." She pressed a kiss to the old injury.

"Quite the idiot. The guy was linebacker huge. Blood everywhere. My mother offered to have the bump repaired, but I refused." He pried his wrists from her grip and pulled her down for a proper kiss. "My one rebellion against the family standards."

"Well, I like it." She kissed the spot again, and were he a younger man, the press of her breasts against his bare chest would've triggered another round of glorious sex.

Instead, she rolled off him and nestled to his side, her head propped up on her elbow. "I'll bet your fiancée was impressed."

"Actually, she was pissed. Told me she could've handled it herself." He chuckled. "The whole incident was wildly out of character for me. Instead of stepping back to analyze my options, I just acted on instinct. Not my usual M.O."

She dropped a kiss on his bare shoulder. "Well, maybe you should give your instincts more credit." She rolled out of bed and, beckoning, backed toward the bathroom door, a saucy grin on her glowing face. "What do you say to a shower for two?"

How could he refuse?

Following a steamy, slippery interlude in her claw-foot tub, Michael hacked up carrots, onions, celery root, and potatoes while Annie browned hunks of beef and filled her electric pressure cooker with wine, broth, and herbs. After assembling everything to simmer, they set out for a stroll on the beach.

Annie waved to her neighbors, an older gal and a little girl whose corkscrew curls flew with each ka-chonk of her pogo stick.

"Miss Annie!" the little one hollered. "Lookit! Santa got me a jumper stick."

Annie clapped her hands together. "Splendid, Olivia. And you're already an expert jumper." She gave the grandmother a wink before taking Michael's hand and turning toward the beachfront road. That simple touch warmed him right to his core, despite the brisk winter wind off the Pacific.

The child's singsong voice trailed after them. "Miss Annie gots a boyfriend."

"Cute kid." He glanced back over his shoulder. "Friend of yours?"

"Yeah, Olivia's a doll. So's her Grandma. Marion runs the yoga studio over the bakery." Smiling, she shook her head. "Kind of blows my mind to think how, if I'd made different choices, I might be sharing Christmas with grandkids of my own."

Grandkids? Annie? He did a quick mental calculation and realized that, had he not blown his engagement at twenty-two, he might be a new grandfather as well. Talk about the path not taken…

An image flashed in his mind's eye—hunched over his MacBook Pro, working up investment proposals while a cute little tyke clambered onto his lap, knocking over his coffee. "Play with me, Grampa!"

Kaboom! Mind blown.

When they reached the wooden boardwalk fronting the beach, Annie leaned her elbows on the railing and gazed out at the waving dune grass. Pale winter sunlight glinted off the water and burnished Annie's wind-blown hair.

Looping his arm around her shoulders, he snugged her closer. She leaned into him and sighed, a wistful, shaky sound.

"You okay, Annie?"

Her chuckle rang Sahara dry. "I should be over this by now, but sometimes it just—ambushes me."

Right—she'd mentioned miscarriages. What a heartache to carry all these years. With her no-nonsense manner and wide-open heart, Annie would've made a splendid mother.

He'd endured his own moments of regret, like at their last company picnic, when laughing, squealing kids chased each other along the shoreline of Lake Washington. But he'd never come close to becoming a dad, not really. To have wanted a child, begun to bond with a new life, then lose it—that must be devastating.

Still staring out to sea, she nuzzled his shoulder. "Matt and I were so damn young, so confident of our future. We'd have three kids. He'd teach at the high school, and I'd run a boutique." Her voice quavered. "Every time I got pregnant, I was sure this one would stick, you know?" She raised her teary eyes to his. "So much loss—it broke us."

"I can't begin to imagine, Annie." He wrapped his arms around her shoulders and rocked her slowly, giving her time to breathe through her grief.

Baring her private heartache was a gift more precious than any physical object—an act of vulnerability and trust.

After a long moment of swaying together, she snuffled and laid her head on his shoulder. "I've loved watching my nieces and nephew grow up, but it's not the same, you know? There are things in life you want dearly and just don't get. And I'm so fortunate. I have a thriving business, good friends, a lovely home. I should be content."

He hugged her tight. "Maybe it's not our nature to be content. I haven't mastered that trick yet."

"You?" Twisting in his embrace, she pinned him with her tear-bright eyes.

Sheepish, he shrugged. "I know, who am I to complain? On the surface, I'm beyond privileged. But sometimes I can't help wanting more—I don't know, substance? Fostering tech start-ups made me feel like my work mattered, and now I'm probably losing that."

"Midlife crisis?"

"Yeah. Textbook case." He pressed a kiss to her temple. "Shall we walk?"

"Yeah, let's." She slipped her hand into his and started down the wood-plank path over the dunes. "The sea breeze is an excellent cure for the blues. Blows away the detritus. Scrubs you clean."

When they reached the stairs, she kicked off her shoes and tucked them beneath a bench. He followed suit and trotted behind her down the sun-warmed wooden steps and onto smooth, cool sand. Side by side in companionable silence, they picked their way around driftwood shards and sharp shell fragments to the hard-packed damp sand where, arm in arm, they watched the mesmerizing rise and fall of Mother Ocean's breath…whoosh in, sigh out, on and on forever.

A squadron of pelicans glided low over the water. Michael fought the urge to scoop up a pebble and toss it at them like the sandy-footed boy who loved this beach long ago.

He chuckled. "You're right about how the sea cuts through the bullshit. For a minute there, I time-travelled back to childhood summers here." Digging in with his toe, he sketched a heart in the damp sand, then used a bit of driftwood to carve *AS + MG 4 ever*.

"Whoa now, slow your roll, rich boy." She shoved his shoulder, knocking him off balance. "We hardly know each other."

"Easy, woman. Don't destroy my masterpiece."

But the surf took care of that, washing over their feet and blurring his message.

"Come on, Romeo. Let's walk to the rock wall." She pointed to the line of boulders that separated the main beach from Ivan's Hollow, the cliff-framed cove only accessible during low tide. Back when he was small, local kids convinced him that secret beach was a magical place full of hidden treasure.

They set off at an easy pace, waving greetings to beach walkers and anglers.

"Oh wow, I remember this rock." He pointed to a lone boulder with indentations the perfect size for a pair of kid-size butts. He and Violet had perched here, spinning tales of pirates, ghosts, and friendly sea monsters. He sat and patted the spot beside him.

She sat and speared him with a probing look. "So, you know about my miserable love life. Tell me about this foolish girlfriend who—how did you put it—kicked you to the curb?"

She remembered that? Interesting.

"Her name's Crystal. She's in finance, like me. Nice woman."

Annie waited, eyebrows raised.

"It's no big deal. We parted amicably."

"Because?"

"She fell for someone else."

"Ouch." She rubbed his arm as if soothing a bruise. "Did you love her?"

"No, ours was an arrangement of convenience. But I like her, and I wish her the best." He shifted to take both her hands, rubbing his thumbs over the fine bones. "If she has the chance to find love, she should go for it."

Annie nodded slowly, her lips in a tight line. "I see. So I'm your rebound crush?"

His breath whooshed out as if she'd punched him right in the solar plexus. How could she think so little of their amazing chemistry? He was spending Christmas with her, for chrissake. Ever since his arrival in Trappers Cove, he'd been following her around like a lovesick puppy. How much proof did she need before she'd believe the devotion he poured into every kiss, every word, every touch?

"Annie." He kissed her knuckles. "You are so much more than a crush. Meeting you tumbled my world on its ass. With you by my side, I feel like I'm finally looking in the right direction. The fog is lifting.

Knots are untying. All the cheesy metaphors." He stroked a damp curl back from her forehead. "I know you don't trust me yet, but hear me out, okay?"

She nodded, eyes wide.

"What we have is significant." He arced a hand overhead. "Like, kismet-level important. And I have no intention of disappearing from your life after the new year. I want to know you, share experiences with you, build a future." He cupped her jaw and traced the curve of her mouth with his thumb. "Please, Annie, don't write me off as just a fling."

Biting her lip, she stared at her bare feet. "Michael, sometimes good sex is just good sex."

"And sometimes, phenomenal sex is an opening door. A glimpse of something so much better." Gripping her elbows, he pressed his forehead to hers. "I've built a fortune on my intuition, and what we have has so much potential, Annie. Will you at least give us a try?"

Her piercing blue eyes speared him. "You're asking a lot."

"I know. But there it is—my beating heart on a platter, yours to take or squash."

"Gross." She wrinkled her nose. "And you were being so poetic."

"Hey, my gig's finance, not lovey-dovey words." Grateful for her gift of comic relief, he took her hand. "Come on, let's go climb the rock wall for old times' sake."

As they padded on the damp sand, he wondered—was it the magic of this place, the memory of intense childhood emotion that ramped up his emotions? He hardly recognized himself, but there was no denying the irresistible tug behind his ribs whenever Annie turned those impossibly blue eyes on him. His feelings for this confounding, frustrating, fascinating woman encompassed so much more than lust.

Chalk it up to Christmas magic, or Zora's magic crystal in his pocket, but Trappers Cove and Annie Scott had gifted him the best present ever.

Michael Garwood believed in love again.

Build a future with me? What the hell does that mean?

Listlessly, Annie pushed a chunk of beef around her plate, tracing spirals in the wine-rich gravy. Ironic—this was probably the best boeuf bourguignon she'd ever made, but she couldn't force an appetite around the mob of butterflies in her stomach.

Michael's soft hand fell over her restless one, stilling its motion. "Annie, what's wrong? You've hardly touched your food."

She dropped her fork with a clatter. "Oh, I uh...guess I ate too much breakfast."

She knew she was spoiling their cozy Christmas dinner with her mood, but her acting skills had dried up along with her appetite. Sucking in a deep breath, she forced her clenched jaws into a smile.

Michael pushed his empty plate away, refilled her wine glass with Columbia Valley cabernet, then leaned on his elbow and searched her face, his gaze probing deep.

"Bullshit," he said at last, his soft expression belying the harsh word. "We walked in the cold wind for hours. There's no way you're not hungry." He tapped her nose with his forefinger. "You're hiding from me."

Why did he have to be so damn perceptive?

Normally the queen of straight talk, here she sat, playing with the food she'd so carefully prepared. Dithering, that's what she was doing. And she hated dithering.

She slid her plate to the side and took his hand. "Okay, you're right. What you said out there, about us, about the future—I'm having a hard time wrapping my head around that."

Grasping her hand, he pressed his soft lips to her knuckles, a move that always echoed between her thighs. Every single time. "What about your heart?"

Pressure swelled in her chest, her throat, behind her eyes. "Honestly, my heart is still pretty shredded."

He nodded slowly. "That's why you keep it under wraps."

"Michael, I—argh!" She knotted her free hand in her salt-stiffened hair. "I'd love to believe in a future with you, but I can't help feeling like a ginormous fool, falling for a man who's so... unsuitable."

Up flew his eyebrows. "Says who?"

"Years of painful experience."

Emotion flickered over his face. For a long moment, he chewed his lower lip, a sexy gesture that wasn't helping her concentration at all. But of course, Michael Garwood, apex business tycoon and master negotiator, wasn't about to give up.

He released her and folded his hands on the table. "*The Courage to Change* disagrees. I mean, that's what the whole book is about—how we have to unshackle ourselves from the past to build a better future, a life worthy of our spirit and potential." He scooted his chair closer and trailed a finger over her collarbone, then tapped her sternum, right over her thundering heart. "And the Annie Scott I'm coming to know is not afraid to face hard things."

She gaped at him, then spluttered with laughter.

His cheeks reddened. "Gah. That's not what I meant."

"Wasn't it, though?" She wiped a tear of mirth.

He looped one arm around her waist, the other around her shoulders, and dipped her backward, tango style. A playful grin twitched on his lips. "That's one of the many things I love about you, Annie. You see right through me." He kissed one the corner of her mouth, then the other, a teasing touch that tempted her to drop the thorny topic and drag him back to her bedroom.

But this was too important to brush away with the breadcrumbs. Her heart was on the line. Ditto her self-concept and her future.

"And you see through me, Michael. Which scares the shit out of me, quite frankly."

He righted her and laced their fingers together on the tablecloth, his eyes enormous, his lips gently parted, waiting for the answer he needed and deserved.

Annie gave a sigh that emptied her lungs. "Right before meeting you, I'd finally admitted a hard truth to myself—despite my free-spirit, sex-positive blah blah blah, what I really crave is a partner, someone I can count on. Short-term flings once lifted my spirit, but now they drag it down."

He enfolded her hand in both of his. Around and around, his magic thumb stroked her skin, soothing and addictive. "I've told you again and again, Annie, I want us to share much more than a brief fling."

"Hearing it is one thing. Believing it is another."

"Then why are you sharing your Christmas with me?"

Embarrassed, she chewed her lip. "I told myself this would be my final fling, an ego-boosting treat for the holidays. I thought you were safe, because once you returned home, you'd forget about me."

He shook his head slowly. "Not gonna happen, Annie. Whether you let me in or not, you've already carved your name all over my heart." He pressed her palm to his chest, right over the strong, steady heart that vibrated her bones with every beat. "And I know you care for me. Even though your words speak of fear, your actions speak of hope. You shared your holiday with me, for God's sake. You introduced me to your town, your friends. Is that what you do with someone you don't care about?"

Struck dumb by his logic, she could only shake her head.

He wound a strand of her hair around his finger, his gaze as wide-open as the endless sea. "We both know how amazing we could be together. And if you can't say it out loud yet, that's okay. I can wait until you trust me. But know this—even if you send me away, I'm not going to forget about you. Not ever."

Her throat tightened as her aching, foolish heart duked it out with common sense.

"Michael, you're a wonderful guy, but we both know there's no way I could ever fit into your world."

He reared back. His nostrils flared on a deep inhalation. "You don't seem like the type to give up so easily. Was I wrong about that?"

"I'm not giving up, Michael, I just—" Sorrow weighted her shoulders, her brow, the corners of her mouth. "I'm old and wise enough to know who I am, through and through. And I won't contort myself to fit in where I don't belong."

His brow rumpled. "Why would you let anyone tell you where you belong?"

She threw up her hands. "You've never had to smile through all the little digs that let you know you're out of place, not good enough, not welcome. After a while, it feels like the death of a thousand cuts. I lived that when I, daughter of humble, hardworking people, dared to set up shop in Bellevue. I won't subject myself to that again." Sorrow closed up her throat as she stroked his cheek with her fingertips. "Not even for you."

He slumped in his seat. "Okay. I hear you. Forget about my parents' New Year's Eve party. I was selfish to ask. I see that now." Shoulders slumped, he reached for her hand again. "I'll make an appearance, smile nice and press the flesh, then fly back in time to kiss you at midnight."

"Michael, Trappers Cove doesn't have an airport."

He flapped a hand. "I'll figure it out."

Clearly, he was losing his mind if he thought that would work.

She rubbed the tightly corded muscles of his forearm. "You need to be there, don't you?"

With a soft grunt, he closed his eyes and leaned into her touch. "My disappearance over the holidays has sparked rumors—they say I'm having a midlife meltdown. I can't be trusted." His lips twisted in a wry grin. "So I'll go alone. I'll endure the come-ons and make nice with the movers and shakers. The board has to see me as stable, reliable, or they'll believe the rumors, and I'll lose everything I've built." He placed his broad, warm hand over hers. "You understand, don't you? Can you imagine someone moving in to steal your shop and turn it into something else entirely? Something more profitable but soulless?"

Shame burned behind her breastbone. Of course she understood. Michael might be rich as Croesus, but he was every bit as passionate about his business as she was about hers. Her wounded pride had nearly made her forget one of her most fundamental values—being a good friend. After all Michael had done for her and Trappers Cove, she owed him far more than enduring one uncomfortable evening, even if their connection burned out after the holidays.

She clasped his hand. "I do understand where you're coming from. If my business were threatened with a hostile takeover, I'd do whatever it took to protect it. So I'll go to the party with you and be your moral support. I'm a woman of my word, Michael, and no matter how ill-matched we are, I care about you." She swallowed the spiky lump in her throat. "But please don't build fantasies about me fitting into your life—because I won't."

His dark eyes sparkled with determination. "Then we'll build a new world, Annie—one where we can be ourselves and be together. We've both endured so much and accomplished so much. We can figure this out." He wove his fingers through hers. "I know we can."

Oh, this darling, frustrating, unrelenting man! She desperately wanted to believe him, but she couldn't fight reality, and reality has a cruel way of dulling the brightest hopes.

Tears choked her. "How can you be sure? Once you go back, how do you keep real life from washing away this feeling like that heart you drew in the sand?"

His dark eyes burned into her, sharp and merciless. "Because, beauty, I've built my success on knowing when something is right."

Her gaze fell to her lap. "Your parents' fortune also had something to do with it."

"The money thing again." He cupped her jaw in both hands and waited until she lifted her eyes to his. "Annie, can't you see me through all that?"

The thing was, she did. Even with tears blurring her vision, she saw him, clear and bright and so perfect he pierced her armored heart.

And he saw *her*.

Did their differences really matter that much? She was resourceful and strong, and he seemed so sure.

Maybe this time she really could shake off her past and see the world through new eyes. She'd asked the universe for a partner, and here he was, a sweet, loving man offering her his heart. All she needed was the courage to accept this best-ever Christmas gift.

"Yes, Michael. I see you." Surrendering to his gravity, she pressed her lips to his in a tender kiss, savoring the sweetness of this man, this moment, this lucky accident.

Please, God, let it last.

Chapter Eighteen

♥

Maybe the helicopter was a mistake.

Michael had thought it would be a fun surprise, whisking Annie into the sky for a quick flight to Bellevue—an expression of his gratitude and affection, especially since she'd agreed to brave his parents' boring New Year's Eve party. And even a way to prove how easily and quickly they could bridge the distance between his home base and hers.

But when the chopper landed on the beach, Annie turned green and clutched him like a drowning woman. Damn, he should've asked first, should've known she was deathly afraid of flying. Assuming she'd enjoy what he enjoyed was a bonehead move for a guy already skating on thin ice.

After sending the pilot back, he packed their bags into his Jeep and headed for the interstate. The cold snap had lifted, replaced by a typical winter drizzle. As they rounded a sharp turn through dripping pines, he set a tentative hand on her knee.

"Again, I'm sorry, Annie. I should have asked, not assumed."

She flashed a thin, brittle smile. "It's okay, honestly. You couldn't have known about my thing with flying. And flimsy death traps."

"For what it's worth, I'm looking forward to learning all your hot buttons." He squeezed her knee. "As soon as this party is behind us, I plan to memorize all your likes and dislikes."

She leaned her head against the window and exhaled a sigh that fogged the glass.

"And the party will be fine, I promise. If anyone is rude to you, I'll smack them down." He was too diplomatic to dismiss Annie's concerns outright, but honestly, he couldn't imagine even his parents' stiff friends being overtly rude to a party guest. They might drink too much, perhaps let slip indiscrete details about someone's affair, but bald-faced snobbery? He'd never seen that kind of behavior.

Annie patted his hand. "Still playing the knight in shining armor, even outside the castle."

Holiday traffic slowed their arrival, and by the time they reached the Bellevue turnoff, dusk was falling. The concrete and glass canyon he called home glowed with white twinkle lights. Funny, he hadn't noticed before this December how bland it all looked—elegant and polished, but lacking Trappers Cove's color and spirit. In comparison, these sophisticated storefronts felt sterile, impersonal, dull.

He parked in his underground spot, leaned over the center console, and pulled Annie into a kiss. "I give you my solemn promise. I'm going to make tonight as painless as possible." Her spicy-rose perfume teased his nose as he nuzzled the satiny skin behind her ear. "And afterward, I'll give you so much pleasure, you'll be glad you put up with my stuffy work associates."

That won him a smile with real warmth. She traced his jawline with her lips. "Will you have to shave?"

"Afraid so. To convince the board, I'll have to look like my old self—sharp, clean cut, focused." He pressed a kiss into her palm. "The minute I accomplish the mission, I'll let it grow again."

"The sacrifices we make for love."

He huffed a wry laugh. "I assure you, tonight's party is purely business."

She patted his cheek. "And you love your business. Nothing wrong with that. Now, let's go gird our loins for battle."

They rode up to the marble lobby, then took the private elevator to his penthouse apartment. As the numbers ticked upward, he watched Annie chew her lip.

He nudged her with his elbow. "Nervous?"

"Honestly, I'm still a little nauseated. You know, from the helicopter." She flashed a wan smile and wound her arm through his. "But it'll be fine. I mean, parties are fun, right? I'll drink champagne and enjoy the view, and if anyone gets snooty, I'll imagine them in their underwear."

The door slid open. Annie stepped into the foyer and clapped her hands to her mouth. "This is—um—it's very—"

He chuckled. "Go ahead, be honest."

She entered the great room and executed a slow spin, taking in the wall of windows, the sleek gas fireplace, the spare modern furnishings. When he moved up here ten years ago, he hired a popular decorator who filled the space with low sofas and chairs in neutral tones of beige-gray, lots of chrome, glass, and grayish wood. He'd never given much thought to the abstract art objects and paintings she installed. They gave the apartment a finished look, and that was enough for him. But compared to Annie's eclectic, colorful, cozy home, his place looked and felt as sterile as a hospital waiting room.

Annie skated her fingertips over the copper-colored artistic blob on the mantelpiece, then turned and sighed. "I don't see any of you in here."

He shrugged. "My office shows more of me than my apartment." Which was true, thanks to Nancy's attention to detail. What a sad commentary on his life.

Moving to the open-plan kitchen, he checked the contents of the fridge. Thank God, his housekeeper had dumped the wilted leftover takeout and stocked fresh fruit, veggies, his favorite organic hummus, and enough cheese for a sizeable cocktail party. Not that he ate much cheese, but his housekeeper did.

He assembled a selection of nibbles on the breakfast bar. "Glass of wine?"

She wrinkled her nose.

God, he hated seeing her look so stiff and uncomfortable in his home. Maybe his sister would help him spruce up the place, give it a woman's touch. Or perhaps Annie could...

She scooped up her garment bag and overnight case. "Thanks, but I'd like plenty of time to get ready. Which way?"

He led her into his bedroom, where she laid her bag on the bed. He winced as another embarrassing truth smacked him—Annie was the only spot of color in this gray and ivory room.

Note to self: order some green plants, stat. And buy some colorful pillows. Looks like a morgue in here.

Annie unzipped her bag, revealing a flash of brilliant blue. "I'll go freshen up. You know what I would love, though?"

He stepped closer, his fingers itching to touch her soft curves.

"A cup of coffee. It's going to be a long night."

"Coming right up." Disappointed, he left her to her ablutions while he fired up his electric kettle and ground fresh Kenya AA beans. The metallic chime of his doorbell cut through the grinder's din.

He peeped through the spyhole, then threw open the door. "Violet!"

"Happy New Year!" His sister flashed her usual mischievous grin, lifted a paper noisemaker to her lips, and blew, bopping him on the nose.

"Come in. I was expecting to see you." Throwing an arm around her shoulders, he pulled her inside. "You're not here for the party, are you?"

"'Fraid so, big bro." She dropped a duffle bag at her feet and hugged him tight. "Love the whiskers."

"Enjoy them while you can." He held her at arm's length and drank in her familiar, funky vibe. "Looking good, kiddo. Life on the road suits you."

She hadn't changed in the six months since they'd last stood face to face. Same plump hips—a rebellion against their mother's strict diet and exercise regimen. Ears, neck, wrists and fingers piled with ethnic jewelry, a loose, chunky sweater over faded leggings and ankle boots. She'd be right at home in Trappers Cove. Between Zora's hippie-dippy shop and Annie's place, she'd find everything she needed.

He pulled her into another tight hug. "Man, I've missed you. It's been too long."

"True." She patted his cheek. "Hey, can I crash with you tonight? Randy's off saving the rain forest."

"And you're not with him?"

She pinched the bridge of her nose. "Yeah, well—my van died. Mom offered me a new one, but that gift comes with a whole net of strings."

He furrowed his brow. "You know you can always ask me."

"I know, but I don't like to take advantage. Anyway, I cut a deal with Dad—he'll pay for repairs in exchange for showing my face at their party. I figure, why not? Just a couple hours, a few shrimp cocktails, and I'll be on my way."

"Um, okay, sure. But I should warn you—"

"Mamma Mia!" Violet's dark eyes bugged out. "Who's the hottie?"

Annie stood in the bedroom doorway holding up two gowns, both in blazing bright colors. "Michael, which do you—" Taken aback, she gaped as her gaze darted from him to Violet and back.

Violet poked his shoulder. "Introduce me."

He sent up a silent prayer that his sister and new love would get along.

"Annie, this is my sister. Violet, meet my friend Annie Scott from Trappers Cove."

Grinning, Violet elbowed his ribs. "Friend or girlfriend?"

"I'm working on that," he said under his breath.

Annie laid the gowns over a chair and stepped forward, hand extended. Never one to stand on ceremony, Violet pulled her in for a hug.

"Awfully brave of you to face a party with the 'rents. You must like my brother a lot."

Annie shot him a wary glance. "I do."

Violet clapped Annie's shoulder. "Don't worry, hon. We'll take good care of you. Is this what you're wearing? She lifted one dress, then the other, both flashy vintage gowns—the first an eighties style with big, puffed sleeves and a deep V back, the other an Audrey Hepburn-esque number covered in emerald sequins.

His sister whistled. "Hubba hubba. What do you think, Michael?"

He suppressed a frown, knowing that Annie would stand out in either choice. To the best of his recollection, most of the women would be dressed in black. He could hear the microaggressions fly as she entered the party glittering like Christmas.

He cleared his throat. "Did you bring anything more... um... conservative?"

Violet clucked her tongue. "You mean more boring? These gowns are fabulous. Way more elegant than the boho schmatta I'm wearing." She flashed a grin at Annie. "You'd think at almost fifty I'd be over pushing our parents' buttons, but it's still fun. Come on, let's get fancy."

She scooped up her bag and trotted to the guest room.

Annie started after her, then turned back, brows lowered, eyes narrowed. "In Trappers Cove, you told me you liked my style. Now it's a problem?" She held the sequined green dress to her chest. "This is who I am, Michael. Unconventional. Bright and shiny. Definitely not a follower. Take it or leave it."

Yikes. Introducing Annie to his social circle would require as much finesse as persuading the board.

Grasping her hips, he pulled her close and pressed his forehead to hers. "I'll take it. Whatever you wear, you'll be the belle of the ball."

She gave a sultry chuckle, her eyes sparkling with sapphire devilry. "Play your cards right, mister, and I'll ring your bell." She brushed her fingertip over his fly, flung the gowns over her shoulder, and sashayed down the hall to join Violet.

Before she closed the door, his sister's always-too-loud voice rang out. "My brother has a huge heart under all that polish. He just needs a good woman like you to loosen him up."

Michael retired to his bathroom to shave, grimacing as his workday face re-emerged from beneath the foam.

Violet was right. He did need loosening up. Here he was, removing the beard Annie found sexy in order to impress his colleagues and, let's face it, his parents.

They loved him, in their stiff, limited way—of that he had no doubt. And he loved them. Until this recent crisis at GRA Capital, he'd dismissed their expectations as no big deal, just the way the game was played—show up in the requisite black tie, press the flesh, and flatter the movers and shakers whose money and influence he needed to do good things in the world. Without the funds Mother and Dad gifted him after earning his MBA, the firm wouldn't be where it was today. And though he'd repaid them long ago, he was still grateful. After all, Dad's ultra-wealthy father hadn't given him a dime until his death at ninety-two.

But at age fifty-four, it was high time he stopped dancing to their tune, much less dragging his new girlfriend into their status-building rituals. After tonight, Mother and Dad would have to party without him.

A merry peal of laughter jerked his attention from his slippery cufflinks to the guest room down the hall.

The women emerged, Annie in the curve-skimming emerald sequined gown, her hair in an artful up-do with golden tendrils floating around her face. Like a catwalk model, she slunk toward him, her face arranged in elegant boredom.

He gave a low whistle. "Audrey Hepburn never looked as luscious as you."

The chandelier's light glittered in the rhinestones surrounding her vintage pearl earrings. If she were his, those would be real diamonds.

Vamping comically, Violet followed in a floaty purple caftan embroidered in silver thread, her dark hair upswept to show off big dangly earrings. Her armful of colorful bangles jingled as she straightened his bow tie. "Don't know why you insist on wearing these choke collars. How can you breathe?"

Annie tweaked his pocket square. "I think he looks dashing. Very James Bond. But I do miss the beard."

"I'll let it grow again, starting tomorrow."

Though he'd only known her less than two weeks, he was learning her little tells and recognized the nerves simmering behind her smile. He cupped her elbows and gave her a smooch. "You are stunning. All the other guys will be jealous."

"The women too," Violet added, "though they'll never admit it."

Annie gave a delicate snort. "Here, let me help you with those cuf-flinks." She fiddled with the tricky clasps, and the spicy-floral perfume wafting from her cleavage was enough to make a man dizzy.

"Will I meet your partners tonight?" she asked as his left cufflink clicked into place.

"No, schmoozing is my job. Jose will be with his family, and I think Rick is skiing. I'd never ask them to endure this."

Frowning, she cocked a hip. "You're not exactly instilling confi-dence here."

"Don't worry," Violet assured her, "you'll have me and Michael to shield you from the worst of it." She stepped to the bar and poured them each a shot of Extra Añejo Tequila, then raised her glass. "Trust me, these parties are more fun if you pre-game. Cheers!"

Annie downed her drink, shuddered, looped her arm through his, and faced him with a tight-lipped smile.

He pressed a kiss to her perfumed temple. "Ready?"

"As I'll ever be. Let's do this."

Chapter Nineteen

♥

From her plush seat in the limo Michael's parents sent to collect them, Annie glanced sideways at Michael, flipping through his phone and muttering under his breath as he reviewed his talking points. Tension radiated from his stiff posture. They'd be having so much more fun at the VFW pajama party back in Trappers Cove, but her sacrifice would be worth it if her presence helped steady him—and kept the vultures away.

She gripped his biceps and squeezed gently. "You've got this, Michael."

Visibly relaxing, he smooched her cheek. "Thanks again, angel."

"My pleasure." Funny how after only two weeks together, she felt so protective of him. Possessive too. Though she wasn't at all proud to acknowledge it, the thought of him battling come-ons filled her belly with sick heat.

Those snooty bitches better keep their diamond-crusted fingers off my man.

She huffed a chuckle and fanned herself. *Defensive much?*

Past experiences aside, she shouldn't assume Michael's friends were a bunch of rude snobs—and if she walked into the party expecting that, her expectations would probably manifest. Best to put on the most genuine smile she could muster and enter the scene with a positive attitude.

I've been reading too many self-help books.

And who knows? Maybe she'd meet more people like Violet—authentic, down to earth, and hilarious. Annie couldn't wait for her new friend to visit Trappers Cove after the holidays.

Michael bumped her shoulder with his. "What's funny?"

"Well, for one thing, we've only been together for two weeks and I'm meeting your parents."

Sprawled on the short end of the limo's L-shaped bench, Violet wiggled her bare, purple-tipped toes. "Props to you, Annie. My brother must trust you big-time."

He shot his sister a glare, then patted Annie's hand. "It'll be fine. Just three hours, a midnight kiss, and you're off the hook."

His reassurance didn't exactly boost her confidence. Neither did the long line of ridiculously expensive cars in front of the gleaming high rise.

As they glided to the entrance, Annie clenched her jaw to keep from gawking. Like a troupe of well-rehearsed ballet dancers, uniformed valets opened doors and handed passengers out of Lamborghinis, Ferraris, Porsches, Bentleys, Lotuses, and other sleek machines she couldn't begin to identify.

Their driver met Annie's eye in the rearview mirror and smiled. "Good luck, hon."

While Michael gallantly helped Annie to her feet, Violet bounced from the limo. "Evening, Fred," she chirped to the doorman, a stiff older gentleman dressed to lead a marching band. "How's Aurora?"

"She's very well indeed, miss," he intoned. "I'll tell her you inquired."

"Please do. Happy New Year!"

Falling in with the other guests, they passed a three-story lobby waterfall on their way to a bank of mirror-fronted elevators. Once inside, a silver-haired, tuxedoed gent greeted Michael with a hearty handshake and gave Annie a cool nod. His female companion, wrapped in vintage mink, showed what might be generously interpreted as a smile before turning her attention to the front of the elevator.

Annie straightened her shoulders and tightened her grip on Michael's arm. *Just three hours for his sake. Breathe in, breathe out.*

Someone whispered behind her. Someone else tittered. Annie gritted her teeth, fighting a wave of paranoia. This time would be different. Her business no longer depended on the good will of anyone here, and she was arriving on the arm of the hosts' son, for goodness' sake.

The elevator zoomed upward. Annie's stomach swooped downward.

Michael inclined his head and whispered, "You look beautiful."

She'd caught the tightness in his expression when she showed him her gown, a carefully chosen compromise—color and glitz to stand out, classic lines to blend in. But now, surrounded by sleek, expensive dresses right off the pages of *Vogue*, she kicked herself. Should've worn the basic black Givenchy, but she couldn't resist the urge to tweak their stuffy expectations. Bad call. Instead of propping up her confidence, this dress made her feel like a neon sign in an art gallery.

When the doors whooshed open, she glanced at Michael, whose smile had taken on a plastic sheen—a mask she didn't recognize and didn't like.

In the mirrored foyer that reflected a crystal chandelier above and an ornate marble mosaic floor below, a slim, middle-aged man with a pencil-thin mustache greeted guests and discretely checked his tablet before gesturing them inside. He nodded to Michael before giving a huge hug to Violet, who kissed him on both cheeks. Seems Michael's sister had a gift for making people break protocol.

The majordomo's appraising glance raked Annie from head to toe. He cocked an eyebrow. When she did the same to him, he cracked a smile.

Michael cleared his throat. "Dixon, this is my dear friend Annie Scott." He leaned a little harder on "dear," a warning to treat her with care.

"Welcome, Ms. Scott," the man drawled. "I wish you a pleasant evening."

"Thanks, same to you."

As she passed, she caught his murmured reply— "Not bloody likely."

The elder Garwoods' glass and chrome apartment reminded her of a fairytale ice palace complete with chandeliers like frozen waterfalls. Beside a wall of windows overlooking the sparkling cityscape, a jazz trio tinkled—baby grand piano, drums, upright bass. Blue flames danced in a wide, ultramodern gas fireplace. Black and white clad servers circulated with trays of elegant canapes, which most guests ignored.

Violet waylaid a server. "Hold up, sis." She snatched a tiny roast potato topped with sour cream and caviar and popped it into her mouth. "Mmm. Love these. Who's cooking tonight?"

"Starlight Catering, miss."

"Marvelous! Tell Chef Sergio Violet says hi." Grabbing another, she nudged Annie, who shook her head.

Her appetite was AWOL.

Michael's hand settled on the small of her back, a turn-on despite the high-stakes atmosphere, and he murmured in her ear, "Ready to press the flesh?"

She nuzzled his freshly shaved jaw. "Is that an option?"

His sexy, rumbling laugh lit up her nerves like heat lightning. "As soon as I accomplish what I came here to do, I'm going to take you home, peel off that sparkly dress, and make some New Year's fireworks of our own."

He led her through the crowd, greeting guests along the way, until they reached an elegant, white-haired couple holding court near the baby grand, him in an impeccable tux, her in a steel gray gown with discreet sparkle on the ruched collar. Both wore faint, regal smiles. The woman regarded Annie with her son's sharp dark eyes before spreading her impressively toned arms, her smile widening into genuine warmth at Michael's approach. "Well, well, well. The prodigal son finally returns." Completely ignoring Annie, she grasped his shoulders and pressed a kiss to each cheek.

His father gave him a handshake and a hearty pat on the back. "Michael, at last." As handsome as his son despite his advanced age, he turned to Annie and raised an eyebrow. "And you've brought a new friend?"

Michael took her hand and wove his fingers through hers. "Annie Scott, these are my parents, Edward and Clarissa Garwood."

Mrs. Garwood blinked in what she suspected was false confusion. "What happened to Crystal?"

Annie's stomach tightened. Not even a hello. She hadn't yet opened her mouth, and already she wasn't good enough for Michael's ice-queen mama.

"Mother." His voice sounded tight. "You know that Crystal and I are no longer seeing each other."

"I see." The older woman gave Annie a saccharine smile. "Forgive me, my dear. At my age, it's hard to keep track of Michael's girlfriends. Are you in finance too?"

Annie's muscles stiffened. Here it came, evaluation via net worth, a competition she could never win. Not that she cared to, but for Michael's sake, she'd hoped to fit in for the next few hours.

"Annie's in vintage fashion," he interjected smoothly. "She's quite talented at matching customers with beautiful, classic pieces. In fact, she found me the perfect navy peacoat to keep me warm out on the coast." If she read his mischievous smile correctly, he was thinking of other things she'd done to keep him warm.

Mrs. Garwood fingered the ribbon belt at Annie's waist. "Interesting choice. You know, I had a dress like this many years ago."

Annie forced her shoulders down. "It's a 1965 Norman Norell."

"Is that so?" The older woman's gaze shifted to the middle distance, and her smile lost its tightness, as if she were recalling a pleasant memory.

Perhaps she'd found an ally.

A cloud of exquisite perfume enveloped her as the older woman leaned close and whispered, "I wouldn't go back to those days for all the tea in China."

"Clarissa," Mr. Garwood purred through clenched teeth. "We'll talk later, son, about these rumors I'm hearing of changes at your firm. If you ask me, it's high time you focused on sounder investments."

Michael stiffened beside her. "I've got it handled, Dad."

"Of course you do." He inclined his head. "A pleasure to meet you, Annette." Taking his wife's arm, he glided away to greet other guests.

"Ugh." Michael scraped a hand down his face. "I'm sorry, Annie. They're miffed at me for skipping out on Christmas." He signaled a passing server and took two flutes of champagne.

"Uh huh." She sipped, willing herself to focus on the nose-tickling bubbles and not the sting of wounded pride. So what if his parents didn't like her? She doubted she'd ever see them again after tonight.

"Michael," a florid man in a too-tight dinner jacket boomed as he jostled a server in his haste to join them. "Where the hell have you been?"

"Away," he replied, his jaw muscle ticking with tension. "How was your holiday, Bruce?"

"Would've been better if we'd knocked that board meeting out after Christmas, but Rick and Jose wouldn't hear of it. 'Gotta have Michael at the table.'" He turned his oily grin on Annie. "Would you excuse us for a sec, little lady?"

Michael shot her an apologetic glance and whispered, "Here comes the boring part."

"I'll be fine." She extended her hand to the sexist swine. "And nice to meet you too, Mr.—"

The overstuffed suit grabbed her hand with his sticky paw and pumped it like he was inflating a bike tire. "Bruce Blevins. Michael and I go way back."

"Sorry," Michael mouthed, and held up five fingers before moving off with the blathering boor.

"Sure." Annie gulped down half her drink. She was a grown-ass woman. She could handle a few minutes of unescorted small talk.

Except no one seemed interested in talking to her. She approached a group of guests, then another, then a third, but each time she met frosty smiles and very cold shoulders.

Might as well be invisible.

She nabbed a mini crab quesadilla and watched Michael do battle with Mr. Sticky, who slapped his shoulder repeatedly. In Michael's shoes, she'd smack the blowhard back, good and hard.

But ever the diplomat, Michael maintained a tense smile as two more men joined their confab. Over his shoulder, he held up five fingers again.

"Ugh." Claiming another glass from a passing waiter, she tossed down half its contents and sashayed into the crowd, determined to force conversation with someone. Anyone. After all, connecting with people was her specialty, her strength, the foundation of her business. If she could handle a cutthroat vintage clothing auction, she could handle this boring party.

Putting a little extra sway in her step, she approached a trio of women around her age who were giggling over cocktails. "Evening. Lovely party, isn't it?"

"I suppose so," a sleek brunette drawled. "And you are?"

"Annie Scott. I'm here with Michael."

"Does he know that?" The short one curled her lip ever so slightly.

"Doesn't look like it," the tall one replied over the rim of her martini glass.

Annie glanced over her shoulder to where Michael had been, but he'd moved on. Scanning the crowd, she spotted him by the fireplace in close conversation with a plump young man in a snazzy sharkskin suit. A sinewy woman with slicked-back hair slunk to Michael's side, draped herself over his shoulder, and whispered in his ear. Without acknowledging her, he stepped aside and continued his discussion. She followed, this time toying with the hair behind his ear, that special curl that Annie loved to stroke.

The heat and pressure filling her chest stung like broken glass.

Michael angled his head and said something to the woman, then glanced at Annie.

That's right, bitch. He's with me.

The predator sauntered away.

And another woman sidled up to bat her eyes at Michael.

The martini trio tittered, and the short one patted Annie's shoulder. "News travels fast in this crowd. By now, everyone knows Michael's on the market again."

"On the market?" She blinked in astonishment. "He's a person, not a commodity."

The tall one snort-laughed. "Oh honey, you're cute."

And there it was, laid out in black and white for all to see. Nobody here saw her as serious competition for Bellevue's most eligible bachelor. No matter how much confidence she bluffed or how many glasses of champagne she swilled, she'd always be an outsider.

She gave her inner critic a hard slap, squared her shoulders, and started across the vast room toward Michael, now leaning in and gesturing emphatically to a cluster of suits. Halfway there, an elegant, androgynous person in a satin suit and shiny pompadour slithered into her path.

"Fabulous dress, doll. Are you with the band?"

"No, I'm with Michael Garwood." *Not that anyone cares.*

"Oh?" They raised their perfectly arched eyebrows. "Sorry to assume. With this vintage look, I thought..." They waved a hand and sauntered off.

At last, she reached Michael's side. Without missing a beat, he encircled her waist with his arm. For a moment, his bracing touch turned down the volume on her inner doubts.

"... but really, you must see the benefit of a more secure and profitable focus," his colleague insisted, ignoring her completely.

Michael hugged her closer. Though his posture seemed relaxed, his muscles were as tight as steel cables beneath his Armani tux. "Steve, Charles, Monte, let's continue this conversation on the fourth. I've neglected my lady long enough."

As they made their way to the buffet, he pressed a kiss to her temple. "I'm so sorry, beauty. I'd hoped to make some inroads tonight, but I might as well talk to a brick wall."

She forced her jaw to unclench. "I know exactly how you feel."

She didn't, though, not really. Because Michael was clearly at ease among these stiff, arrogant people, and she felt like an imposter.

She'd sworn she'd never let anyone make her feel this way again. Yet here she was, the invisible woman despite her neck-to-toe sequins. Was his sweet affection worth being treated like gum on their shoes?

"Mmm. This tuna tartare is kick-ass." Michael licked wasabi sauce from his thumb, then extended his hand. "May I have this dance?"

She cast a sidelong glance around the room. "No one's dancing."

"They will once we start." Just like at Casa Francesca, he towed her to an empty spot near the piano and swayed her to the music, his hand on her hip, his cheek pressed to her hair. "Dancing out the old year with my lady. What could be better?"

She could think of lots of things, but his warmth and nearness eased the sting of rejection. Who cared what these people thought of her? Michael adored her, and that was all that mattered.

As long as we stay far away from these snobs.

But how were they going to do that? Michael's home was here, ditto the business he cared so passionately about protecting. Faced with the cold, glittering reality of his life, Trappers Cove seemed a million miles away.

A bejeweled hand reached over her shoulder and tapped Michael's arm.

"May I cut in?" the raven-haired, model-perfect interloper cooed.

Heat climbed Annie's cheeks and tightened her jaw. People really did that? How incredibly rude.

"Not tonight, Aurora," Michael told the woman.

Her ice-smooth brow didn't move, but the rest of her face screwed into a scowl. "Oh come on. Surely Ms. Thrift Shop here can spare you for a few minutes."

A titter sounded behind her, then another, blooming into a wave of mocking laughter.

Annie's ribs squeezed. She stumbled out of Michael's hold. "I need air."

"This way." With a hand on the small of her back, he guided her through glass doors to the balcony, where propane heaters barely eased the chill.

Face contracted in a grimace, he pulled her into his arms. "I'm so sorry, Annie. I should've never asked you to endure this farce."

The inescapable truth knotted her gut.

"You didn't mean any harm, Michael." She jerked her head toward the party inside. "But they do. That's why I left Bellevue for Trappers Cove. The humiliation isn't worth it. Besides," she cleared her throat to cover the wobble in her voice. "It's plain I'm a liability for you. You need to focus on saving your business, not protecting me from their scorn."

Summoning the last shreds of her pride, she lifted tear-blurred eyes to his. "We had fun, Michael, but our holiday fling has reached its end. I wish you all the best in the new year."

Despite his spluttered protests, she pressed a farewell kiss to his cheek and walked away—shoulders back, head held high, steps slow and regal as she crossed the crowded room. No way would she let them see her flinch. Her tears could wait until she'd reached the shelter of—

Shit. My things are at his apartment. How will I get home?

"One step at a time," she whispered. "First escape, then take a breath and make a plan."

"Annie, wait," Michael's deep voice boomed behind her.

She quickened her steps, unwilling and unable to bear the sight of his beautiful, anguished face.

Just her luck, the rest of the Garwood clan clustered near the foyer. To leave, she'd have to pass them. She raised her chin higher and strode toward the door.

But Violet turned with a swooping gesture, sloshing her drink onto the marble floor. "Annie? What's wrong?"

"Let her go, dear," Mrs. Garwood warned.

"I will not." Defiance snapped in Violet's voice as, in a flurry of paisley and sequins, she rushed to Annie's side. "Are you leaving?"

She nodded, blinking hard to hold back brimming tears. To her utter humiliation, one broke free and slid down her cheek.

Shoving aside onlookers, Michael skidded to a stop, his eyes so full of pleading misery that she nearly crumpled to the floor at his feet.

"Please, Annie, you can't just"—he flapped a hand at the crowd. "I don't give a flying fuck about these people."

"Michael," his mother hissed, "don't make a scene."

Bright spots of color blotched Mr. Garwood's tan cheeks. "Is this your doing, Violet? Teaching your brother to burn bridges?"

Violet looped her arm through Annie's. "You know, Mother, Dad, I thought by now we'd all be mature enough to share a family celebration without all this venom and drama. But I was wrong. You still care more about your standing than you do about your children. Come on, Annie. Let's go."

Michael stepped forward. "I'll get us a car."

"No, Michael." Annie placed her palm on his chest, right above his pounding heart. "It's time to let me go."

Half-blind with tears, she stumbled through the door and into the dying old year. Just as she'd predicted, all their sweet kisses and hopeful promises had shattered.

And she was the biggest fool of all for believing they'd ever had a chance.

Chapter Twenty

♥

Rain pattered the mullioned library windows, as unrelenting and gray as Michael's mood. Unable to focus at home and haunted by the echoes of Annie's tearful goodbye, he'd fled once again to the castle, where two more days remained on his holiday rental. But the change of scene wasn't helping him prepare for his presentation to the board, and neither was the feedback from his partners, video conferencing from their cozy homes.

"Man, I've been turning my brain inside out, and I still can't find an angle that'll budge the board's position." Rick leaned on his desk and steepled his fingers. A fat gray tabby hopped up beside him and aimed its fluffy butt at the camera. "Dusty, that's rude." He scooped the intruder onto his lap.

Jose guffawed and chugged from his "Super Dad" mug. How many of those things did he have? In the background, his lanky teenage son slouched past, nose in his phone.

"Homework, Nico," Jose called over his shoulder.

The kid grunted and waved at the screen. "Hey, Uncle Mike."

When the coast was clear, Jose leaned closer to his camera and lowered his voice. "I took Barstow and Yang out for coffee yesterday.

I figured they were the most likely to change their minds, but..." He heaved a sigh. "Sorry, I got nothing."

Rick nodded from his square on the screen. "I tried Walters and Williams over sushi. Nada. Pamela Martin got to them first."

Rick and Jose exchanged a tense glance—except from Michael's viewpoint, each appeared to be studying a different corner of the screen.

Michael hit *Mute* to cover his groan of defeat. His partners had done their best. Now it was on him to pull a solution from this flaming dumpster.

He forced a smile. "Thanks, guys. I appreciate your efforts. I'll see you on Wednesday."

He poked the *Leave Meeting* tab and tried to massage away the ache in his temples.

It didn't help, of course. Not when everything was crumbling around him.

First Annie, now the firm. What's next?

An unwelcome vision flashed before his eyes—the castle disintegrating, its stone walls toppling into the sea.

He downed the last of the bourbon he'd shared with Annie. If he hadn't taken her to that God-forsaken party, they'd be finishing the bottle together while they made out in front of this goddamn picturesque fireplace. Or in the cozy-as-fuck window seat. Or beneath the blighted Christmas tree.

Everywhere he looked, another memory of Annie struck him—blow after blow of bitter regret. All those sweet memories could be his present reality if he hadn't been so damn cocky. And inattentive. He'd promised to protect her from the other guests' snobbery, but instead he got so caught up in defending his position to board members that he neglected her, leaving her to flounder alone.

It wasn't like she hadn't warned him. She predicted how she'd be treated by those sneering snobs. But they'd never treated him that way, so he'd disregarded her concerns and betrayed her trust. And for what? Attending his parents' party had accomplished exactly nothing.

Moving to the window, he sank onto the bench seat and pressed his throbbing forehead against the cold glass.

Until now, he'd prided himself on his talent for choosing the right risks—a skill that increased his wealth and reach with each successful start-up he backed. But this time, he picked disastrously wrong, and it had cost him Annie's love.

Because that was the painful truth of it—he loved her, and he was pretty sure she'd loved him too, or very nearly so. But now—how could she love someone who promised to keep her safe only to lead her into humiliation?

Never before had he so wanted to Hulk smash a party. Desperate to make things right, he'd rushed home. But by the time he got there, Violet and Annie had already left.

And now, she wasn't answering his calls or texts—except for that last message that shredded his heart.

Let it go, Michael. Let me cherish the memory of our time together.

A sonorous gong sounded from somewhere below.

"What the ever-loving fuck?" He stalked to the door and poked his head into the hallway. Oh, right. The doorbell. He'd like to strangle the designer who chose that sound to announce visitors.

And who the hell would be visiting on a dreary Tuesday morning? Unless...

Heart tripping, he bolted down the stairs, praying that she'd changed her mind.

He flung open the giant door, wrenching his shoulder in the process, only to find his sister wrapped in one of her raggedy Renaissance Faire cloaks, her pink nose peeping from beneath the hood, and a greasy paper bag clutched to her chest.

"Vi? What—why?"

She shook her head, causing the hood to drop back, and grinned. "I brought kebabs."

He tugged her inside, scooped up the duffel bag at her feet, and slammed the door behind them.

She hung up her cape and did a slow pirouette, mouth gaping in a wide grin. "Look at this shit. It's glorious! Well done, you."

"Wasn't my doing, it was the cold snap that busted pipes in my first rental. And why are you here?"

She heaved a dramatic sigh. "After dropping Annie off, I meant to drive back to Portland, but my conscience wouldn't let me leave without talking to you first." Her stern gaze reminded him painfully of their dad's lecture mode. "And this isn't the kind of talk you have via text."

Alarm pounded through him. He gripped her arm. "You drove Annie down here in that rolling death trap?"

She jutted her chin. "I'll have you know Gertie has new brake pads, a new transmission, and she passed inspection with flying colors. You didn't think I'd let the 'rents renege on their promise, did you? Especially after they were such snots to Annie." She snatched up her bag. "Now, take me to a room with a fireplace."

"Ugh. Come on up." As they climbed the stairs, he peppered her with questions.

"Where did you two go after the party?"

"We crashed at a friend's place."

"How did she seem?"

"How do you think, numbnuts?"

"Vi, please."

She turned on the top stair. "Sad. Tired. Kind of—empty, I guess."

He growled in frustration, every instinct urging him to rush to Annie's side, wipe away her tears and kiss the bitter taste from her mouth.

But going against her wishes would make him just another asshole who disrespected her.

Violet stepped through the open library door and whistled. "Right out of a freakin' fairytale. And this Christmas tree!" She set the food on the desk atop his notes for the board meeting. He snatched it up, but too late—grease had already smeared his flow chart.

She spun back to him, her hands clasped over her heart. "Let me guess—Annie did this."

"We did it together." His voice cracked on the last word.

"Oh, Michael." She threw her arms around him and hugged him tight.

That simple gesture of affection broke the dam. He clung to his sister, his shoulders shaking with ragged sobs, his body and mind wracked by pain and grief and hopelessness.

"I lost her, Vi. I loved her and now she's gone."

Cooing softly, she rubbed between his shoulder blades. "I've got you. Let it all out."

So he did, pouring out all the self-recrimination and regret. And when he could breathe again, he shivered in his sister's arms, exhausted and empty.

Violet grasped his shoulders and peered up at him, her jaw set. "You're hurting. She's hurting. We've gotta fix this."

He snuffled. "We?"

"I'll help, of course. 'Cause clearly, left to your own devices, you'll botch it again."

He fished a paper napkin from her takeout bag and blotted his swollen eyes. "You've never ridden to my rescue before."

"You never needed my help before. Now, let's fuel up before we strategize."

After purging his pent-up emotion, he was surprised to find himself ravenous.

When they'd decimated two deluxe kebab plates, a large order of garlic fries, and gooey, crispy squares of baklava, Michael pushed away from the tea cart they'd used as a dining table and patted his distended belly. Turns out eating his feelings helped a little. So did Violet's comforting coos and clucks.

Even if she thought he was an idiotic oaf, she was on his side.

She rubbed her hands together, scattering crumbs on the pseudo-Persian carpet. "So, we're agreed. You write the letter, and I'll deliver it." She poked his arm with her plastic fork. "This is your best chance, bro. She needs space and time to think it over, so lay it all out for her—what you're sorry for, what you'll do differently going forward, how you're going to weave your life together with hers." She smacked the table. "Tell her what you told me—all the stuff about your aching, empty heart. I've seen you persuade misers to invest big bucks in your techie schemes, so I'm sure you'll convince Annie to sit down with you over coffee." She pushed to her feet and brushed still more crumbs onto the floor. "See you in a few hours."

"Where are you going?"

"Into town. I haven't seen Madame Zora's shop since last year. Think I'll get a reading."

He tilted his head. "You were here last year?"

"I come through at least a couple of times each year." She flashed a wistful smile. "So many fond memories of Trappers Cove. Isn't that why you came?"

He shook his head. "I'm not sure. I just needed to escape for a while, find space to think, and this was the first place that came to mind. It sort of—felt right, you know?"

She nodded, her smile brimming with warmth and understanding, and walked to the door.

He called after her, "Are you happy, Vi?"

Turning, she cocked her head. "Usually. Why?"

"Do you ever miss the life you had before?"

She chuckled. "Only when my van breaks down."

He rose and gathered her into a hug. "You can always come to me if you need help."

"I know." She smooched his cheek. "And yeah, sometimes I miss the little luxuries—jetting to the Caribbean in the middle of winter, kicking back while someone else drives, getting tickets to sold-out shows. But that God-awful party reminded me I wouldn't trade my freedom for any of that shit." She squeezed his shoulders. "Don't worry, this artist isn't starving. I have everything I need."

He flicked her dangly beaded earring with his fingertip. "You always were resourceful."

"And so are you, Mike. That's your superpower. Whenever you get into a tight spot, you always find your way out."

He sank back into his armchair with a sigh of defeat. "Not this time. This was going to be my year of clarity—for the firm, for me, for building something real with Annie. But now, two days in, it's all a pile of wreckage."

She crouched at his feet and gazed up at him, her eyes soft with compassion. "You can't have it both ways, Michael. You can't be your own man and follow Mom and Dad's path. They don't know how to love without strings attached. Their whole world rests on what other people think of them." She patted his knee. "I thought you'd moved beyond that."

"Ouch." He rubbed his sternum.

"Truth hurts, bro. Now, pour your heart out. This calls for a grand gesture."

She left him alone with his stack of grease-stained paper.

He lifted his pen. *Dearest Annie...*

No words came. Grunting in frustration, he rose to pace from fireplace to window to Christmas tree, where each quirky ornament reminded him of the happiness they shared—like this sequined mermaid, a twin to one hanging on Annie's tree in that cute cottage he'd probably never see again.

He unhooked the little siren and carried her to the window seat Annie loved so much.

Funny—when he first rented the castle, he braced himself to hate it. Now that his time here was almost up, he found its weird charm has grown on him. The thought of going back to his empty, sterile apartment filled him with dread.

"Words. I need words."

He picked up his copy of *The Courage to Change* and opened to the spot he'd bookmarked with a raffle ticket stub from the Christmas banquet. "Forgiveness is the key to positive change," he read aloud. "Forgive your past self for making choices that no longer serve you. You did the best with what you knew back then. Now you know better."

Hmm. What if...

A slow smile stretched his lips. What if he combined the best of what he'd learned from his career and what he'd learned from his time with Annie?

He darted back to the desk, swept his presentation notes to the floor, and fired up his tablet. This would take research, careful negotiation, and a huge helping of luck, as well as guidance from an expert, but it could work.

A giddy buzz filled his chest, the same ring of promise he experienced when pitching his most successful startups.

Time to forge a new path.

He picked up his phone.

Annie couldn't decide which part hurt more—packing up the holiday merchandise and decorations, or opening her bins of Valentine's stuff. All that glittering, mocking pink and red curdled her stomach. But the retail calendar didn't give two hoots for her battered feelings, and it was time to arrange the shop for the next big holiday push.

The front doorbell tinkled as Cheryl entered, bearing to-go cups and a bag of treats from Garrett's bakery. Ever since Annie's return from the Bellevue disaster, her bestie had been extra solicitous, putting her own business on hold to keep Annie company through these dark, dreary post-breakup days.

She set down her load. "They were out of bear claws, so I got apple fritters, blueberry muffins, and a couple slices of lemon-poppy seed cake."

"Bless you, angel of caffeine and carbs." She snatched up a still-warm muffin, inhaled its sweet, buttery aroma, and took a big chomp.

Cheryl pried the lid off her coffee and doctored it with sweetener. "It's the least I can do. I never should've pushed that snooty rich guy into your path."

"He's not snooty, just clueless." She wiped crumbs from her 1950s mohair sweater. "And I don't blame you one tiny bit. This one's all on me."

Cheryl rubbed Annie's arm, her touch soothing. "Listen, we can put the whole online dating thing on hold."

"Nope." She gulped her coffee. "Tonight, after work, I'm activating my profile. Annie Scott is officially on the market."

"You sure?"

Not one tiny bit. In fact, she was dreading the whole ordeal, but getting back on the horse would help her heal faster than stewing in heartache and wounded pride.

At least she wasn't blindsided this time. She'd seen heartbreak coming as soon as she relaxed into Michael's embrace. That New Year's Eve debacle only confirmed her worst fears, the ones that kept her from giving away her whole heart. She'd patch it back together again, eventually.

Finished with her snack, she turned her attention to a case of antique perfume bottles, hairbrushes, and hand mirrors. Grouped with fancy soaps and lotions, these would lure baffled boyfriends with no clue what to gift their Valentines.

At the bottom of the storage bin, she found a mispacked item—a velvet jewelry box containing onyx cuff links just like the ones she'd helped Michael fasten before the party. She ran her thumb over the smooth, cool stone, and it all came flooding back. His nearness, his warmth, the low rumble of his voice, his dark eyes sparkling with desire and the promise of love that died on the vine, wilted by forces neither of them could defeat.

The room tilted. She grasped the glass counter to keep from tumbling to the floor.

"Hey now." Cheryl rushed to her side and looped her arm through Annie's. "Let's get you to a chair."

Ignoring her protestations, Cheryl settled her on a tufted velvet ottoman and crouched before her, eyes full of concern as she patted and chafed Annie's hands.

"I'm okay," Annie insisted. "Just a little aftershock." She blew out a breath between pursed lips. "See? All gone now."

"Bullshit." Cheryl pulled up a wrought-iron garden chair and sat close, her knees touching Annie's. "You're hurting bad, lovie. It's to be expected. That man was charm and sex and money, all rolled up into a perfect, poisonous bonbon. I'd like to smack him upside his handsome head."

"You'll do no such thing." She extricated her hands from Cheryl's grip. "He's a good person. I can't hold him responsible for his friends' behavior. Besides, my time with him taught me a hard lesson—hooking up with men who don't value me and trying to impress hostile strangers are two sides of the same coin. I need to get clear on what I want out of a relationship."

She closed her eyes and knuckled her tear-swollen lids. "I let my feelings for Michael override the obvious truth. We don't fit together, and we never will. Hell, he might as well be from a different planet, and all the chemistry in the world won't change that."

The doorway bell tinkled as a customer entered.

"Be right with you, hon," Cheryl called out.

"That's cool," the woman answered. "I'm just browsing."

Cheryl squeezed her hand. "Now, you sit here, drink your coffee, and let me play shopkeeper for a while. Bet you I can sell something."

"Be my guest." Closing her eyes, she let herself drift, buffeted by waves of memory and regret. That damn audiobook talked about leaning into your fears as the best path into a better life. Did leaning into pain work the same way? Perhaps it was like meditation, where you watched the shadows pass through you unheeded. How the hell did a person even do that?

Images flashed through her—Michael asleep, his heavy arm draped over her waist, his breath soft on her bare shoulder. The sweet, sexy groan he'd make when she kissed him awake before leaving for work. The way his chestnut eyes darkened when she returned to the castle and stripped out of her clothes. His drugging kisses as they tumbled back into bed. His hand warm in hers as they strolled along the shoreline. Their footprints pressed into the damp sand. Teasing banter, easy laughter, companionable silence as, arm in arm, they stared out to sea...

Stop! Shooting to her feet, she shook off the flood of memories. This meditation bullshit was only digging her deeper into misery. She needed a distraction to keep her grounded.

She followed the sound of feminine giggles and found Cheryl and another woman behind a scarf-draped wicker screen, laughing at their reflections as they tried on vintage cocktail hats. Catching sight of her, the visitor spun and greeted her with a wide grin.

"Annie, your shop is amazing! So many treasures. I can't believe, during all these years of visiting Trappers Cove, I've never come in here."

Annie blinked in surprise. "Violet. What are you—uh...?"

"Killing time while my brother figures out how to grovel. He's very methodical, that one. Gotta have a plan for everything."

"I've noticed." She furrowed her brow. "Wait, he's here?"

"Up in the castle, moping." Her voice softened. "He's miserable without you."

Cheryl clucked her tongue. "And Annie's miserable without him."

The two women exchanged a knowing look, then turned on Annie, clearly expecting a response.

She shook her head. "He'd be miserable with me. I don't fit into his world."

Violet shrugged. "I hear ya. I keep away from that crowd as much as possible. But I suspect Mike would rather fit into your world."

Annie snorted. "Right. He's going to leave behind the company he built, the one he's spent the past two weeks trying to save."

Cheryl poked her shoulder. "Ever heard of telework?"

Annie poked back. "Ever heard of leaving well enough alone?"

Violet flashed an over-bright smile and pushed a floppy-brimmed felt hat into Annie's hands. "I'll take this one."

They moved to the register.

"Here's something to consider," Violet continued as she dug through her pockets for cash. "Maybe Mike doesn't fit into that life anymore. I'm sorry those people were assholes to you. I guess my brother had to see it with his own eyes to believe it. He can be stubborn that way. But he's stubbornly attached to you, and I'm sure if you gave him another chance, he'd move heaven and earth to make it work between you." Her earnest, dark-eyed gaze was so like her brother's.

Annie's heart squeezed like a fist. "Please, Violet, right now, I just can't."

"Okay." She nodded. "I don't want to cause you pain. But think about it, okay?"

As if she had an ice cube's chance in hell of thinking about anything else.

She watched the two women leave, whispering and glancing back over their shoulders. Still scheming, probably.

Alone in the shop, she groaned and draped herself over the glass counter. Roscoe, her ceramic panther, gazed down at her with flat, glittering eyes.

"Don't look at me like that. It's the right decision for both of us."

The big cat seemed to curl its lip—a trick of the light, no doubt, but a shiver danced down Annie's spine nevertheless.

"Okay, so maybe I was hasty, running away from the party." She pushed onto her elbows. "Not my most mature moment. I suppose I should hear him out."

Or was that just her libido urging her toward one last night with Michael? Knowing he was so near, all alone in the castle and probably as wretched as she was, made holding her ground seem stubborn and pointless. Didn't he deserve a proper goodbye, after saving Trappers Cove's Christmas ball?

She pulled her phone from beneath the counter and stared as if the answer lurked behind her beach sunset wallpaper.

"Arrgh!" Screwing up her face, she tapped the screen to life. Her finger hovered over the phone icon, then slid to the audiobook app above it. Perhaps *The Courage to Change* had an answer.

The narrator's velvet voice intoned, "Forgiveness is the key to positive change. Forgive your past self for making choices that no longer serve you. You did the best with what you knew back then. Now you know more."

She pressed *Pause*. "Okay, Roscoe, what do I know now that I didn't know before meeting Michael?" She stroked the statue's elegantly curved haunch. "I didn't know I could make a billionaire fall for me." She huffed a bitter laugh. "Imagine that. He could snag a model-perfect trophy wife without even trying, but he fell for me. And I didn't know I could feel so much for someone like him. Which means"—She pressed her forehead to the cat's—"I let my prejudices blind me to a really wonderful guy."

A heavy chill settled over her. "He wants me, Roscoe. And I want him desperately. Knowing he's up there, so close, and I can't touch him, it's killing me." She traced the cat's curled tail with her fingertip. "But if I spend one more night with him, I'll fall so deep in love I'll never climb back out. And I can't see a way forward. Tell me what to do, puss."

The beautiful cat only stared, cold and silent.

Chapter Twenty-One

*B*lah, blah, blah. *Get on with it.*

Feeling his lip start to curl, Michael forced a nonchalant mask and tapped his Montblanc pen on the long conference table as Pamela Martin, chair of GRA Capital's executive board, took her sweet, smarmy time tallying the votes. Each "aye" tipped him closer to the point of no return.

What a colossal mistake he'd made five years ago, letting that business coach talk him, Rick, and Jose into adopting a traditional corporate structure. Ironically, it was he who convinced his partners to make the change, freeing them up to focus on hunting down hot start-ups.

So here he sat, helpless to stop this train wreck. Rick fished a faded bandana from his pocket, blotted his sweaty forehead, and flashed Michael a look of pure dread as their turn crept closer. Jose gnawed a cuticle and kept his gaze on his notes.

He hated seeing his friends like this, but having given up their controlling interest in GRA in return for an expanded pool of capital, they had only two choices: go with the board's decision or strike out on their own—and neither could afford that.

"Mr. Alvarez?" the chairwoman repeated, "your vote?"

A drop of sweat trickled down Jose's temple as he raised his pleading gaze to Michael.

His gut roiled with guilt over placing his friends in this awful position.

"It's okay," he whispered. "Do what you need to do."

Jose scrunched his eyes shut and croaked, "Aye."

Murmurs and whispers swept the table like ripples in a pond.

Pamela's eyebrows crept up, but she betrayed no other sign of gloating—yet. An outsider would never guess the heart of a ruthless mercenary beat behind that boxy tweed jacket.

"Mr. Roth?" she asked.

Ruck stared at his clasped hands and mumbled, "Aye."

A tinge of smugness twisted Pamela's thin lips. "And that brings us to Mr. Garwood."

His plush leather chair rolled smoothly across the carpet as he pushed to his feet. He'd miss that chair, and this room, with its sweeping view of the skyline and Lake Washington beyond. He'd miss late-night strategy sessions here, and team breakfasts with Nancy's superb coffee. He'd miss watching young tech pioneers' jaws drop when he, Rick, and Jose welcomed them to this table and pitched their buy-in offer.

But most of all, he'd miss his best friends. They'd built this firm together, and now he was losing it.

Squaring his shoulders, he fixed each board member in turn with an unblinking stare. "For the record, I vote nay."

Pamela's oily smile could lubricate an eighteen-wheeler. "I'm sorry to hear that, Michael. We'd hoped for a unanimous endorsement of GRA's new direction."

"About that." He smiled with lots of teeth. "You'll need to change the name of the firm."

"Pardon?" The chair's smug grin faltered.

"The board has chosen to focus on increased profits, but for me, it's more important to align my investments with my values. After consulting with my attorney, I'm exercising my option to leave the firm, and I'm taking my clients with me."

Ignoring spluttered protests, he pressed his intercom button. The door swung open, and Nancy strode in, stiff and proud as a general in her navy blazer with gold trim. She gave him a sad nod, then swept the board with a withering glare. God, he was going to miss her.

"My assistant has emailed you all a copy of our articles of incorporation with the pertinent portion highlighted in—" He draped his arm around her shoulders. "What color did you choose, Nancy?"

"Spring green." She grinned up at him. "The color of new beginnings."

A surprise smile stretched his lips. He had braced himself for the bitterness of defeat, but instead, a strange, giddy lightness filled his chest. Weird, considering that between his breakup with Annie and this debacle, he'd hardly slept since New Year's Eve, and he still faced a litany of phone calls and meetings. But for now, he'd bask in this victory.

Even if she never gave him another chance to make things right, he would be forever grateful to Annie for opening his eyes. Their two weeks together had changed him for the better. Armed with new-found courage, plus long-cultivated skills, connections, and resources, he'd finally found his own path.

God and Cheryl Rossi willing, that path would lead him back to Trappers Cove. Two days after sending that pathetic letter of apology to Annie, and still no response. Not that he blamed her—why should she believe him? Words alone weren't enough—he needed something bigger, grander, something to prove the new Michael Garwood was here to stay.

While the board lost their ever-lovin' shit, he sauntered to the door and held it open for Nancy, who sailed through with a self-satisfied "Hmmph."

"Mike, wait." Jose hustled out behind them, followed by a slack-jawed Rick, who leaned against the wall and raked shaking fingers through his sparse hair.

"Holy shit. Are you for real?"

Dizzy with relief, Michael drew a deep breath. "You know, I actually am. This change has been coming for a long time." He grasped his friends' shoulders. "There's no one better equipped than you guys to steer this ship. So, what'll you call it? Rothalva Capital? Alvaroth Investments?"

"Holy shit," Rick hooted, his eyes crinkling with laughter. The three of them exchanged back-slapping hugs until Michael pulled away. "Gotta go. We'll catch up soon."

"Where are you going?" Jose asked.

"I've gotta see a lady about a castle." He pointed to the closed door. "Now, get in there and take the wheel."

His two best friends exchanged determined nods, then strode back into the boardroom to do just that. He had no doubt they'd do a magnificent job.

Nancy gave his hand a motherly squeeze. "I'm so proud of you, Michael."

"For being stubborn?"

"For following your conscience." Smile lines crinkled at the corners of her glistening eyes. "It's been an honor working with you."

He swiped away his own welling tears and hugged her tight. "The honor was all mine, dear lady." He pulled an envelope from his breast pocket. "A little parting gift from GRA Capital. That should cover a few vacations with your grandkids."

"Oh, Michael, that wasn't necessary." She tore the envelope, peeked inside, and gasped. "Holy cats! I could take them on an around-the-world cruise with this."

He pecked her soft cheek. "Pro tip: Take them to Trappers Cove. And be sure to ring me up when you do. I'll let them beat me at Skee-ball."

Laughing, she gave him a playful shove. "I'll take you up on that. Now, go win the fair lady."

He rubbed his hands together. "Oh, I intend to."

Chapter Twenty-Two

♥

"**F**or fuck's sake, just tell me where we're going!"

Clucking her tongue, Cheryl steered her Outback around a hairpin turn in the rutted road. "Such language. What's got into you, Ms. Cranky Pants?"

"Sorry." Annie thunked her head onto the headrest. "Work stress, I guess. I've got a lot going on at the shop."

"Baloney. I saw exactly zero customers in there. Teresita's got it covered." Cheryl's smug grin made Annie want to smack her.

Her friend was right, though. January was dead time for Trappers Cove's merchants. No tourists braved the blustery weather, and locals hunkered down to recover from holiday overindulgence. She might as well close up for a few weeks and go somewhere warm—maybe bask on a Mexican beach and drown her regrets in tequila. Or splash out for a weekend in Vegas, or visit her cousins in Southern California. Anything to escape the memories that ambushed her at every turn—from the moment she awoke, half-expecting to hear Michael rattling around in the kitchen, to his remembered reflection in store windows as she walked to work. The wind on her cheeks conjured up his touch. Even her own shop wasn't safe—especially the men's coat rack.

But their connection was doomed from the very start. Michael's sweet letter of apology doubled her over with sobs, but once she was all cried out, the truth still glared, inescapable. Mere words could never erase the difference between his world and hers.

Her fingers strayed to her jacket pocket and stroked the folded edge of the heavy cream stationery she couldn't bring herself to throw away.

Cheryl's SUV lurched around a curve, and Annie's stomach sank. Distracted by obsessive regrets, she hadn't recognized the landmarks until it was too late.

She whirled on Cheryl. "The castle? Are you effin' kidding me? You said you wanted to show me a new property."

"No," her friend replied with infuriating calm. "I said I wanted to show you a new *project*." As they bumped along the gravel driveway, she pointed to a construction placard.

Future site of the Phillis Baron Community Center.

"Who the hell is Phillis Baron?"

"Former owner of the castle. I did such a good job of selling her on its potential as a rental, we had to sweeten the pot to convince her to part with the property. Stroking her ego helped, but she still doubled her asking price."

Before Annie could ask more questions, Cheryl parked, hopped out, and jogged up the stone steps to rap on the enormous front door.

Frozen, Annie clutched her seatbelt as if that narrow strap could protect her from the rush of emotion tightening her ribs and speeding her pulse. How could her friend be so cruel?

A woman she didn't recognize opened the door and shook Cheryl's hand. Cheryl pointed to the car.

Annie glared daggers at her friend and hunkered down in her seat. Whatever this was, she wanted no part of it. Hell, she'd hike down the hill and back to town if she had to.

The stranger trotted across the driveway and rapped on Annie's window. Wind whipped her dark hair as she waited, shivering.

Well, shit. Annie cracked the door open. "Can I help you?"

"I hope so. The project manager recommended you as a consultant on this conversion."

"I, uh, wha—?"

"Sorry." She extended a slim hand. "I'm Aiko Sato, of Sato Architecture. We're handling the renovation."

Baffled but intrigued, Annie shook her hand, then followed her into the castle. In the front parlor, a roaring fire eased the chill and illuminated the profile of a man bent over a low table, examining a set of blueprints.

Her heart skidded to a stop. "Michael?"

Slowly, he straightened. Their eyes locked. The air between them hummed and crackled.

He looked like hell—deep shadows beneath his eyes, Oxford shirt wrinkled, scruff darkening his jaw. He looked like heaven, his dark gaze glittering as he drank her in. He looked like everything she'd ever wanted.

"Annie. You came." As irresistible as gravity, his raspy-velvet voice tugged at her heart, but her feet stayed rooted to the floor.

Cheryl hooked her arm through Annie's and towed her toward him. "Told you I'd get her up here even if I had to hogtie her."

"I will kill you," Annie snarled through clenched teeth.

"You'll thank me. Now sit." She shoved her into a chair beside Michael's. "She's all yours."

"Umm." He rubbed the bump on his nose. "Maybe you two could give us a moment?"

"Sure," Cheryl chirped. "We'll go make coffee. Come on, Aiko."

Whispering, the two women withdrew. Annie nearly bolted after them, but Michael gently gripped her shoulder. Breath held, she braced herself, but he merely helped her out of her coat and folded it over a chair, then sat beside her and laid his broad, warm hand over hers.

It took every iota of her strength to keep from climbing onto his lap and claiming the kiss she craved. Instead, she pinched her lips together and waited, her nerves thrumming with tension.

His thumb massaged distracting circles on the back of her hand. "So, I bought the castle."

"You...why?"

His lips curved in a smile. "I decided it's time to—how did you put it?—invest in other sorts of ventures."

"Like real estate?"

"Like community resources. You said Trappers Cove needs more facilities for locals, and the school building on the property was standing empty, so..." He tapped the blueprints. "Lots of potential here."

She yanked her hand from his delicious, distracting hold. "Michael, this makes no sense. You brought me up here to talk about real estate?"

With a tinder-dry chuckle, he shook his head. "Annie, I realize I'm asking a lot of you, but I don't know anyone with a better connection to this community. Will you do it?"

Her frustration bubbled over. "Do what, for God's sake? Quit being so damn cryptic."

He flinched at her harsh tone and raked his fingers through his hair, mussing it adorably. Her core throbbed with the memory of the last time she'd seen him so rumpled—lying beside her, his naked body tangled in the sheets, his satisfied smile reflecting her own...

"Okay, let's start from the top." He leaned in close and captured her hands again, piercing her with his intense gaze. "Annie, I'm in love with you."

Her mouth dropped open, then snapped shut as her poor, overwhelmed brain short-circuited.

Finally, she shook her head. "Michael, why do we keep torturing ourselves? It'll never work between us. We're from two different worlds."

His lips quirked up. "Not anymore. I live here now."

"But your work—"

"The board rejected my proposal." Smiling broadly, he shrugged. "So I quit. And you know what? I feel amazing. Free. Ready to start a new chapter." His eyes sparkled with pure, crystalline hope. "With you, Annie."

Dizzy with delight and disbelief, she could only gawk, speechless.

The light in Michael's eyes dimmed. He straightened, blew out a breath, and slapped his thighs. "Okay then. I gave it my best shot. Guess my gamble didn't pay off."

The defeat in his voice eviscerated her. But he continued, his face a near-perfect mask of poise. "Either way, this goofy castle is my home now, and that school building"—he hooked a thumb over his shoulder—"is going to be Trappers Cove's new community center. Will you help me build it, Annie?" He tapped the faded blueprints spread across the table. "See, we've got six classrooms and a—"

"Michael, stop." She had only seconds to express her jumbled thoughts before melting into a puddle of tears. Of their own volition, her fingers slid up his arm, over his muscled shoulder, into his soft hair. "You uprooted your life to be with me?"

Eyes half-shut, he leaned into her caress. "Meeting you has changed me, Annie. My old life doesn't fit anymore." His fingertip traced her jaw, the curve of her lip. "Your love feels like home. When I'm not with you, I'm homesick. I need to be here. With you."

Each simple, beautiful word pried another plank from her boxed-up heart. She flattened her palms on his chest to feel his thundering pulse, as wild and frantic as her own.

"I'm afraid, Michael. I gave my heart once before, and love wasn't enough to hold us together."

He circled her hips with his strong arms and scooped her onto his lap, nestling her into his solid, sheltering warmth. "I'm not that fool who abandoned you, Annie. Whatever trouble we meet, you'll find me right by your side. I won't fail you." He pressed his forehead to hers. From this close, his eyes were deep, dark pools she wanted to drown in.

His lips brushed hers, a gentle touch that promised everything she'd ever dreamed of. "Say yes, Annie. Be mine. Love me back."

The naked sincerity in his beautiful, simple words crumbled the last of her armor to dust.

"Yes. I will. I do." Throwing her arms around his neck, she smashed her lips to his and grinned into their kiss. "I love you, Michael."

"Really?" He snugged her tight against him.

"Really to the thousandth power." She licked the seam of his lips, and when he opened to her, she drank him in—his sweetness, his heat, his love.

His fist tightened in her hair as he deepened the kiss. If he hadn't held her so tightly, she'd have floated away, lifted by the champagne bubbles fizzing through her veins. Breath and bodies entwined, they kissed and caressed and pressed so close together she felt every shiver that shook him. Every moan and sigh and hum of pleasure echoed deep in her core.

"Annie, you—oh God, I thought—I'm never leaving you."

She broke the kiss and cupped his beautiful, flushed face. "I'm terrified in the best possible way." She pressed a kiss to the bump on his nose.

"Me too." Eyes sparkling, he grinned up at her. "Isn't it awesome?"

"That's the perfect word for it." When she shifted on his lap, her hip nudged a hard, hot ridge.

Moaning, he canted his hips higher. "Upstairs?"

"We've never actually made love in this room, have we?" She kissed along the edge of his jaw, then nipped his tender earlobe.

With a growl, he lifted her in his arms, kicked the chair back and stumbled toward the leather sofa facing the fireplace.

A sharp rap on the doorframe halted his charge. Cheryl stood there, grinning widely while Aiko hovered behind her, eyes averted.

"We'll catch you guys later," Cheryl called, her voice twinkling with barely suppressed laughter.

"Thanks for everything," Michael answered over his shoulder. "We'll get back to you with our preliminary thoughts on the classrooms."

The juxtaposition of his crisp, businesslike tone and his fingers digging into her flank drove Annie into a fit of horny giggles.

"Righto, byeee," Cheryl sang out as the front door scraped closed behind them.

Grunting like the sexy beast he was—God, how she'd missed his feral sounds of pleasure—Michael dropped onto the couch, then pulled her onto his lap to straddle him. He shoved her wool skirt up high, and then hissed through clenched teeth when his fingers reached bare skin.

"What is this magic?"

"Thigh-high wool stockings. Popular in our great-grandmothers' day." She'd worn them on a whim—plus, all her regular tights were in the laundry hamper.

His fingertips hooked beneath the elastic and tugged, but the stockings didn't budge. "How do I take them off?"

"Here." Chuckling, she guided his hand to the garter clip.

On a sharp intake of breath, he lifted her skirt higher. "A lace garter belt? Oh, Annie." He buried his face in the crook of her neck, where his whiskers scratched deliciously against her sensitive skin. "We are going to have so much fun with your wardrobe."

His lips stretched in a wicked smile as he slowly unfastened her blouse buttons. She arched her back and wriggled out of it, loving the way his gaze drank in her every move.

Lips parted, he skated his fingertips over her arms, her ribs, the curve of her waist. Humming deep in his throat, he cupped her breasts through her hot-pink lace bra.

"This is stunning," he murmured, his voice smoky with desire. "You are stunning." Curling forward, he pressed his mouth over her pebbled nipple, heating the cloth with his breath. When he pinched the sensitive nub between his lips, she nearly levitated from the shocking pleasure.

Gripping her nape, he drew her down for a deep, sensuous kiss, exploring her mouth in long, luscious strokes while he rolled and squeezed her nipples.

Impatient to feel his skin on hers, she wriggled out of her bra, then closed her eyes on a moan as he drew each sensitive peak into the wet heat of his mouth, releasing her long enough to murmur, "Staying away from you was agony."

"It was terrible." For a long, sweet moment, she rode the intoxicating sensations, her nerves singing with each caress.

But a woman could only take so much anticipation. She gripped his shoulders and pulled her nipple from his mouth with a champagne cork pop. Growling in protest, he pursued her, then closed his eyes on a hiss as she pressed her wet, aching core to his hardness and rocked against him.

His grip on her hips would probably leave bruises, but right now, she reveled in this loss of control, this edge of pain that heightened her pleasure.

She made quick work of his shirt buttons and ran her hands over his heated skin, loving the rasp of crisp hair against her palms. When she reached for his belt, he arched his hips, an instinctive movement that fired her blood.

She tugged his slacks down his thighs and bent low to kiss his shaft through his tight boxer briefs. His breath shuddered as he thrust upward, and her aching sex clenched in anticipation. It took tremendous strength to hold back now, as she freed his cock from its cloth prison and whispered kisses over him from root to plush crown.

A pearl of pleasure appeared under her lips. She licked it away, swirling her tongue round and round.

Gasping, he jerked free from her mouth. "Angel, I need to feel you coming on my cock." He groped in his pockets. "Shit. Condoms are upstairs."

She gripped his shoulders and pushed him back against the cushions. "Michael, I'm not going to get pregnant. And—" She scrunched her eyes shut—"Argh, why is this so awkward? After my last, erm, encounter, I got tested. I'm healthy. Are you?"

He nodded, a slow smile blooming. "Had a physical right before Christmas. My doc always tests me for—well, you know."

She pressed her lips to his. "Look at us, a couple of middle-aged grown-ups, shy about STIs." She slid her hand down his belly, grasped his cock, and gave it a languid, up and down stroke. "Let me feel you bare inside me."

He yanked her panties to the side and thrust first one finger, then a second, between her slick folds. With expert skill, he alternated tight circles around her clit and deep thrusts into her channel. All the while she stroked him, loving the sensation of velvet skin sliding over hard heat.

On a hiss, he withdrew his fingers and gripped her hips. "Now, Annie. Please." He shifted beneath her, and the plush head of his cock nudged her entrance.

Slowly, breath held, she sank onto his shaft. For a long, delectable moment, they rested there, fully joined, hearts pounding in tandem. Until Michael groaned and began to thrust.

Rocking in rhythm with his thrusts, she rode him as sharp pleasure built, melting her bones and electrifying her nerves until bliss ripped a scream from her throat.

Inside her, his cock grew impossibly harder, thicker, and then he howled her name as his climax crested and broke.

Slowly, slowly, the room reformed around them, hushed except for their panting breaths.

Blissed out, replete, Annie dissolved into laughter, chuckling against his sweaty temple. "That was phenomenal."

He buried his face between her breasts and groaned. "I don't even have words to describe how good you feel."

"Words are overrated." She nuzzled his soft hair and cradled him over her heart. "So, what now, my love?"

He banded his arms around her ribs, propped his chin on her breastbone, and grinned up at her, eyes sparkling with mischief. "Want to help me take down the Christmas tree?"

"It's still up?"

With a laugh, he thrust his still-firm cock deeper. "When you're near, it's up. But yes, it's January sixth. Three Kings' Day."

"Mmmm." She wiggled on his lap, loving the tingling, squishy slide of their joined flesh. "Let's leave it up a bit longer. Our first Christmas tree together. Seems only right we should make love under the tree." She traced the shell of his ear with the tip of her tongue. "And in the conservatory."

"Don't forget the ballroom." He licked a lazy circle around her nipple. "There's so much I want to explore with you, Annie." Pulling back, he fixed her with a serious gaze. "And we'll plan it together, okay? No more assuming what I want will work for you."

"Sounds good." She brushed a damp curl from his temple.

He turned his attention to her other nipple. "For example, do you want to live up here or in your place? Or a little of both?"

"Oh, we're moving in together, are we?" She was only teasing, though, because spending a night anywhere but in Michael's arms was simply out of the question.

His sigh tickled her skin. "God, I hope so."

"We'll work it out, Michael. I'm thinking we'll try a little of both until we find our rhythm." She kissed him, soft and sweet and unhurried, because they had all the time in the world—the world they would build together.

Chapter Twenty-Three

♥

Annie locked the castle's front door, set down her overnight bag, and took a deep breath of the balmy evening breeze. Days like this were a gift, a sweet early foretaste of summer. Soon, April rains would arrive, but right now, the sea gleamed a rich blue, touched with rose-gold as the sun lowered toward the horizon.

A crunch on the gravel driveway drew her attention back to tonight's mystery date. "Dress warm," Michael had told her, his dark eyes sparkling with mischief.

"Fancy or casual?"

"Comfortable." And he refused to elaborate further.

So here she stood in her 80s suede ankle boots, soft jeans, and a light angora sweater, wondering where the hell they were headed tonight.

Curiosity itched like a rash under her skin, but over the past four months, she'd learned that patience paid off when it came to Michael's schemes. He loved surprising her with special treats—massages for two, horseback rides on the beach, a private chef for their first dinner party in the castle. Loving a billionaire definitely had its benefits.

But it was his Jeep, not the Tesla, that rounded the corner from the garage. Huh.

He hopped out and, grinning like a kid with a secret, opened her door and handed her into her seat, then tossed her bag into the back.

"Where are we going?"

His grin looked positively smug. "You'll see." Tires spinning, he took off down the bluff toward town, traversed the length of Main Street, and continued farther south.

"Are we going to Portland?"

"Nope."

"Astoria?"

"Wrong again." He turned toward the shore. They passed the lighthouse parking lot, empty at this late hour, and pulled into the southernmost beach lot.

Okay, a picnic on the beach? But instead of exiting the Jeep, Michael tapped his phone, angling the screen so she couldn't read it. Drat.

He tucked the phone into the breast pocket of his perfectly tailored chambray shirt, then leaned over to kiss her cheek. "Five more minutes, love. What shall we talk about?"

Playing along in moments like this made her squirm with impatience, but she supposed it was a character-building experience. At least, that's what her latest self-help audiobook, *The Power of Patience,* suggested.

"How about the community center?" she suggested. "Cheryl says the electrician is almost done."

"Yes, indeed." He drummed his fingers on the steering wheel, clearly feigning interest. In fact, judging by the speed of his bouncing knee, he was nervous about whatever surprise lay before them.

"Hey." She gave his leg a gentle squeeze. "The renovation is going great. We're right on schedule, and the grand opening event is coming together beautifully."

"Thanks to your connections." His phone pinged. He glanced at the screen and grinned. "Here we go."

She reached for her door, but he steered the Jeep down the drive and onto the beach, now dotted with trucks, cars, and bonfires as tourists and locals alike took advantage of the unseasonably fine weather. She scanned the sand for their picnic site, but he kept on driving until they reached the rock wall separating the main beach from Ivan's Hollow, the picturesque cove surrounded by high cliffs and accessible only during low tide, and... *Holy cow, the tide is waaay out tonight.*

Buzzing with excitement, she bounced in her seat. "We're going to the hollow? I haven't been in years." As a kid, she, her brother, and their friends would wade around the rocks at low tide and enjoy their own secret beach. Once, they forgot to pay attention to the rising tide and got stranded with nothing but a few chocolate bars to sustain them until her dad motored out to rescue them in his aluminum fishing tiller.

As they drew nearer, a big, shiny black pickup zoomed around the seaward boulders, splashing water in its wake. The driver, a dark-haired young man, waved, and his passenger flashed a thumbs up.

"Isn't that Zora's nephew and his girlfriend?" she asked.

"You know Zeke and Lara?"

"Of course," she huffed. "There are very few people in Trappers Cove I don't know. Are they in on this?"

"You'll see." Grinning, he gunned the engine, and they zipped around the rocky point, a rooster tail of surf spouting in their wake.

Her breath hitched as they rolled up to the prettiest campsite she'd ever seen—a yurt-style tent, its flaps tied open to reveal a glowing interior. Fairy lights twinkled from the tie-down lines. Out front, a Persian carpet spread on the sand held two camp chairs draped with sheep fleece and a table set for two with china and crystal. A crackling campfire danced in the stone fire ring.

"Wow. Talk about a picnic with style."

"My lady deserves nothing less." He hopped out, fetched her bag, and trotted around the car to open her door, his arm extended to help her down.

Her feet slid into the soft sand. "This is..." Wandering toward the picture-perfect scene, she did a slow pivot and drank in the stunning details. "You planned all this?"

Grinning sheepishly, he shrugged. "Lara helped. Seems she's a Pinterest addict."

"Remind me to thank her." She threw her arms around his neck and kissed him thoroughly.

He swatted her butt. "Now, go make yourself comfortable while I get started on dinner."

She took her bag from his arm and moved toward the tent. "Wait." She turned back. "You're cooking?"

While Michael's simple breakfasts were excellent, his attempts at fancy cooking had proved, well—less than ideal. She loved him for trying, though.

"Again, I had a little help. The sides and dessert are premade. All I have to do is grill the lamb chops, and I watched five different tutorials." He laced his fingers together and cracked his knuckles.

She poked her head into the tent, then withdrew on a gasp. "Are we spending the night?"

"If you're willing. I did everything I could to make it warm and comfortable. Next low tide is at six-thirty a.m., but we should be able to drive out until seven-thirty."

She smiled so hard her cheeks ached. "Let's stay." How could she possibly pass up the chance to spend the night with Michael on this tall air mattress made up with crisp sheets, warm blankets, and a faux fur throw that promised delicious erotic possibilities? More fairy lights swayed from the interior poles, soft rugs covered the floor, and fat LED candles glowed in hurricane lamps scattered around the perimeter. The perfect setting for seduction—not that she needed persuading at this point. In fact, she was tempted to skip dinner and drag him in here right now.

The pop of a champagne cork drew her back outside to find a side table holding an ornate charcuterie platter and an ice bucket. Michael filled two flutes with Château Ste. Michelle brut—not the most expensive, but her absolute favorite. "To us, love."

She clinked and sipped, loving the tickle of bubbles on her tongue. "What are we celebrating?"

"A fruitful union." He emptied his glass, then nibbled his lip, a tell revealing nerves and deep thought, as she'd come to learn during their time spent pouring over blueprints and contracts. "Why don't you stretch your legs while I grill the chops?"

"Okay, sure." She let him refill her glass, nabbed a cheese-filled pro- sciutto roll, and wandered to the shoreline, stepping over chunks of driftwood and broken crab shells as she munched. When she reached firm, damp sand, she sipped and sighed.

"How did I get this lucky?" she asked a flock of plovers who darted into the retreating surf, then scurried back.

She must've done something especially worthy to earn a perfect moment like this, with a perfect man like Michael. And though she wasn't a religious woman, she wondered if some higher power hadn't guided him across her path. The man she'd nearly tossed away over her prejudices and wounded pride had proved so full of love and integrity, so generous and brave and honest—better than she ever could have hoped for.

And a good sport too. He meant what he said about starting a new chapter in Trappers Cove. Now the tech innovators he fostered came here to present their ideas, meeting Michael over craft beers at the Salty Dog Saloon or coffee in Cassie's Café. He'd joined the library board, the Sons of Italy—turns out he had an ancestor from Trieste—and the TC Road Runners, volunteering at their St. Paddy's Day charity 10K. The memory of how good he looked in those Kelly green running tights was enough to rev her engine.

"Thank you," she whispered as the setting sun flared in a final burst of celestial flame, gilding the sand and surf.

Turning shoreward, she saw that Michael had lit a circle of camping lanterns around the table. She slogged back through the sand and joined him at the fire ring, where lamb fat sizzled onto glowing embers.

The rich scent of roasting meat, garlic, and herbs made her mouth water. "Wow. You've got chef skills."

"Let's not get carried away." He chuckled as he flipped the grill cage holding the chops. "Haven't won any Michelin stars yet."

"Hmm." She rubbed his lower back, then slid her hand under his shirt and teased a fingertip inside his belt, stroking warm, smooth skin. "Getting carried away sounds like my favorite dessert."

Laughing, he wriggled away. "Woman, let me concentrate. I'm trying to make this nice for you."

"You make everything nice for me." She wrapped her arms around his middle and smooched the back of his neck, then sauntered to the table, adding extra hip sway to whet his appetite.

Dinner was amazing—a trio of marinated salads from the Trappers Market deli, plus artisanal cheeses and crusty bread, and lamb that melted on her tongue. Soft blues music wafted from a speaker on their table, and the crackling campfire kept the evening chill at bay as they laughed and talked about everything and anything.

After clearing away their dinner dishes, and refusing her help, Michael brought out a selection of pastries from Garrett's bakery: glistening mini fruit tarts, paper cups of chocolate mousse, and her favorite lemon bars. He refilled their champagne flutes and watched, lips pressed in a tight line as she dug in.

She licked creamy custard from her fork, closed her eyes, and groaned. "Sooo damn delicious." A sudden silence struck her, and she opened her eyes to find him chewing his lip again, his dessert plate untouched.

"Aren't you having any?"

"Later. I—Annie—" His brows rumpled, pleating his forehead. Reflected firelight danced in his dark gaze as he rose from his chair and sank onto one knee.

Chills and heat chased over her skin as her heart stuttered, then raced.

"Annabelle Aurora Scott, love of my heart, light of my life, I..." He winced and shook his head. "Damn it, I've been practicing this all week."

Warmth swelled beneath her ribs and flowed through her veins like honey. Though she'd vowed to take their love day by day, without hurry or expectations, deep down, she'd known this was coming. And now that the moment was here, surrounding them both in golden light, she found herself vibrating with anticipation and delight.

She laid her hand on his cheek and stroked his cheekbone with her thumb. "Just say what's in your heart."

He pressed a kiss into her palm, his lips warm and soft. "I love you, Annie. Until I met you, I didn't really understand what love means, but you've shown me the way to something deeper, stronger, better.

Your smile is my warmth and light. Your arms are my refuge. Your body is my home." He pulled a velvet box from beneath the tablecloth and opened it to reveal a flash of blue flame. "Marry me?"

Her mouth fell open, but no sound emerged. What could she possibly say to match the breathtaking beauty of his words? Heart fluttering, she nodded.

"Yes?"

"Yes," she croaked.

"Oh, Annie." Arms flung wide, he launched himself at her, knocking her camp chair backward as they tumbled into the sand. Sprawled atop her, he fumbled the ring free from its velvet bed and slid it onto her finger.

She held her hand up to catch the light. "It's so beautiful."

"Blue like your eyes, sparkly like your spirit. I'm so glad you love it." He kissed her lips, her throat, her closed eyelids, the tip of her nose, her lips again, sweet and slow, unhurried because they had all the time in the world to spend together.

Annie wrapped her arms and legs around Michael's heavy, warm body, clasping him tight. Her teasing hip wiggle soon had him rocking against her in the sand, his heated shaft pressed to the seam of her jeans.

Dessert forgotten, they stroked and caressed and writhed until, panting on the edge of bliss, she cried out, "Bed. Now."

Inside the tent, he untied the flaps and let them fall, enclosing them in an ivory cocoon. While the sea whispered and sighed outside, they peeled off their sandy clothes and tumbled onto the bouncy air mattress—a new sensation as its rebound magnified each urgent thrust. Wrapped in crisp linens and silky fur, heated skin and strong limbs, she sank deeper and deeper into bliss until pure rapture blasted through her. With a feral growl, he rammed into her body once, twice, then joined her, shuddering his release, whispering her name over and over.

Gasping, laughing, she stroked his damp, soft hair, loving the primal feel of his weight atop her. "That was amazing." She raked her nails over the smooth curve of his ass. "Must be the ring."

"Powerful stuff, right?" He pushed onto his elbow and rained kisses over her face and chest. "Zora says sapphires release mental tension and promote wisdom."

"Is that so?" She kissed his bare shoulder and nibbled along his collar bone. "What else?"

He closed his eyes on a hum. "Something about spiritual clarity? Hard to remember when the most delicious woman in the world is naked beneath me."

She arched into his hypnotic touch. "I'd say the road ahead is totally clear. I see more of this. With you."

"Should I arrange to have this spot to ourselves next spring tide?"

"You arranged..." She blinked up at him. "Michael, did you...?"

Rolling onto his side, he banded his arm over her and nuzzled the crook of her neck. "Zeke and Lara are keeping guard, just in case."

A laugh escaped her lips. "With how fast gossip travels in this town, everyone probably knows by now."

"Shoot, I forgot. Hang on." He stepped into his jeans, shrugged on his jacket, wrapped her in the faux-fur throw, and beckoned her outside.

"What are we..?" She watched him open a tackle box. "We're going fishing?"

"Nope." Grinning wide, he stuck their empty champagne bottle in the sand and inserted a bottle rocket, then flicked a lighter and lit the fuse. The firework soared into the sky and exploded in a shower of silver, green, and gold.

In the distance, someone cheered. Several someones, in fact.

Michael pulled her into a hug. "Now they all know."

"You goof!" Cool wind whipping her hair, warm, happy man holding her tight, she sank into his kiss—grateful, hopeful, and happier than she'd ever thought possible.

Chapter Twenty-Four

♥

Excitement buzzed in Michael's veins as he checked his watch, then Annie's face. Biting her lip, she grinned and waggled her eyebrows. Her playful smile filled him with so much fizzy joy he nearly levitated off the castle's front lawn.

What a splendid spring day. A brisk coastal breeze tempered the heat of brilliant sunshine. Soaring on the cliff-side updrafts, hopeful, laughing gulls hovered over the crowd, searching for tasty morsels—and with this many food vendors, there were plenty of gull snacks to be seized. Funny how a change of perspective softened his view of those squawking sky raccoons.

With his arm around Annie's shoulders, he could happily stand here all day, drinking in the happy scene. But they still had important work to do, so he raised his voice to be heard over the grizzled blues band jamming on the makeshift stage. "Five minutes till launch."

"Finally." She pecked his cheek—a fleeting touch that didn't come close to satisfying his near-constant craving for her. Heedless of the crowd, he dipped her in a torrid kiss. She tasted of lemonade and kettle corn, sunshine and hope.

Giggling, she smacked his shoulder. "Easy now. We're surrounded by children."

"So what?" He squeezed her lush ass. "They've gotta learn about the birds and bees sometime."

"Keep it in your pants till later, love." Her smile sparkled with promise.

God, she was beautiful. This weird, kitschy castle was beautiful. This funky little beach town was beautiful. His cheeks hurt from smiling so much, but he couldn't stop.

Truly, Annie and her squad had worked miracles. Just five months after signing the purchase agreement, the new community center was opening its doors.

Okay, sure—he'd had a hand in it as well, mostly funding renovations and lassoing contractors. But thanks to Annie's connections and amazing power of persuasion, the school building was freshly painted inside and out, including a colorful mural framing the entrance. Pansies, daffodils, and grape hyacinth—Annie's favorite—bloomed in newly planted beds. And Mrs. Zika's fourth grade class had done a marvelous job of transforming that ugly whatsis fountain into a sparkly, tile-covered whatsis burbling a merry welcome to the hundreds of visitors.

Vendor tents lined the gravel drive, their canopies snapping in the crisp ocean breeze. On the newly sodded lawn, little kids squealed and chased each other while adults reclined on folding chairs and blankets, enjoying the food offerings—garlicky kebabs from Ali Baba's, ice cream from Gelateria Paradiso, chowder from the Salty Dog Saloon, cupcakes from Sweet Dreams Bakery, plus corn dogs, cotton candy, saltwater taffy—even Casa Francesca had turned out to serve paper boats of tortellini.

Hand in hand, he and Annie moved toward the community center's entrance, where a wide red ribbon stretched behind a cluster of microphones. As they passed the ice cream stand, Sal Verducci raised his scoop. "Don't forget, Garwood, I'm gonna trounce your butt at cornhole."

"Yeah, yeah. Big talk, signore." He'd developed a deep affection for the old gent who'd commandeered the Sons of Italy to run today's games: cornhole, ring toss, balloon darts, and his favorite—Dunk the Principal. Max Azarian perched on the hot seat now, wearing baggy swim trunks and a TC High School Sharks hoodie.

"That's the best you got, Reyes?" he taunted a muscly kid holding a softball. "Coach needs to drill you on pitching."

The kid's buddies hooted. "Oh, snap. You gonna let Mr. Az talk to you like that?"

The youngster wound up and pitched with deadly accuracy. Sploosh! The principal dropped into the dunk tank.

Annie tugged Michael closer. "Isn't this great? It's like the Fourth of July in April."

"Nearly May." He nodded toward the May pole, where giggling kids danced colorful ribbons into a hopeless knot.

As Mayor Hal Horvat stepped up to the microphone, it shrieked, causing a curly-haired tot to burst into tears and clutch the skirt of Annie's vintage sundress. Michael's heart squeezed when she stooped to comfort the little guy.

Funny how life balances the scales. Neither he nor Annie had kids of their own, but now they had a whole townful of adopted grandkids. He did a slow turn to drink it all in—the smiling faces, the colorful banners dancing in the breeze, the neat, if slightly trampled garden they would wake to all summer long, and the new community center, reborn from ruin thanks to his funding, Annie's resourcefulness, and the deep generosity of Trappers Cove.

Though he'd never been good at poetic language, an image tickled at the edge of his brain. Turning to Annie—his lover, his partner, his inspiration—he grinned. "There's a lesson here. Something about the phoenix rising from the ashes."

"Perfect metaphor. Look at her." She gestured toward the school building. "In fine plumage, bright and shiny, ready to begin her new life."

"Just like you, love." He lifted her left hand and pressed a kiss to her knuckles, right below her sapphire engagement ring—an oval stone as blue as her eyes, flanked with diamond-studded filigree. Classic, sparkling, and nearly as beautiful as his bride to be.

"Cut it out." She elbowed him. "You're gonna make me cry."

"As long as they're happy tears." He smooched her temple. Seeing her proudly fight back tears at his parents' disastrous New Year's Eve party had made him resolve to never again give her a reason to weep. So far, he'd kept that promise, and he intended to keep it until his dying day.

"Very happy," she assured him and tugged him toward the podium. "Come on, it's time."

They followed the others drifting toward the Community Center as the mayor began his opening remarks.

"And now, let's give it up for the man of the hour, Michael Garwood."

Annie gave him a little shove. "Go on. They're expecting a speech."

He looped his arm through hers and towed her to the microphone, ignoring her half-hearted protests. No way was he letting her contribution go unapplauded. Before speaking, he took a moment to just breathe in the happy energy of his new neighbors gathered in front of his new home to launch his most audacious start-up yet—one that wouldn't make him a dime but would pay dividends beyond measure.

"Thank you, Mr. Mayor. And I want to thank the people of Trappers Cove for making me feel so welcome. You truly are family, and I'm honored to be accepted into the fold. Thanks also to Mrs. Baron for sharing her family's legacy in such a meaningful, generous way."

Beside him, Annie gave a little snort. She knew the inflated price the shrewd old gal had demanded.

He wrapped his arm around her shoulders. "And special thanks to my beautiful fiancée, Annie Scott, for her patience and wisdom."

She beamed up at him, her ocean-blue eyes gleaming.

He kissed her temple. "Is there anyone better at twisting arms?"

A smattering of laughter and applause broke out.

"Until I came to Trappers Cove," he continued, "my life was about running from project to project, always searching for the next innovation. Annie taught me the value of going deep, sinking roots. And even though this community center is outside my area of expertise, I've never been so excited about a project." He snugged her tight against his side. "So, Annie, thanks for all the long nights, the meetings and phone calls. Thanks for weaving your magic web of friendship and love. Let's cut the ribbon, then sign up for some classes."

With the mayor's help, they lifted the giant scissors and sliced through the ribbon, declaring the Phillis Baron Community Center officially open. The crowd cheered, photographers snapped photos, and everyone surged toward the tables where instructors stood ready to pitch their offerings.

Annie tugged on his sleeve. "We could sign up online, you know."

"Nah. I like the personal touch." He squeezed her hip, drawing her close enough to whisper over the din. "And I'm looking forward to your personal touch as soon as this crowd clears out. Now, what should I start with—Zumba? Yoga? Watercolors? Bookbinding?"

As a kid, he seldom got to play around with fun, artsy-fartsy pursuits. But this new chapter was all about exploration, not striving, and he looked forward to being a beginner again.

Annie's smile glimmered with sass and mischief. "I'm signing up for whatever woo-woo workshop Zora's offering. And maybe that digital art course. My shop could use some new graphics."

Taking a page from Annie's book of tricks, Michael had sweet-talked a few of his tech mentees into volunteering their time to teach computer basics, coding, and some creative applications as well. Once he sweetened the pot with an honorarium and the promise of networking assistance, enough volunteers lined up to keep Trappers Cove techie into the new year. Nice way to stay in touch with the tech start-ups he continued to sponsor from his new home base.

Violet trotted up, waving a brochure. "Look at all these classes! Lebanese cooking, healing crystal terrariums, living history of the fur trapper days, community theater... I'm gonna have to visit Trappers Cove more often." She landed a playful punch to his shoulder. "Good job, big bro. Hey, Jasper, wait up!" Hippie skirt flapping and bracelets jangling, she skipped off to join her boyfriend in the beer line.

Good thing Annie and Violet had hit it off. This was his sister's third visit since he moved here, another surprise benefit of leaving Bellevue behind. Rick and Jose had come too, along with their families, filling the castle with laughter.

Next week would mark his parents' first visit, though, and he looked forward to that milestone with a mixture of dread and hope. He'd made it clear that, if they wanted a continuing relationship, much less an invitation to the wedding, they must apologize to Annie.

"And not just empty words, Mother," he'd told her on the phone, "the real deal. Major groveling."

He and Violet had a bet going. She thought their parents couldn't pull off an entire snub-free weekend, but Michael was betting they'd come around once they saw what he saw—how amazing this place was, and this community, and especially the woman he was sharing it with from now until forever.

"Auntie A!" Annie's two teen nieces bopped up, each wearing a T-shirt with a tie-dyed alien from Crazy Gus's Souvenir Planet. "Dad says we can come back for the art fair next month."

"Did he now?" She wrapped an arm around each grinning girl. "Well, you're always welcome, but does this sudden interest in art have anything to do with those cute boys I saw you with at the dunking booth?"

The younger girl gave an epic eye roll, but the older one's giggle told the truth. Well, why not? Having her family near made Annie happy, so whatever lured them to Trappers Cove was all right with him.

After pecking their auntie's cheek and giving him shy smiles, the girls linked arms and headed back into the throng in search of their brother.

Michael extended his arm, and Annie nestled into the space he made. "This is truly marvelous, Michael. I'm so glad you came back."

"I'm so glad you let me."

"Pshaw." She poked his ribs. "You could afford to buy the whole town if you wanted to."

He arched an eyebrow. "*We* could, yes, but that's not the point. As wonderful as Trappers Cove is, it's not home without you beside me. Now, are you a hundred percent sure you want to let Cheryl rent out your place?"

"Absolutely." She hugged him tight. "I love my little cottage, and so will the visitors who rent it, but it can't compare to sharing a castle with the man I love."

Though they'd nearly broken the bed that morning, he felt his body stir again at the press of her luscious curves. "We've done our bit, angel. What do you say we take a breather?"

"A breather?" Grinning, she goosed his butt. "Is that what we're calling it now?"

He waggled his eyebrows. "Well, maybe just a short break to make out? I'm dying to see what you've got on under that dress."

Annie's musical laughter rang out as, arm in arm, they left the merry hubbub behind and strolled around the castle to the private garden in back, where he'd installed a cliff-side gazebo as an engagement gift to Annie.

She squealed when his hands slid beneath her fluffy sundress to caress her bare thighs. "Michael, someone might see."

"I can't help it, beautiful. You're just too tempting to resist." Though their lives had meshed into an easy, comfortable rhythm, Annie's flirtatious glances still stirred him up like—well, like this. He couldn't keep his hands off her.

Giggling, wrapped in each other's arms, they made out like teenagers. Finally, Annie sat on the bench and pulled him down beside her. "Feels like I've been on my feet for days."

He scooped her feet onto his lap, slipped off her ballerina flats, and massaged her arches, loving how her low moans of pleasure blended with the soft whoosh of the sea.

Annie nuzzled the crook of his neck. "Have I told you yet today how glad I am you came back to Trappers Cove?"

"Once or twice." He dug his thumbs into the firm muscle of her calf. "But I never get tired of hearing it."

Looking back, he realized his return here was inevitable. His happiest childhood days were spent in this funky little beach town, and when you love a place as deeply as he'd loved Trappers Cove, it always calls you back. Add Annie to the mix, and there simply was no other choice.

Just yesterday, he'd visited Zora's metaphysical shop in search of another book to share with Annie, and Zora insisted on giving him a tarot reading.

"The Four of Wands." She'd patted his hand in her motherly way. "The card of weddings and homecomings."

Perhaps the old hippie mama really did have psychic powers because her words rang true. Here, in Annie's arms, he was finally home.

Thank you for reading! If you enjoyed Michael and Annie's love story, please leave a review! We authors depend on your reviews to help other readers find our books, and I'm oh so grateful for readers who take the time to leave a few kind words.

Don't miss the next Trappers Cove Romance: **Love, Legacy, and Little Green Aliens,** coming 2024.

He's all about the future. She's clinging to the past.

Xander Anagnos is running out of options. His uncle's bequest provides the perfect opportunity to escape the family curse. How hard could it be to transform Crazy Gus's Souvenir Planet into a modern shopping gallery? All he needs is a plan, some cash, and a way to shake off the hot local journalist hell-bent on derailing his improvements to this backward little beach town.

Hannah Leone is determined to save the funky heart of Trappers Cove, and there's no way she's going to let this tempting interloper turn a beloved landmark into a cookie-cutter mini mall—not when she's got the power of the press on her side. If she can stir up enough outrage, not only will she save a huge tourist magnet, she might even rescue her dying local newspaper.

Weird occurrences in the old shop stir up suspicions that Gus's alien obsession wasn't just a marketing gimmick. When disaster strikes, it'll take Xander's innovation and Hannah's connections to rise from the ashes. But if these hard-headed foes don't lay down their arms, the town they've both come to love will pay the price. Their hearts and livelihoods are on the line.

Come back to Trappers Cove for a steamy, laugh-out-loud rivals-to-lovers romance full of found family, beachy fun, and out-of-this-world mystery.

For new releases, plus Sadira Stone's other steamy, swoony books, visit https://www.sadirastone.com and sign up for Sadira's monthly reader newsletter. Subscribers get a free sizzling Valentine's Day over-40 romance novella, ***Cupid's Silver Spark***.

About the Author

Award-winning contemporary romance author Sadira Stone spins steamy, smoochy tales set in small businesses—a quirky bookstore, a neighborhood bar, a vintage boutique. Set in the U.S. Pacific Northwest, her stories highlight found family, friendship, and the sizzling chemistry that pulls unlikely partners together. When she emerges from her writing cave in Las Vegas, Nevada (which she seldom does), she can be found in dance class, strumming her ukulele, exploring the Western U.S. with her charming husband, cooking up a storm, and gobbling all the romance books. For a guaranteed HEA (and no cliffhangers!) visit Sadira at sadirastone.com.

Visit Sadira on All the Socials!
https://linktr.ee/SadiraStone

Also by Sadira Stone

The Trappers Cove Romance Series

Welcome to Trappers Cove, a quirky Washington State beach town nestled among the pines. Here you'll find steamy, small-town romance, laughter and tears, Madame Zora's Psychic Emporium, all the best beachy fun, heart-warming chosen family, and guaranteed HEAs with no cliffhangers ever! (That last bit goes for all my books.)

The Bangers Tavern Romance Series

Sizzling romance set in a neighborhood bar in Tacoma, Washington. Come to Bangers Tavern for chosen family, holiday bar bashes (Christmas, Valentine's Day, St. Patrick's Day, Cinco de Mayo, Halloween), all the feels, and the best tater tots in Tacoma!

The Book Nirvana Series

Three steamy romance novels set in a quirky bookshop in Eugene, Oregon—because bookshops are sexy! Do you dare peek behind the red door? That's where shop owner Clara keeps her collection of naughty books. Come to Book Nirvana for chosen family, artistic characters, bookish delights, and Lulu the shop cat!

Gelato Surprise

A sizzling standalone older woman/younger man beach romance novella. She came to the beach to find herself—and found him!

Acknowledgements

This story was sparked by the real-life castle in Ben Lomond, California, up in the Santa Cruz Mountains—such a pretty town nestled among the coastal redwoods. If you get the chance, go!

Thanks to Dar Albert of Wicked Smart Designs for her inspired book covers, to my editor Saya of Red Quill Editing, LLC for her sharp eyes, to my oh-so-patient husband for supporting me on my writing journey, and to my beloved readers whose support keeps me writing.

Special thanks to my beta readers Michelle McCraw, Payton Harley, and Cindy Kehagiaras, fabulous authors all! Your insight helped make Michael and Annie's story shine.